PLAY THE DEVIL'S TUNE

BY

JOHN ROACH

DEDICATION

My first debt is to all the musicians and writers, too many to list here, who have nurtured my love of music and reading.

A special thanks to the following people:

Rob Nisbett, who encouraged me to expand upon what began as a short story about a mysterious Mrs. Francis.

Jay Austin of Devine Destinies/eXtasy Books, who believed my story was worth reading.

Debbie Nygaard and Larriane Wills, whose editing skills encouraged me to get it right and ready for release.

Muriel Carpenter, who enlightened me regarding the tonal beauty of 'Hoing' violins.

All my friends, from our writing group, who I am delighted to say, have continually supported each other's writing adventures.

My wife Jenny, for her patience and support.

A big thanks to all of you, for buying this book. I hope you enjoy reading it.

CHAPTER ONE

Sunday, 27 September, 2009

Engrossed in the intensity of Shostakovich's piano quintet, Josh Stoller waited for his entry. He glanced over at Sophie, absorbed in her playing. With two bars of rests on his score, his bow ready to attack the next motif, another tune interrupted him.

Josh's attention focused on the unexpected sound, and he forced open his eyes. His phone's ringtone, Elgar's *Chanson de Matin*, brought him to his senses. Someone wanted to contact him.

His dream of the concert with his ensemble in London disturbed, he sat up.

Who the hell's ringing me up this morning?

He turned his head to see the time display on his bedside clock. No-one rang him at nine o'clock, not even his boss, but his phone's vibration on the small table demanded to be answered. Without checking the caller's identity, he pressed the accept call button, ready to display his annoyance, when a tense female voice grabbed his attention.

"Is that Josh Stoller?"

"Yes." He paused for a few seconds. "How can I help you?" He heard the caller exhaling breath, and assumed she was relieved she'd rung the correct number.

"We've moved to the area and I'm looking for a violin teacher for my ten-year-old son. I saw your advert at the local newsagent."

1

"Oh, yes. Has he played before?"

"Sean's been playing for three years, and he's passed his grade five."

"When do you want to start? Sorry, what did you say your name was?"

"I didn't." The caller remained silent for a few seconds. "It's Mrs. Francis. Do you teach in the evenings?"

"Yes, most are free, apart from Mondays or the weekends. How about Wednesday, half an hour?"

"Yes, fine. How much do you charge?"

"Shall we call it a tenner to begin with? We can make a decision later, based upon how long he wants a lesson to last. You'd better have my address."

"I've got it. Sean will be over this Wednesday at six-thirty."

Josh sensed her hesitation to elaborate any further.

"Does he have his own violin?" he asked.

"Yes, it's a Hoing."

"Oh. They're excellent. I used to have one." He remembered the hand-crafted instrument he'd owned as a teenager, its excellent tone more than acceptable. He'd used it at the start of his professional career. Mrs. Francis didn't comment. Josh assumed she wanted to finish the conversation without further discussion. "I'll look forward to seeing Sean on Wednesday."

"Yes," she said, and the phone went dead.

The number had been withheld. He dropped his phone on the bed, puzzled by her haste to finish the call. The revelation the boy had a Hoing violin intrigued him. It was an unusual instrument for a youngster to be playing

Although he was free on Wednesday at six-thirty, the conversation was over before he had a chance to discuss if time was a convenient allow him time to prepare after a day's work.

Sean Francis sounded ready to progress, since he'd passed

grade five. Josh had achieved grade six with distinction at primary school, and he assumed Mrs. Francis had similar aspirations for her son.

Once Josh found his diary, he made a note of when to expect Sean and wrote a question mark next to his name. He was surprised the woman hadn't asked about his qualifications, but she seemed happy for her son to be taught by a stranger on the strength of an advert at a newsagent's.

Although Mrs. Francis claimed to know where he lived, he knew he'd not written his address on the card he had asked the newsagent to display.

All his pupils in the South Wales town were either young teenagers preparing for external exams who wanted more instruction to improve their chances of success or students about to leave home for university. Sean Francis would be the youngest pupil he'd ever taught, and he wondered how he should approach the boy. Josh hoped the child wouldn't be as antisocial as his mother.

Josh was curious, though. He'd not met anyone throughout his career with another Hoing violin. Clifford Hoing had only produced six to eight in any given year. They took an age to construct from over seventy separate parts. He'd then added twelve coats of varnish and allowed them to dry under natural conditions. It would be interesting to see the instrument, irrespective of the mother's attitude.

In a previous life, Josh had played the classics in prestigious venues, but he was no longer able to claim that privilege. He currently worked in retail and played in a semi-professional folk-rock band in the Cardiff area. Opportunities in the disciplined genre of music for which he'd trained had eluded him for many years. A recent curious phone call from a supposed ex-colleague to his mother regarding orchestral work in the Midlands had raised his hopes, but it had amounted to nothing.

Mrs. Francis' call had thrown him. Her clipped tone and approach weren't what he'd expected from a complete stranger eager for a violin teacher.

Before he took his customary morning shower, he looked at his reflection. The abrupt interruption to his sleep, showed in his unkempt blond hair and tired eyes. His mind wandered back to Sean Francis as he showered. He hoped he wouldn't regret accepting the boy as a pupil.

Josh needed a distraction from Mrs. Francis' evasive manner and he opened his book of Bach's Partitas. The Chaconne was a favourite of his. It brought back memories of his former career, when he performed the piece with the ensemble in which he'd played, before his career had begun to diminish as a result of his self-destructive personality. His ability to still play it with no discrepancies allowed him to re-affirm his existence as a competent musician.

Twenty minutes later, after repeating several phrases, he closed the book and placed his violin in its case. In need of a coffee, he filled the kettle in his small galley kitchen and put back into the correct cupboards several pieces of crockery he'd left to dry the previous afternoon.

His ground floor flat contained just enough furniture to guarantee his basic comfort. His music stand, a permanent feature, always held a sheet of music. The remainder of his collection he kept in a small cupboard on which his television stood. His living space, with plain painted walls, was bare of any memories. He'd not taken time to decorate it with photographs to celebrate his previous musical successes, of which most had been lost.

After he finished his coffee, his mind wandered again to some music he wanted to work on. He wanted to perfect several phrases in an instrumental break of a new song his band had decided to include in its repertoire.

He played, then adjusted several intervals and note values

on manuscript paper until he felt satisfied. Happy with what he'd achieved, he placed his violin back in its case again.

The cool air of late September prompted him to venture out to clear his head. He walked to one of the several woodland paths in his neighbourhood. The blue sky, with the occasional wisp of cloud, allowed him to enjoy the welcome change of weather. Summer's premature departure had prompted the deciduous leaves to begin their autumnal change.

Twigs and leaves, victims of a September wind, carpeted the path underneath his feet. At other times, his movements would provide the rhythm to accompany the birdsong of the native blackbirds and finches to inspire musical ideas. Yet with the early phone call foremost on his mind, he ignored these sounds.

Several families, with children he estimated were the same age as his new pupil, passed him. Boys with sticks, slashing at tall grasses, caused him to wonder what level of indiscipline his new pupil would display.

After an hour, he returned the way he'd come and called in at his local pub, busy with lunchtime regulars who took advantage of the cheap Sunday roast dinners on offer. As he waited to be served, he looked around the bar area for anyone with whom he could socialise. Loud banter between several customers caused him to smile, but he wanted to be served and moved away from the joviality.

Most tables were full of diners, a respite from cooking which attracted families as busy barmen relieved customers of their credit cards in exchange for meal orders. Some regulars acknowledged him. They recognised him from the shop where he worked and his infrequent visits for a drink, but no-one initiated any conversation of more than a few sentences.

Once served, he walked through the dining area and spotted two of the locals with whom he frequently socialised. As he approached them, one pulled an empty chair from underneath another table, and he sat to join them.

The men were in discussion about the weekend's sports events, highlighting the successes and failures of the local rugby and football teams. Although he'd not played rugby since his teenage years, he maintained a level of interest in the game and joined in the conversation, albeit on a superficial level.

The conversation moved to the Premiership football teams and became too repetitive to maintain his interest. He glanced at his watch and explained he had to return to his flat for lunch. As he reached the door, he spotted the newsagent who'd agreed to display his card and approached him on the off chance he'd mention Mrs. Francis. The newsagent appeared eager to see Josh, to relay information about the interest in the advertisement.

"I think you might have a new pupil."

Josh didn't tell him he'd already been contacted. He hoped the newsagent would provide more information about the mysterious woman and allowed him to continue. "Lady came in yesterday afternoon, saw your card. She asked me about you. I told her you had a few pupils. She said it wasn't for her but her son. You'll have a phone call, probably tomorrow."

"What was she like?"

"Early thirties, at a guess. She came in to look for a magazine. Don't think she was looking for a violin teacher. When she came to pay for the magazine, she saw your card behind the counter. She asked what you did. I told her where you worked and taught the violin part-time. She seemed surprised for some reason."

"Was she local?"

"No, English. Northern, I'd say. I haven't seen her before. She asked where you lived, so I told her, and she took your number. The strange thing is she left the magazine on the counter."

"Thanks, I'll wait for her call."

Puzzled by Mrs. Francis' impatience to phone him, he began the short walk home. At least the conversation had enlightened him regarding her knowledge of his address.

It took him several minutes to reach his street of terraced houses, most of which had been converted into flats. Outside his own, he saw a white BMW parked. The near silent purr and smoky vapour escaping from its exhaust indicated the driver was possibly waiting for someone. He noticed the new registration-plate and wondered if the driver was lost. Two people were visible in the front, the driver taller than the passenger, who he half expected to open the window to ask directions As he drew level, the driver manoeuvred the vehicle away from the kerb and drove away to disappear around the bend fifty metres or so down the street. He continued to look in the direction the car had taken, even after it was out of sight.

With Mrs. Francis' phone call still on his mind, he wondered if the driver had been her. Wednesday's lesson might prove more interesting than he'd anticipated.

CHAPTER TWO

Two Years Earlier

Soon after Josh relocated to the Cardiff area in 2007, he'd answered an advert for a rhythm guitarist in a band. He'd spotted it in a music shop in the city centre and quickly telephoned the mobile number on the off chance the musicians would accept his violin playing as an integral part of their line-up.

Chris, the drummer, answered the call and told Josh the band rehearsed in a barn on a farm owned by the guitarist's uncle. The location was a twenty-minute drive from his flat. As he had no transport of his own, he asked Chris if he was willing to collect him for the audition.

He carried both his acoustic guitar and violin to the car. Chris looked intrigued and asked why Josh had no amplifier, the least he would have expected from a potential guitarist. Josh asked if he could use the band's PA for the audition, hoping they would overlook the discrepancy.

As they drove to the barn, Josh announced he'd played in several bands in London. He made no mention of his orchestral experience, information he wished to keep to himself until an appropriate time.

They arrived to find the equipment had already been set up, apart from Chris' hi-hat cymbals and snare drum. Those he carried into the barn before he introduced Josh.

The building, no longer used for storing crops, had been converted into an admin office which held various box files on shelves. It had enough room for each musician to make use of his own personal space.

Josh placed his violin and guitar cases on the floor and removed *his acoustic guitar. As he did so, he noticed the puzzled look on the other guitarist's face. Although his instrument had a detachable pick-up to amplify its sound, Josh was aware the band members would have expected an electric model. He checked the tuning before he plugged it into the PA and ignored his violin.*

Dave, the guitarist and vocalist, checked they were both in tune, and Rob adjusted his bass before he suggested a song for Josh to accompany. It had an easy chord structure, and after one verse, Josh added the rhythm part without any discrepancy.

"Don't you have an electric guitar?" Dave asked afterwards. He appeared disappointed but seemed to recognise Josh's immaculate timing and chord progression. Josh admitted the acoustic one in his hands was all he owned.

"But I do have this," Josh said, as he knelt to open his violin case.

They all watched with interest as he placed the violin under his chin, adjusting the fine tuners as he flicked each string with the middle finger of his left hand. He picked up the bow and drew it across the top string.

"More rosin needed," he said, his deliberate movements designed to create an element of suspense. From their expressions, the band members wondered if he had the proficiency to impress.

Chris and Rob began a slow blues tune, and Josh accompanied with the appropriate pentatonic scale. Dave began to play at the beginning of the second verse, which inspired the other two to take the tune to a different level. Josh listened with interest, and as they finished the twelve bars in preparation to lead into a third verse, he bowed his head. The intensity and clarity in the music he produced stopped Dave in his tracks. Chris smiled but didn't miss a beat.

When the blues jam ended, the band members congratulated Josh on his ability.

"Well, I think this solves the vacancy. What else do you play?" Chris asked.

"Jazz, world, and rock, but I'm classically trained."

"What grade?" Dave asked, as if it made a difference.

"Degree, Music College in Cardiff."

"What, the music college?" Rob asked.

"Yes, back in the nineties. It's a long story, maybe another time."

The band performed in the Cardiff and Newport areas twice or three times a month. They played covers in their own style along with several of their own compositions. With a virtuoso violinist to augment their sound, they gained the appreciation of audiences wherever they played.

However, breaking through to a full-time professional status still eluded them. At first, Josh had been happy with their progress, as he knew the sacrifices demanded to become full-time musicians. However, the rock scene was as competitive a field as the classical one, and he'd begun to feel frustrated. His job in the clothes shop didn't interest him. It had been a means to an end to regain his solvency. He now felt the urge to move on to look for other musical opportunities.

Although his regular practice sessions at home were part of his self-discipline, he had to consider the neighbours. The sound of a mixture of Kurt Weil, Stephane Grappelli, Tchaikovsky, Bach, and an array of world and modern rock music had raised a few eyebrows on occasions in the safe environment of his neighbourhood.

CHAPTER THREE

The Violin

Monday, 28 September, 2009

Josh introduced some of his new arrangements at the band's rehearsal, but with the conversation with Mrs. Francis still on his mind, he felt distant.

Chris, who always transported him to practices and gigs, had noticed his failure to connect with the other musicians on a social level and asked, "Everything okay, Josh?"

"Yes, I think so. I had a call yesterday morning from someone wanting violin lessons for her son. Sounds as if he's very good. Strange woman though, she seemed reluctant to speak openly with me." He didn't mention the conversation he'd had with the newsagent or the presence of the white BMW with its mysterious occupants. The vision had stuck, and he couldn't understand why. The situation seemed illogical.

"Don't worry. You don't have to teach her," Chris said.

Josh hoped Wednesday's lesson with Sean Francis would be a straightforward one and his concern amount to nothing.

Before Sean arrived for his lesson on Wednesday, Josh placed *Chanson de Matin* by Edward Elgar, on his music stand. He wanted to discover if his new pupil was as good as his mother had claimed. The doorbell rang, and Josh opened the door.

"You must be Sean. Come in." The boy thrust his hand

towards Josh, who acknowledged his good manners and beckoned the boy to follow him into his flat.

"Your mum not coming?"

"No, she'll call for me at seven o'clock. She's had to go to the supermarket."

"No worries. Have you brought any music with you?"

"My grade five pieces, Mozart and Vivaldi."

"Let me see your violin, Sean."

The boy opened the case and pulled out the bow and rosin. He then lifted a red cloth to reveal the instrument.

The violin lay before Josh, almost begging to be played by him. Unable to believe his eyes, he was impatient to see Sean lift it out. It appeared identical to the one — with his parents' help — he'd bought as a teenager when he was selected to play in the county youth orchestra in Swansea.

"Do you like my violin?" Sean asked. "It belongs to my Mum's partner. He said he used to play. My three-quarter sized one is all right, but I want to try this one now."

Josh was impatient to hear the instrument being played. He was also interested to find out its history.

"Do you know where he bought it?"

"No. Mum plays it now and again, but she's got her own."

Sean placed his Mozart piece on the music stand and played it as if a natural. The instrument's distinct tone demonstrated its quality. It was the same as he remembered his old violin sounding. The combination of the instrument and the boy's skills — both intonation and tempo — were impressive. Sean had passed his grade five exam at ten, with grade six achievable by the spring, if his knowledge of musical theory matched his practical ability.

"Try this," Josh said, as he placed the Elgar piece on the stand. "It's in G major, but trickier than you think. Be careful with the dynamics."

Sean played the first twenty-four bars almost note-perfect,

and Josh suspected he wasn't sight reading.

"Do you know this piece?"

"It's my mum's favourite. She often plays it on her violin. We've got a CD of Elgar's music with this and *Chanson de Nuit* on it, so I know them both quite well."

"One of my favourites, too. May I try your violin?" Josh had great difficulty concealing his eagerness to play the violin as Sean handed the instrument to him. He placed it under his chin and drew the bow across each string. The beauty of its sound was evident as it quietened. Although the strings had ceased to vibrate, the atmosphere in the room contained a hypnotic silence.

As he played *Chanson de Nuit* from memory, he lost himself in the tone and passion of the music. A minute went by, and he continued to play as if in a trance, ignoring Sean's presence.

He stopped at the end of a phrase and studied the body of the violin, looking for clues regarding its history and possible previous owners. Yes, it was familiar, but the label inside had been scribbled over, as if to delete its past.

"So, your mother plays?" He continued to examine the instrument and stroked the body with the affection reserved for a lover. He saw a slight scratch on the scroll and another on the back, testament to good use by someone. He remembered his old instrument also had a scratch on the back, but he didn't comment. "And you've got this?"

Josh continued to study the instrument as he spoke. He looked again at the back. Unlike many quality violins, the back had been made from one piece, but it didn't diminish the quality of sound. Clifford Hoing's instruments were well crafted.

Sean looked but answered in a calm voice. "Yes, she does play, really well, and helps me a lot. She pushes me to practise and helps me with the theory. She plays the piano, too, but we haven't got one here yet. She hopes we'll get one soon, so she can accompany me."

"Do you want to learn this piece in its entirety, or do you want to start on the grade six pieces?"

"I'd like a break from exam pieces for a couple of months."

"How about your mother? What does she say? Have you discussed it with her? We could look at the grade six Handel or Schumann pieces if you like."

"This Elgar is a grade five piece, isn't it?" Sean asked.

Josh was surprised by Sean's knowledge of exam pieces. "Yes, but not used a great deal now. It's a good piece to practise tricky intervals. I'm happy to take you through it."

"It's seven o' clock. I'd better go," Sean said, changing the subject without warning. Taken aback by Sean's abruptness, Josh said, "Next week okay?"

"I'll check with my mum. Thank you." Sean took little time to pack his violin and bow into the case. He closed the lid and pulled an envelope from his pocket, which he gave to Josh.

Josh placed the envelope on his table and offered Sean the photocopy of Elgar's music.

"I've got a copy at home, but thank you."

"Of course, you don't need this. You play well. I look forward to seeing you again." Josh added, attempting to hide his confusion.

He opened the outside door to see a stationery BMW, its engine running, parked twenty metres up the road. As soon as Sean reached the vehicle and got in, the car pulled away. It moved down the street, and Josh gazed after it until it disappeared.

After he stepped into his flat, Josh pushed the music stand to the corner of the room. He walked over to the sink where his dinner plate lay, waiting to be washed. His mind centred on the events of the last half hour, and he dropped the plate. Now in three pieces, it was only fit for the bin. The knife and fork he left where they were.

"I'll wash them later," he said as he picked up the envelope. He read his name written in neat script and tore it open to see a crispy new ten-pound note.

The atmosphere surrounding Sean took him out of his comfort zone. Nothing appeared straightforward, and seeing the violin had thrown him. Had it been part of a collection of similar instruments placed before him, he would have assumed it was his old one. It felt like his and responded to him in the same way his old one had. He remembered writing his initials-JS-on the label of his instrument as a fifteen-year-old, but that was in the past.

He often reflected on how he'd not had the strength and tenacity to overcome the tragedies and disappointments he'd experienced in London. With his skills, he should be performing at the highest level, but certain lifestyles had their consequences. His lack of resilience to various temptations had left him in this regretful position, willing to accept a meagre sum from pupils.

The millennium year had not provided him with the hope and expectations of a new century the media had encouraged everyone to embrace. A predicted glittering career in music had been dashed within the space of a few months. The death of a close friend and the break-up of a relationship had left him vulnerable and isolated. He'd subsequently turned to alcohol and became less than adequate in the competitive world of classical music.

A similar orchestral post hadn't lasted any length of time, and he'd ended up finding work in music shops to help pay his way. To exist in London required a healthy and regular income. As a result, it had become necessary to play a more contemporary style of music with local musicians in the evenings, the only work available in his chosen discipline. It meant survival.

15

He picked up his violin and began to play, then placed it back in its case after less than thirty seconds. Memories of the millennium summer interrupted his train of thought, reducing his concentration level.

At work the next morning, Josh was in a pensive mood. His boss asked him if he had any worries. Terry knew Josh didn't suffer from a habit of excess. Several times when they'd gone for a drink after work, Josh had always refused alcohol. He claimed he didn't like the taste. His boss had never questioned this.

Eventually, Josh opened up, "A new pupil turned up for a lesson last night."

"Any good?"

"Yes, better than most I've taught. He reminded me of what I was like as a youngster. His instrument was familiar as well. It was as if I'd seen it before."

"How could you tell?"

"Sometimes you can. I used to own one of a similar make."

Towards the end of the afternoon, a stranger entered the shop and approached Josh. The man ignored Josh's friendly manner and said, "I want a seventeen-inch wing collar shirt."

"Here we are, sir." Josh said as he took one from a drawer beneath the counter. "Would you like one of our bow ties as well? We have a few different types."

"No, it's all I want. Here's my card." He held his credit card in front of Josh.

"Thank you, twenty-five pounds, ninety-five pence please." Josh typed in the relevant information on the card machine and asked the customer to enter his PIN. Josh removed the card to complete the transaction, and glanced at it to see the customer's name.

"Thank you, Mr. Simpson," he said and thought no more about it.

The man walked toward the door without a thank you. As

he opened it, he turned and looked at Josh. Their eyes met. For a split second, the look the customer gave Josh suggested an element of malice.

Josh felt relieved to see Terry turn the closed sign on the door at five o'clock.

Chapter Four

The band met for a final rehearsal before Friday's gig at a venue in Cardiff, the first since the middle of September.

"How did Wednesday's lesson go?" Chris asked on the way.

"Strange. I thought I recognised the boy's violin. It was identical to one I used to own. I even played it, and it felt the same. You know what it's like. You always know your own instrument, like your drums or trumpet. I'd sold it to buy a more expensive one when I lived in London. I must be mistaken about this one." Josh had not divulged the details of how his life had descended from the heady experiences of those days. All he'd originally said was he'd not been ready for the competitiveness of performing at the highest level.

"How much was it worth?"

"A thousand, the new one was over four."

"You must have been earning a bit. The one you've got isn't worth more than two hundred."

"Things didn't work out."

"Yes, I gathered. Is the boy coming again?"

"This Wednesday, I hope."

"What about the mother?"

"Didn't see her. Just dropped him off and picked him up afterward."

"Strange. Didn't she want to meet and find out about you?"

"She must have assumed I was qualified to take him

18

further than grade five."

On Tuesday afternoon, his one afternoon off work, Josh went to Cardiff to trawl through the music shops. He looked for unique tunes to teach his new pupil. He wanted to introduce Sean to a variety of styles of music, as he felt the boy had the potential to progress at a rapid pace. As a youngster, Josh had appreciated the opportunity to explore different genres of music, and for some reason, he wanted his new pupil to have the same experience.

On his way back to his flat, his phone rang. The display indicated a withheld number. He accepted the call, but before he could respond, he heard Sean's voice.

"It's Sean, about tomorrow's lesson. Can I come at seven? I've got rugger practice after school. Do you mind?"

"No, it's fine," Josh said, aware he'd have more time to prepare food after work. "Seven will be fine. Do you play rugby at school?"

"I've just started since moving down here this term. I used to play in my old school and wanted to carry on."

"Great. I used to play for school when I was your age. You'll have to tell me all about it when you come tomorrow. See you at seven."

Sean arrived on time, and the first few minutes were spent discussing his interest in rugby. Josh was eager to begin the lesson, and asked, "How did you get on with the Edward Elgar?"

"My mum helped me a lot with this," Sean said as he took his copy of the music from his bag. He placed it on the stand and played the first twenty-four bars, dynamics and note values as written, with no discrepancy or hesitation. Josh smiled, impressed by the quality of Sean's musicianship.

"Excellent. You've spent a lot of time over the piece." Sean ignored the compliment and said,

"Can we go on now?"

"Is your mum a good musician?"

"Yes, she used to teach music in a primary school where I used to go. It's where I started playing the violin, but after she met my stepfather a couple of years ago, we moved in with him. My stepfather decided to send me to a private school. My mum came in to teach part-time as well. She's really pleased I enjoy the violin. She's helped me a lot this week."

Josh hadn't meant to pry, but Sean had given him more information about his family in those few seconds than he realised.

"Great. We'll move on, shall we?" They went through the intricacies of the next twenty-four bars and played through it a couple of times.

Josh noticed Sean looking at his watch several times during the lesson. Without warning, Sean announced, "It's half past seven. I'll have to go. My mum will be waiting. She's always on time." He put his violin into his case and gave Josh an envelope before he put his music in his bag.

"I'll just let you out." Josh beat Sean to the door. He hoped to see the elusive Mrs. Francis. The car was parked along the street as before. As Sean reached it, he turned and waved to Josh. The car pulled away as soon as the boy closed the door.

Sean appeared to be a talented boy who enjoyed a variety of hobbies—both music and rugby, or rugger as he called it. He was the product of a public-school education from the other side of the border, or so his accent suggested.

Josh turned to his attention to a few songs to perfect some of the solos before Friday's gig. He hadn't been happy with what he'd played at the last rehearsal. The classical training and his eclectic tastes had allowed him to experiment with a variety of unusual progressions, but the short five-minute songs they'd rehearsed didn't normally allow the self-indulgent excursions into the unknown he sometimes played as a means of escape.

The chord sequences and harmonies were imprinted in his memory. He wanted to impress at Friday's gig, not just his fellow band members, but anyone with influence in the music business who might come to watch. He didn't want to have to rely on pleasing pupils' awkward families. Once recognition of his talent was established, he knew he'd have more freedom to experiment.

He made sure he finished his practice before his neighbours complained. A young family with a small baby lived upstairs, and playing any later would be considered antisocial. It was another reason he had to make an impression and secure a better future.

On the way home from the gig on Friday, Josh felt delighted with how the band had performed. It was a cohesive unit and had the potential to attract the interest of someone influential in the music industry.

"When are we going to see your new violin? Mind you, you gave the old one some stick tonight, a bit different to Monday," Chris said, breaking the silence.

"I've still got to play it in, get used to it before I try it out on the public."

"The old one sounded good."

"Yes, the PA's very forgiving."

He arrived at his flat before midnight, not too late for a good night's sleep before work the next morning. But as he lay in bed, he thought about Sean's violin. It still played on his mind.

CHAPTER FIVE

Monday, 12 October, 2009

Josh's telephone rang as he arrived home from work. Although it was a withheld number, he answered it, believing it was Mrs. Francis, confirming the time of Sean's next lesson.

"Siwmae, pwy sy'n galw?" He usually responded in Welsh to anonymous callers, asking who was calling. He hadn't been brought up to speak Welsh but had decided to learn its basics since he'd returned to South Wales. He'd realised it would be advantageous if he wanted some work with the local television and radio companies. Why shouldn't he answer in this manner?

"Is that Josh Stoller? Don't you speak English? Sean won't be with you for a lesson next Wednesday. He won't be available."

Intrigued to be speaking to Sean's stepfather, however rude he was, Josh hoped the conversation would continue and perhaps enlighten him about the violin's history.

"Oh, right, thanks for letting me know. How's he getting on with the Edward Elgar piece?"

"Fine." The phone went dead. Josh was taken aback by the manner of the call. He'd not met anyone in the small town who'd displayed such arrogance. However, since Sean had begun lessons with him, he now had to deal with a family whose members appeared to treat people differently. Mr. Francis, if that was his name, must have been a proficient musician if he owned a Hoing violin.

Although the man's accent gave the impression of a refined background, his brusque manner lacked finesse. Maybe he regarded part-time musicians beneath him. Josh had often experienced the attitude they should give their services for free or at least for a minimal sum. His band had often turned down gigs when an acceptable fee hadn't been agreed. He hoped the meagre ten pounds he charged for Sean's lesson wouldn't be compromised.

His mobile phone rang again within minutes. His mother's name appeared on the display. "You don't normally ring on Mondays. Is everything okay?"

"I just wanted to let you know we've had a visitor this afternoon. Someone you used to know. Your old girlfriend, Bethan Williams. She wondered how you were."

The mention of her name took Josh by surprise.

"She's looking well, been teaching back in Swansea for years. Settled down and married now."

Josh had not seen or heard from Bethan for over nine years. He'd been attracted to her as a teenager. Their paths had also crossed in Cardiff, as they had in London some years later. She'd been one of a few girls who had penetrated his guarded persona, but they'd parted on bad terms. She wasn't a person he had any enthusiasm about meeting again. He remembered how she'd treated him.

"She called in to see us. Just wanted to be remembered to you. We told her you were working near Cardiff. She was pleased you were okay."

"Did she say she'd call again?"

"No, she didn't mention it. She was up this way for a meeting of some sort. Anyway, I promised her I'd let you know she'd called to see us. You busy?"

"Non-stop, I've got a rehearsal soon. Give Dad my regards. I've got to go now, Mum. Sorry, I can't stay on any longer. Chris will be here any minute."

He turned off his phone, packed his violin in its case, and waited for his lift. Memories of his relationship with Bethan flooded back in the silence as he waited. She was married. Of course, she would be. Her affections had been directed elsewhere the fateful summer of the Millennium year, and he'd lost touch with her. He'd attempted to blot her out and had pushed the memories of their relationship to the back of his mind. If he did think about her, it was always with an element of animosity.

Josh was in a pensive mood when Chris arrived. He made no conversation for the duration of the twenty-minute journey with memories from his past on his mind. Apart from learning new pieces for the band, his concentration level slipped from time to time, and he forgot on a few occasions to play what had been arranged.

As Chris drove him back to his flat, he asked him if he had any other worries.

"Not really, just someone I never expected to hear from called in at my parents this afternoon."

"Your past turning up?"

"Sort of, a past girlfriend."

"Seems to have thrown you. I assume she was important at one time."

"Very."

"Where does she live?"

"Swansea."

"Do you want to see her again?"

Josh didn't answer.

Chris continued. "Bridges are meant for burning. Last week a violin you thought might have been yours. Now a girl who was. If you ever need to talk . . ." He glanced at Josh and then back to the road.

Chris had recognised Josh's introverted character within weeks of his joining the band. Apart from his enthusiasm for music, Josh often appeared distant. Once or twice, they'd discussed his ability to take improvisations to a higher spiritual level. Josh had maintained his ideas were wholly cerebral. He didn't adhere to the belief a higher being controlled him. Cynical about such things, he found music to be an intellectual abstraction to take him from the reality of his life whenever he felt it necessary.

Memories of his time with Bethan manifested themselves as he attempted to sleep. As he lay awake, he remembered the good times as well as the bad. Every so often, he'd look over at his digital clock and watch the minutes flip over. He turned onto his back to stare up at the ceiling and blame himself for not having forgiven her. There were too many what-ifs to allow him to relax and sleep. The street light illuminated his room and disturbed him. He hadn't noticed it before.

The following day was his half-day off from work. He left the shop at twelve to catch a train into Cardiff, where he wandered around some of the music shops. He often played some of the instruments to the delight of the shop owners. When he demonstrated his skills, other customers would often stop to listen and then buy something on his recommendation.

This particular Tuesday, he looked for music he used to play in the youth orchestra as a teenager. It reminded him of times with Bethan. Since she'd reappeared, his melancholic side began to manifest itself. In an earlier time, his solace would have come from a bottle, but not anymore. It wasn't worth the risk. He knew he should take heed of Chris' advice about burning bridges. Although, he'd done so after most other failed relationships. Bethan had been different. Their parting had been a painful experience.

A teenage pupil arrived for a lesson at seven o'clock and Josh had to repeat the basic fingering he'd taught the previous week. Josh concealed his frustration with difficulty.

He spent the remainder of the evening rehearsing pieces for the band until he felt satisfied — the violin mute, a useful accessory. His classical training dictated he should practise until he didn't get it wrong, so he could be relied on to augment the band's cohesive attack.

On Wednesday evening he played through the pieces he'd bought the previous day. Sean's cancellation had meant no preparations had to be made. He kept telling himself to forget Bethan. It was easier said than done. How dare she intrude into his life!

CHAPTER SIX

Earlier in the summer of 2009

The visiting room of Swansea Prison was full. Prisoners, deep in discussion with either long suffering partners or hopeful mothers, were eager to make physical contact. But warders watched their every move, vigilant in their observations to prevent the smuggling of illicit goods for later use.

Likewise, Tom Parker faced his cousin Julian. Tom was still intent to exact his revenge on the people who'd caused his incarceration, even after nine years. His violent streak, however, had resulted in an extension to his sentence. He should have been free two years earlier, but his altercation with a warder resulted in an increase in his sentence. Not even his father's influence could guarantee any clemency after too many incidents.

His cousin, Julian, visited him regularly in this, his final year. Julian's tall, confident frame displayed an adherence to regular exercise and the appearance of being nurtured in an affluent environment.

Tom, a good fifteen centimetres shorter, but no less athletic in appearance, was impatient to hear Julian's intentions for the future, with his release imminent. Due out at the end of the month, Tom was anxious to find out the location of the two people they continually suspected of being responsible for his arrest. He hoped his cousin had some news about them. Whether their suspicions were correct or not, they didn't care. There had been too many unexplained coincidences before Tom Parker's arrest.

"You've still got their phone numbers? Have you found them yet?" he asked.

"They're safe. His old mobile's no longer available, but I had his parents' number. I got hold of his mother last week. It was too easy."

"What about the girl's?"

"Not yet. Just stay calm. We don't want you serving extra time, do we? You can sort it out once you've been released."

"Does he still live in London?"

"No, he's in the Cardiff area. Not in music any longer, which is perfect for what I have in mind. When I spoke to his mother, I pretended to be an ex-colleague and promised him orchestral work in the Midlands. She was so gullible, she told me where he worked. Said she'd phone him as soon as I'd finished the call. She even gave me his new number. I'll move down to find him and then use him to find the bitch."

"My father owns property north of Cardiff. Give him a call."

"I know. I'll sort it out tonight. Where he works might prove useful as well." Tom understood the comment didn't require further explanation for the time being.

He returned to his cell, confident his revenge would be easier than he'd anticipated. His cousin wouldn't be under any suspicion. Other people were always paid to carry out Julian's wishes.

Julian made the planned move to a village north of Cardiff. Once settled, he began to explore the surrounding area to discover more about the person he wanted to find.

One afternoon in September, he visited a newsagent in the town where the musician lived. An advert on a pin-board behind the counter attracted his attention — one he knew would interest his partner. Several days later, he suggested she should visit the shop to buy a magazine under the pretence he wanted to find out more about the area. He knew everything else would fall into place.

CHAPTER SEVEN

Initial Attractions

1985 to 1993

Josh grew up in a small town on the outskirts of Swansea. Violin lessons available at school gave him a reason to escape to his bedroom, to practise at every opportunity, much to the discomfort of his parents.

An only child, he found the attention they showered upon him claustrophobic. The instrument proved to be the correct choice for him. It felt second nature to him to place his fingers in the correct position on the fingerboard. Whether it was his innate skills as a quick learner or his natural ear and intuition, he never did find out. It didn't bother him. His fluidity on the instrument impressed his teacher, and he raced through his exams, with distinction, by the time he was fourteen.

Neither of his parents demonstrated an interest in music apart from his father's claimed love of his heavy metal albums and his mother's odd collection of country music, both of which gathered more dust than appreciation at home.

With money Josh saved from a paper round, he bought a cheap acoustic guitar to learn chord progressions with the help of Owen, one of his friends. They met on a regular basis at Owen's house where they practised and explored different styles of music. Josh felt comfortable in the environment. His friend's father, Tony, a local jazz musician, encouraged the two teenagers. He'd recognised Josh's gift for music.

At fifteen, Josh began playing in the Swansea schools' youth orchestra. The rehearsals were held several miles from his home, so that he was obliged to travel by bus. This embarrassed him, as all his fellow players were escorted and collected by their parents.

He took his place next to Bethan Williams, an attractive brunette almost his height who appeared more than pleased to welcome him. Only one of two young males in the string section, his inclusion aroused her interest. Impressed with his musical skills and self-effacing personality, she appeared happy to invade his personal space in a tactile manner when they spoke.

He hadn't experienced this approach from anyone of the opposite sex before, and his adolescent hormones raced around his body. He'd never developed a close friendship with any girls at school and was unsure how to react. This male-female interaction was a new experience for him and left him both exhilarated and confused.

However, Bethan had another admirer, Tom Parker, a cellist. Tom was confident with both contemporaries and tutors alike, an attractive feature to impressionable adolescents. He wanted Bethan and saw himself as the odds-on winner in the competition.

Tom often took advantage of his perceived social superiority and would say. "It's one of those cheap eastern European ones isn't it, Josh? I'm amazed how good you make it sound." Unsure if it was a compliment, Josh didn't respond. He wasn't used to sarcasm.

Another comment from Tom, however, touched a nerve.

"Hope you don't mind me saying, but it'll never sound good, Josh. Doesn't matter how hard you try." His pulse raced, and he wanted to react, to leave the cellist on the floor feeling sorry for himself, but as a newcomer, he didn't want to alienate the staff. Any aggressive response and he would be forced to leave the orchestra. The staff appeared wary of Tom.

After one such derogatory comment from Tom, Josh asked his parents if they would to help him buy a new violin of superior quality. He'd delivered newspapers for three years and through his frugality, had saved over four hundred pounds, but persuading his parents to help him buy a new instrument proved difficult. For several weeks, he persevered with his old violin, irrespective of the barbed comments he endured at most rehearsals.

Eventually, they agreed to match Josh's savings. When added to the value of his old violin, it was enough to buy a new one worth one thousand pounds.

The music shop assistant recognised Josh's skills as soon as he tried various instruments and suggested he try one being sold for another customer. The instrument, a sixty-year-old hand-made violin, felt perfect in his hands. The tone suited his ability.

The assistant allowed Josh plenty of time to make his decision, delighted to hear the youngster play. Other customers stopped looking for their intended purchases to listen to him. They, too, appreciated his musicianship. Eventually, pleased with the instrument's tone, Josh demonstrated his enthusiasm to buy it.

"I like this one," he said.

"You've made a good choice. I've not heard any in this shop sound like that before. It seems made for you."

Josh became the proud owner of a Hoing violin. This should shut Tom Parker's mouth. His improved confidence was evident to everyone in the orchestra. In his hands, the instrument responded as though an extension of his dextrous fingers. It obeyed each command without hesitation or question.

Bethan's increased interest in Josh was evident to Tom. She wanted to play this new violin at every opportunity, her own instrument a quarter of its value. She desired it and would flatter him and his musicianship to allow her access to the instrument.

As Tom Parker hadn't commented on his new violin, Josh believed the cellist's attitude towards him had changed. At one rehearsal, Tom invited him to a party at his home in The Mumbles, an affluent area of Swansea.

"Come down next Saturday afternoon. Get the bus. I can meet you. Others from the orchestra will be here. So will Bethan. You get on well with her."

Josh, aware of Tom's affluent background, felt apprehensive about attending, but as Bethan had also been invited, he assumed this would be an opportunity to get to know her better.

Tom promised to meet him at the bus, but when Josh arrived, he could see no sign of Tom. A passer-by directed him to the correct street, where he saw a different world than the one he knew. He counted the ascending even numbers as he passed each house. Expensive cars in immaculate paved driveways. Their headlamps appeared to glare at him in a judgemental manner. Josh began to regret agreeing to meet up with Tom Parker. He now understood why the cellist displayed an annoying level of confidence.

The house he assumed belonged to Tom's family appeared to be a bigger property than the others in the street and failed to have a number on either of the gate's pillars. Only a name, Manor House, was engraved in brass mounted onto one of the pillars. He hesitated at the closed gate, wondering if the invite had been a cruel hoax. As he pushed open the intricate metal side gate, he spotted a large car outside the front door.

The sun lit up the front windows, but their vertical blinds were closed, so he couldn't look in as he walked toward the door. Although he could hear the chime when he pressed the doorbell, he heard no movement in response. He checked his watch, waited for a minute, and rang again. No-one answered.

He turned to retrace his steps to the gates, suspecting he'd been tricked. As he did so, he saw the two larger ones open. A car was waiting to come onto the drive.

As soon as it had stopped, he saw Tom get out from the passenger side. Bethan emerged from the rear, and an attractive blonde woman, who appeared to be in her mid-forties, stepped out onto the driveway.

"This is Josh from the orchestra. Josh, this is my mother," Tom said. The woman smiled without emotion and Josh went to shake her hand, which she offered with little expression and even less to say. She led the way to the door. It was the last time Josh saw her.

A familiarity between Tom and Bethan Josh hadn't noticed before made him feel even more insecure. Josh wondered if the invite had been made to put him in his place regarding Bethan.

Tom led both to what Josh assumed was the living room. Josh stared at the expensive furnishings. A large oriental rug he estimated would have cost thousands of pounds lay on the solid oak floor.

Bethan sat on a large three-seater settee, and Tom moved beside her before Josh could. The closeness Tom and Bethan displayed became even more obvious than before. Josh found a place on a two-seater and looked about the room, wishing he could be somewhere else. He stumbled through a variety of topics he thought would allow his acceptance until Tom spoke

"I've got some stuff here. Do you smoke?"

Bethan's eyes lit up.

Josh had never considered smoking marijuana, wary of the

outcome. Some of the lads at school had tried grass a few times, but like his parents, he'd not even smoked cigarettes.

"What about your mother?" Josh asked.

"Oh, she's busy. She'll be upstairs."

"Your dad?"

"He's at and won't be back until seven at least. I'll just roll up a couple of spliffs, and we'll go down to the beach and smoke them."

Josh looked on with a mixture of nervousness and interest as Tom took a record sleeve from a shelf and put some cigarette papers and a packet of cigarettes on it.

"I've never smoked. What do I do?" Josh whispered.

"Don't worry, I'll show you," Bethan said as she turned to face him. "I've done it before."

The three went to the beach, where they found a secluded spot. With little chance of discovery, Tom lit up the first and passed it to Josh. With encouragement from Bethan, he managed to inhale the smoke, but not without a great deal of coughing Tom looked on, amused by Josh's efforts.

Bethan took her turn when Tom told her. To Josh, neither he nor Tom appeared affected by the dope, but he saw the drug's effect on Bethan, who'd become withdrawn. Her behaviour was the complete opposite to what she'd displayed before.

Once they'd finished the third joint, they walked back to the house. Josh realised how much the drug had affected Bethan and took her arm to support her. Tom led the way, ignoring the pair who lagged behind. When they arrived back at the house, neither of Tom's parents appeared to be at home. The car in which his mother had arrived earlier had gone, as had the other vehicle.

"You okay, Bethan?" It was all he could think to say, as they sat together on the settee.

"Fine, Josh, I'm fine," she said, appearing frustrated with his naivety. Bethan's slurred response led to his confusion about her. It prompted him to wish again that he'd not agreed to attend the party.

Within minutes of them reaching the house, a number of Tom's school friends arrived. Josh noticed several of these whispering and looking in his direction. Josh suspected he was the object of ridicule. This situation was alien to him.

Someone said, "I've got a bottle of tequila in my bag. Have you got the dope?" Tom took out a plastic bag from a rucksack. It contained a large block that turned out to be cannabis resin. He led everyone to the kitchen, where he placed it on a table. He heated a sharp knife on the hob's gas flame and cut the cannabis into several smaller blocks. Several youngsters took cash from their pockets to give to him in exchange for the smaller blocks.

Josh estimated about four to five hundred pounds had changed hands. To be in the presence of someone who demanded this amount of money in a matter of minutes added to his annoyance. It had taken him three years to save the same amount to put toward his treasured instrument.

After the dope had been distributed, the youngsters began to roll joints, heating up the resin to mix with tobacco. The rooms were soon filled with the sweet smell of cannabis.

Josh realised he'd been invited to be embarrassed in front of Bethan. He returned to Bethan's side, but she remained distant, and he continued to find it difficult to make conversation with her.

Thirsty from the smoke clouding the room, he returned to the kitchen to get a drink. Someone offered him a joint at the back door, but he declined. When he returned to his seat, Bethan had disappeared.

"She went somewhere with Tom," someone said in response to his question regarding her whereabouts.

He continued to feel uncomfortable, and went upstairs to look for a toilet, to be on his own, to gather his thoughts. As he walked past one of the bedrooms, a muffled noise came from behind the partly open door. He heard Bethan's voice and pushed it open. He wanted to speak to her but didn't realise what he would witness.

Tom and Bethan were in an embrace on the bed, her skirt up around her waist and his trousers around his knees. Two pairs of hands caressing bare flesh left nothing to the imagination. She looked up to see who had disturbed them, and through the haze that must have been her state of mind, saw Josh in the doorway.

"Oh, Josh, what are you doing here? I'm sorry. Tom what's happening?" she slurred. Tom had also turned around to reveal himself. "What are you fucking doing in here? Piss off."

Josh slammed the door and raced downstairs. Upset, his emotions in turmoil, he had to get away. He searched through his pockets for money for the bus to get home, but in his panic, failed to find enough. He thought he'd have to walk, a journey that would take hours. He looked around for a phone and found one by the front door. He didn't care if Tom would try to stop him using it. To his relief, his father agreed to collect him.

He left the house before anyone had noticed and walked to the seafront. His father collected him half an hour later. As they drove home, Josh claimed he felt unwell.

CHAPTER EIGHT

Josh's Frustration

1993

Josh and Owen had developed a repertoire of songs and entertained at the local rugby club most Friday nights. On the nights they played, Josh stay over with his friend.

Friday nights in the club were quiet affairs and normally a safe atmosphere. Team members enjoyed a quiet night out with their partners and limited themselves to low levels of alcohol in preparation for Saturday's matches.

On one such evening, two weeks after the incident at Tom's party, Josh almost had a disaster with his treasured instrument and another side of his personality reared its head. He and Owen had begun their second set when a funeral party entered the club. A member of the community had died, and mourners from the wake appeared determined to drown their sorrows. It was evident an excessive amount of drinking had already taken place.

The party of ten or so hardened drinkers, who seemed to have lost control of their senses, drifted into the club and invaded the barroom to disturb the audience. They staggered in a rowdy manner toward the bar as Josh was developing a solo on his violin, lost in the improvisation.

Needless shouts from some of the incomers, directed toward the stage, cast a shadow on the atmosphere. The music all but stopped. Josh relaxed his hold on the bow and placed it at his side as Owen continued to strum his guitar but without any emotion. Josh walked over to the case and put his violin away, the tension rising inside him. Neither he nor Owen had experienced any form of criticism or heckling before.

Before anyone had a chance to intervene, Josh shouted, "Who the fuck do you think you are?" The sheltered environment of an orchestra hadn't prepared him for this lack of finesse and ignorance. The room erupted into a blaze of anger and heated tempers. One of the drunken mourners, caught up in the emotion of the day, turned on Josh.

"What's so special about you? You bastard!"

The man walked towards Josh and grabbed his shirt. He ripped it off and threw Josh to the floor. In an instant the room erupted. One of the young women moved toward the stage and picked up the violin in its case and gave it to the barman to store behind the bar.

Owen put down his guitar at the rear of the small stage and leapt onto the back of Josh's attacker but was thrown off. One of the drunks aimed a kick at Josh and caught his hand, jamming it between his boot and the leg of a table. Several of the members intervened to protect the teenagers. Gary Thomas, recently retired from the game, picked up one of the drunks and wrapped his hand around the man's throat. His feet dangled as if suspended from a hangman's noose. Gary's hand ensured no sound could be made.

"Unless you lot get out now, this one stays here until his last breath. Got it?" he shouted. The other drunks stopped, unsure about the seriousness of the threat. Gary released his grip, and the body crumpled to the floor. He picked up the near lifeless shape by the scruff and held him eyeball to eyeball.

"Get and stay out. These are youngsters who are entertaining us. If you had one hundredth of their talent, you could be regarded as human. You're supposed to be mourning Billy

Jones. It looks more like an excuse for a piss-up. Have some respect." Gary dropped the man onto his backside again, and one of the man's friends helped him to his feet.

The mourners left in a subdued manner, but Josh remained on the floor and nursed his right hand. He stared at the blood running down the palm from cuts on two of his fingers. "I can't move them." His nose and lips were bleeding, but his concern centred on the injury to his hand. The barman produced some ice cubes from the freezer, wrapped them in a towel, and placed the compress on the injury.

"I'm so sorry, I caused all this didn't I?" Josh sobbed, "I didn't mean it."

"It's all right son. What's your dad's number? We'll ring him to get you home," Gary said.

Josh's father arrived within fifteen minutes, and Gary suggested Josh should have his hand examined at the hospital.

Once Josh and his father had left, Gary approached Owen and commented on Josh's outburst.

"Never seen him lose it He never even swears. About the only one who doesn't, not even when it's just us lads."

"They were out of order, Owen."

"He never loses it. Something's not right."

"I noticed he seemed quiet earlier. He just wanted to play his violin and looked as if he was away with the fairies. He hasn't taken anything has he?"

"No, I'm sure of it. Sometimes you can't get through to him. Worse lately."

CHAPTER NINE

Summer 1993

The youth orchestra resumed its rehearsals after the Easter break, but neither Tom nor Bethan attended for several weeks. Josh's hand recovered, but his pride didn't.

Another musician, Susan Ellis, from the woodwind section, noticed both Bethan's absence and Josh's return to his unassuming nature. She was opposite to Bethan, blonde, petite, and far less tactile. Susan appeared happy to take her time to get to know him. Josh was glad someone from the opposite sex was demonstrating an interest in him, and they agreed to exchange contact details.

The incident at the party continued to haunt him, and he wondered how far he wanted his emotions to lead him with Susan. In his confusion, Bethan still held a greater attraction. When she returned to the youth orchestra, Susan made a point of approaching Josh before he had a chance to speak to Bethan. She made sure he spent time in her company during breaks in the rehearsals. Bethan could only look on in embarrassment. She regretted the incident at Tom's party, aware he had taken advantage of her.

When Tom Parker returned, he ignored Bethan. Josh had no idea if this was merely to annoy her. He had neither the inclination nor the opportunity to offer her any sympathy.

As he grew more secure with Susan, his relationship with her intensified. They began to see each other on a regular basis. Her interest in literature and poetry fascinated him, and he often asked her to write lyrics to his compositions.

A folk music festival held in a neighbouring town every summer attracted musicians from different parts of the world. Josh was eager to attend, having been introduced to the eclectic styles played there by Owen's father. He and Susan agreed to visit the festival with Owen, and his girlfriend had arranged to camp on the festival field over the weekend. Owen, aware where Josh and Susan's relationship was leading, advised his friend to buy a pack of condoms.

Josh and Susan slept in their tent, but were both unsure how to approach this next level of intimacy. Their first night together, they agreed to rearrange the sleeping bags to allow them to sleep together. Susan confirmed she'd not had sex with anyone before, which allowed to Josh to relax and admit neither had he.

They both returned to the orchestra in September and demonstrated their affection for each other openly. Even though Josh and Bethan played in the same section of the orchestra, they maintained a mutual silence. In the privacy of his bedroom however, he still thought about her.

In the final year of their A levels, Josh still failed to get Bethan off his mind. To release his frustration, he played his beloved violin for hours, improvising in the wildest manner possible.

CHAPTER TEN

September 1995 to Spring 1996

Both Josh and Susan moved to Cardiff to begin their higher education, he to the college of music and she to study English at the university. Susan could quote Keats and Shakespeare with confidence and discuss the themes and plots of Joseph Conrad's books with authority. Although their relationship continued, he made excuses not to see her as regularly as she'd hoped, mainly due to his enthusiasm for his course. He wanted to take advantage of every opportunity to play with a variety of musicians he met. Secretly, however, in the back of his mind, he wondered if he'd bump into Bethan. Consequently, his relationship with Susan became strained, and they bickered when they did meet. With his head in the clouds, he soaked up the demands of his studies, eager to learn from all around him. He no longer felt insecure in the company of the more privileged.

Josh's accent became less an identity of his background, and he adopted a more pseudo-refined manner to communicate with his peers. Although his violin had placed a financial demand on him and his parents, he wished for a more expensive one, to keep up with some of the students he came across at the college.

One Saturday afternoon he and Susan arranged to meet in a café in one of the arcades near the castle. On his way, he bought a book on Stephan Grappelli's *Hot Club of Paris* violin and arrived twenty minutes earlier than agreed to browse through the book. Although the café was full, he ordered a coffee in the hope he could find a spare seat. When he turned around with book and coffee in hand, he saw Bethan alone at a table. She smiled at him, and he joined her without hesitation.

"What are you doing in Cardiff?" he asked, as he sat next to her.

"I'm training to be a teacher. It's what I always wanted to do. I didn't want to stay in Swansea and study. I'd have probably lived at home with my parents. It would have been the only option had I stayed there. I suppose you're studying music. You were always going to."

"Yes, at the music college."

"You seem to have changed, lost your accent a bit, trying to impress Susan. Don't think she'll swallow it though. You're still with her, I take it. What's she doing?"

"She's in the Uni, studying English. We see each other from time to time."

He didn't want to make it obvious they were still in a relationship. Seeing Bethan changed his focus of attention that afternoon, and he forgot about the arrangement to meet up with Susan.

"I know we haven't spoken for a while, and I'm sorry for what happened at the party. I didn't know what I was doing, and when I went downstairs, I couldn't find you. You'd gone. I tried to talk to you in the orchestra, but you avoided me every time, and then you and Susan became an item. Tom was a real bastard, you know. He was jealous because you're such a good musician. We didn't do it anyway. I think the dope had affected me more than it had you, but I came to my senses and realised what was happening. He tried to get my knickers off. Suddenly you were in the doorway. It stopped him."

She didn't allow Josh to comment. He assumed she needed to explain her actions.

"He was so angry. I thought that stuff was supposed to calm you down. I phoned my mum, and she came to get me. Parker was such a shit. He just ignored me when we were next in the orchestra and got off with someone else. He told me I was too much of a prude. Bastard."

Her hand reached out to touch his. The sensation was warm, and they stood without a word, leaving their unfinished coffees on the table. As they walked through Bute Park, she placed her arm through his. He didn't resist.

They turned and looked at each other and embraced.

No longer angry, he said, "Hindsight is a marvellous thing."

"What do you mean?"

"If I'd hit him then, it would all have been better."

"Josh?"

"I'd assumed you'd been a willing accomplice. I thought your hands were all over him. His trousers were around his knees. He couldn't have got up to protect himself, could he?"

Bethan said no more about the incident as they walked toward her hall of residence.

They stayed in her room all afternoon, where the sex was passionate. For a few hours, they were unable to resist each other's bodies, touching, probing, and satisfying each other. He hadn't taken any precautions, and she, caught up in the excitement of the moment, hadn't insisted.

Once he left Bethan's room, he remembered the arrangement to meet Susan and made for her flat. He concocted an excuse, but when he arrived Susan was prepared for him.

"Where were you today? We were supposed to meet in the arcade at three."

"Oh, sorry, Sue. I forgot. I went to the music shop and saw someone on my—Shit, where did I put the book I bought?"

"Yes, you did forget. I asked in the café if they'd seen you. The girl behind the counter recognised you. She said you'd left in a hurry with someone, a girl. Well, is it true?"

"She must have been mistaken."

"This yours? You left it in the café in the bag in your hurry to go, you bastard."

"But Sue."

"You liar. Who is she?"

He'd expected criticism for not meeting her as arranged, but to have been found out hadn't crossed his mind.

The relationship ended. Both Josh and Susan knew it would have been pointless to continue. He wasn't upset. He'd treated her as a convenient alternative to Bethan, and hadn't allowed himself to become too close. Josh discovered many years later, she'd remained angry and bitter. She'd wasted two and a half years of her youth.

Spring/Summer 1996

Abortions put a strain on the closest of relationships. Bethan and Josh had difficulty maintaining any level of friendship with each other afterward, even though they continued to see each other for several weeks.

He failed to support her, reluctant to make a commitment. He'd never had to make one to anybody on their terms before. Without siblings, he had difficulty empathising with others, and his selfish streak became evident due to the stress of the situation. His behaviour and attitude towards her endorsed this.

The future with him was pointless, even though the ambivalence of her feelings for him churned away inside her. They had both taken advantage of the situation without any forethought. When she needed him most, he ignored her predicament, in spite of the magnet that pulled them to each other. What she'd hoped would have been a mutual empathy didn't materialise, and the relationship ended.

In his lucid phases, for the remainder of the first year, Josh had several short-term relationships. They lasted at most a fortnight, some just a day or two, others less. He wasn't any more selfish than many of his contemporaries, just immature.

From time to time, he dabbled in concoctions of stimulating substances and alcohol, which when mixed together, would leave him less than effective for days. Severe vomiting and excruciating headaches amused his fellow students. Jealous of his prestigious talent and his former popularity, they were in no hurry to help him reform his habits. His appearance deteriorated, and instead of a trendy scruffiness, he displayed an unkempt appearance.

One night while out in a drunken state, Josh saw Susan with several of her friends in a bar. He approached her to be sociable, but she wasn't interested and ignored him. A bouncer intervened as he continued to pester her, and he found himself in a heap on the pavement outside.

The following morning, he heard several loud knocks on his bedroom door. He heard his housemate Pete's voice.

"Are you awake, Josh? Someone's here to see you." Without warning his door flew open. He propped his head up against his pillow and saw Liz, a fellow student at his college he'd arranged to meet the previous night.

"Where the hell were you? We were supposed to be meeting at eight. You obviously had better things to do. At least, you've got no-one else in your bed."

Although his head ached from the effects of the previous night's excesses, his body hurt as if he'd been in a fight. He managed to get out of bed to reach for his filthy jeans. As he searched through his pockets, he saw his wallet on the floor.

Liz noticed bruises on his thighs. "God, what happened to you? Have you been mugged?"

"I don't know."

She eased off his T-shirt and laid him back on his bed.

"You'd better have a shower."

"In a minute."

"No, now. You're filthy as well." She pulled him up and pushed him toward the bathroom.

Within ten minutes, he staggered back and lay on the bed.

"Get up, you stupid bastard. You're a mess. Dry yourself and put some clothes on. He got dressed as she looked on. Impatient with him, she said, "You and I aren't going to get on, are we? You're totally unreliable, and you drink too much as well as everything else you shove down your throat."

Although he protested his innocence, she said, "Don't look at me pretending you don't know what I mean. I remember when you came to Cardiff last September. You were different. You were pleasant. I also found out about you and the girl from the teachers' training department last night, the way you treated her. You're not going to earn you many points in the bedroom stakes. Thank God you haven't been able to get it up with me yet. You're a shit disaster, and unless you change, you'll always be a disaster. I'm off."

"Liz, come on, I meant to see you last night, but I don't know what happened. Look at me, I might have been mugged."

"Liar, you were pissed. You stink like a brewery. Anyone would think you've had a burglary in here. See you around."

"Why did you come around?"

"To tell you to get lost," she said and slammed the door.

He sat alone in his room unable to work out how he'd got home in the drunken state his hangover confirmed. After ten minutes contemplating the depths to which he'd sunk, he pushed himself up and gathered the mess from the floor.

He descended the stairs, dragging a bag of dirty clothes after him and left it in the hallway before going into the kitchen. As he opened the door, he saw Pete placing a pizza on his plate.

"She didn't stay?" asked Josh.

"Of course not. What do you expect? I found you on the doorstep, totally off your head, rambling on about Susan, and Bethan, you dick. Just leave them alone. They're not interested." He wasn't interested in Josh either and walked into the living room with his food to join Marc, who also shared the house.

The term was due to finish two weeks later, and spending a few months at home in Swansea appeared to be a good idea. His housemates had distanced themselves from him, and he needed to get away, to hopefully catch up with old friends. However, as he'd not bothered to keep in touch with them over the year in Cardiff, he wondered if they'd want to resume their friendship.

He needed an escape from his indulgences, in preparation for the beginning of the new academic year. Otherwise, his precocious talent would be wasted. He looked at his hands. His fingers could produce a quality of tone most others only dreamt of achieving. Too much time had been spent attempting to escape from his emotional immaturity.

One evening Josh called at Owen's house, but his friend was out. Owen's father, Tony, was pleased to see his son's friend and invited him in.

"Owen's gone to practise with his band," he said. "They're coming on well and have made quite a name for themselves in the Swansea area. They've got a date to record some of their songs for a CD. How are things in Cardiff?"

"It's good. I'm learning lots of new techniques and music by different composers and enjoying some of Bach's lesser known music."

"Have you come across Jacques Loussier? He plays Bach's music in a jazz style. You should listen out for him. I've got some of his stuff on CD. I'll just put it on."

After several minutes just listening to the music, Josh began to feel uncomfortable with the lack of conversation. He made an excuse to leave and stood. Tony picked up the remote control and turned down the volume.

"Sit down, boy. What's happened to you? Cardiff hasn't done you any good has it?"

Josh feigned ignorance but didn't protest.

Tony, an astute character, added, "Look at you, listen to yourself, you don't sound like you used to. You're very talented, but it's gone to your head. Who the hell are you mixing with? I know some of the lecturers, and they've been looking out for you. I don't like what they're saying. You've managed to get yourself involved in things you shouldn't. I've seen it before, too many times, and don't pretend you don't know what I mean. If your mum and dad found out, they'd be mortified. Don't disappoint them."

Josh listened to a number of home truths before Tony drove him home.

"Spend this holiday thinking about what I've said," was Tony's parting shot.

Tony's observation convinced Josh he should keep away from the indulgences that had blighted his first year in university.

Josh worked in a pub over the summer break, but he was determined to stay sober, for fear of losing his job. His studies the following year had to be funded, and loans were limited. He only saw his old school friends a few times and spent his free time catching up on the practice he'd ignored due to his excesses.

Josh's housemates arranged to meet up with him, to tidy their accommodation over the summer break, in preparation for the second year. All three had decided to stay in the house to save the inconvenience of moving. However, Pete and Marc had become apprehensive about the arrangement toward the end of the summer term. Josh's self-destructive habits caused them some concern. They both enjoyed a few beers, but excesses, other than alcohol, were habits they veered away from.

They were relieved to see the improvement in Josh's sobriety and spent the whole of the morning cleaning the house. At lunch time, the three went to the local pub for a sandwich and a pint, where they discussed their future plans for the second year and beyond. By seven, the house was the tidiest it had been since the previous September. Once they'd finished, they visited their local for a final drink.

During the day, Josh had found some grass in his bedroom and had put it to one side. On their return to the house that evening, he rolled up a joint in the silence of his room and tiptoed downstairs to go to the garden to smoke it. Hoping Marc and Pete wouldn't hear him, he closed the back door he lit-up.

Each time he inhaled, he reflected on Tony's advice, but again, he was indulging in substances which contributed to his distorted frame of mind. The more he thought about the two girls who'd entered his life, the more muddled his mind became. In his introspective mood, he contemplated his lifestyle. His ambition to become a professional musician had to be his primary aim. Once he finished the joint, he flicked the cardboard filter into the hedge. He assumed it would be lost in the foliage.

After a disturbed night, deep in thought about his future, he decided to throw away the remainder of his dope. He placed the remaining drug paraphernalia into a plastic bag and walked to a shop at the end of the street to buy some milk.

As he reached the shop, he pushed the bag as far as he could into a near-full bin outside. He hoped it wouldn't spring back. Somehow, it didn't overflow, and he left it to go into the shop.

As he came out, he saw the bag on the floor. He chose to ignore it and looked along each direction of the pavement. In one he saw two policemen walk toward him. He turned the other way and began walking toward his house.

"Excuse me, sir." he heard. He stopped and turned around. The two officers stood ten metres away, facing him.

"I believe you tried to push this rubbish into the bin, which was obviously too full, sir," one said, pointing at the bag on the pavement. "Pick it up and place it in another one. You'll find another about two streets away, unless you take it home. I take it you live around here. Student are you?"

"It's a bit of rubbish we had in the house. We're only here for a day or two tidying up, and the bins aren't collected until Monday."

"Then find another bin. This one's full."

Josh picked up the bag, now greasy, and carried it back to the house. Once there, he ran upstairs to wash his hands and find another bag into which he placed the first. He hated the feel of grease or anything and wiped the bag with some toilet paper before joining his housemates downstairs.

Pete greeted him, but he didn't look pleased.

"Just been out to the garden to tidy and look what I found. Yours?" He held up the end of the joint Josh had flicked into the garden hedge the previous night.

"No, I don't do it anymore."

"You were outside last night, smoking." Marc added.

"Yes, but it was just tobacco, I bought in the corner shop on the way to the pub, remember?"

"What are you putting in the bag?" Pete asked.

"Just some more rubbish from upstairs. I'll put it all in a bin on the way to the station."

"Just make sure you do," Marc said.

The letting agent arrived at midday to inspect the house and confirmed he was happy for the students to continue living in the property for another year. Once he left, the three returned to their parents for the remainder of the summer. Josh, still jumpy after the morning's episode, was glad to leave Cardiff for the remainder of the holidays.

At home, he continued to work in the pub but failed to re-establish the camaraderie he'd had with his friends. Although he practised his violin every day, he failed to take his playing to emotional heights and satisfy his desire for improvement. His improvisations were mediocre, so he'd spend no more than ten minutes attempting, in frustration, to escape from his loneliness. Sometimes he blamed himself, but more often than not, he blamed his violin. It was a lump of wood. It would never change.

However, as time on his own progressed into September, he regained his enthusiasm and produced haunting melodies to escape his solitude. The improvements took him to danger-ous, unconventional places, but his ability allowed him to re-trace his steps by intuition, to discover suitable conclusions. After a satisfying journey into the maze of his complex imag-ination, he was pleased he possessed such a responsive in-strument and forgot his desire to emulate some of his fellow students. He didn't need them. He had his music, with which he could seal off outside influences.

CHAPTER ELEVEN

September 1996 to July 1998

Eager to begin his second year of study, to return to his course and to the inspiration the college would provide, he was determined to make a fresh start. The enthusiasm he demonstrated on his return to Cardiff was obvious to his tutors. The fusions of different types of music interested him. To explore the endless possibilities of improvisation would improve his skills even further. He trawled the local music shops to look for advertisements wanting musicians.

The attraction of live music in bars drew him in to explore the cosmopolitan mix of styles played in the city. His enthusiasm to join in the sessions with all ages of musicians, earned him the respect of the experienced stalwarts. He became adept at both improvisation and the disciplined compositions and finished his studies having gained a great deal of respect from his tutors, who were prepared to write impressive references.

Pete and Marc were happy to share the accommodation with him for the final two years of study, happy he'd reformed his lifestyle. They never understood Josh's personality, and accepted him as their eccentric third housemate, willing to pay his share of the rent on time. He maintained an emotional distance from them and, try as they might to understand him, they only got so far, and then a wall went up. He wasn't anybody's best friend and didn't regard anyone as his.

Josh did have one long-term relationship in his final year. One night, playing with a band in one of Cardiff's pubs, he was approached by a student intrigued with his musical ability. As a violinist, Vicky wanted to find out where his musical influences came from. They arranged to meet for a drink the following evening as they were both free, and a relationship began.

They appeared to care for each other and enjoyed each other's company whenever together, which became more and more frequent. For once he was contented. He'd found someone with whom he felt comfortable, somebody he put first. It was the first time he felt eager to discuss topics other than music. She would push her arm through his when out walking, and he would turn to face her and rub her cheeks with his fingers. When they spent their nights together, they slept facing each other, with one holding the other's hand. Josh was infatuated with her, and she appeared to be with him.

However, Vicky went home to Manchester once every month, where she had a long-term boyfriend. Josh accepted the arrangement, and when this occurred, he would make every effort to find an impromptu music session in a bar. Only once did he end up in someone else's bed.

One weekend, her boyfriend from Manchester visited her in Cardiff. Vicky took him to a pub, unaware Josh had been booked to play there with a jazz band. The situation created a few awkward moments. Although jealous at seeing the boyfriend, Josh coped and played as well as ever.

They met again on Monday, and Vicky's guilt was obvious. Although the arrangement had been an open one, Josh realised he did not want to be the other man any longer. He wanted her undivided attention, but what could he do?

"You knew about Nick. I've always been honest with you," she said.

"I didn't expect to see you two together. It was okay when he was at a distance. I could handle it. I didn't think I'd feel like this." Tears trickled down his cheeks. He walked out of his room, down the stairs, and out to the back yard, where he rolled up a joint from a small supply he'd recently bought.

Five minutes later, she appeared at his side. "I didn't think you cared so much, Josh, or is it about you?"

"What do you mean?"

"Well, you're pretty self-centred, or so I've been told by others who know you. I must admit I haven't seen that side of you."

"Who?"

"I met a girl in our bar at UWIC. Bethan . . ."

"It was two years ago, someone from home I'd met. There's more to it."

"Yes, she told me."

Josh felt protesting was futile. The dope had begun to affect his senses. He didn't want to hear any more.

"Let's go inside when I finish this. Do you want some?"

This was a habit they shared from time to time, especially after Vicky's trips to Manchester. The situation appeared more acceptable when they shared a joint or two. Josh could accept being the other man, and his jealousy was eradicated. Their senses would be heightened to such a degree that when they made love, it was a passionate experience. Afterwards they would sleep in contentment.

When Josh and Vicky parted at the end of the summer term, they both attempted to display an element of stoicism at the end of the relationship. It wasn't how he felt inside. He'd spent eight months in the company of someone who'd made no great demands upon him but had treated him with affection. He'd miss her.

A fortnight after the end of term, Vicky returned to Cardiff to visit friends and called at his house on the off chance he'd not moved out. Josh was packing his belongings, ready to be transported home, and they went to his room.

"I've been asked to an audition to play in an orchestra in London next week. Do you fancy coming up with me?" he asked, more in hope than expectation.

"We've had a lovely time this last year, but I can't. I've arranged to look at a couple of flats in Manchester next Monday and Tuesday. I start teaching there in September. They want me to help out with music and drama as well as my own class of ten-year-olds. I've come down to see a few and wanted to see if you were still here. Have you got any dope? I could do with a smoke now."

"No, I haven't had any since the end of term." He sensed Vicky's disappointment and assumed she felt going out to the world of work was an intimidating prospect.

She sat as close as she could beside him, and he put his arm around her. They looked at each other, and their lips met. They lay down, and her hand stroked his back and touched his thigh. He sat up to remove his T-shirt, and she unzipped his jeans. Within no time, they both lay naked on the bed, wrapped in each other's arms. The rhythm of their lovemaking was steeped in a passion Josh would remember with affection for a long time.

When they'd both dressed, they embraced. Josh sensed she was reluctant to leave him for the last time. Eventually they walked to the front door, where they kissed. As they said their 'goodbyes', he saw her eyes glisten. She left after one last kiss and walked away without turning back. Josh gazed after her until she had gone out of sight, and returned to the house.

"It's over then. Do you want a coffee? You look as if you could do with one." Pete said.

"She got to you, didn't she?" Marc's observation was astute

but sympathetic. "The only one I know to have done so. The forbidden fruit is always the most precious."

CHAPTER TWELVE

The Devil Came Down

Monday, 19 October, 2009

Josh's mobile phone rang as Chris pulled up beside him. The display indicated withheld. He answered in Welsh as he got into the car, and Chris smiled. He approved of his friend's tactics but suspected he'd be caught out one day. Too many anonymous callers had become an annoying consequence of modern technology. Chris ignored these.

"Mr. Stoller? It's about Sean's lessons." Mrs. Francis made no comment regarding his response in Welsh. He assumed her partner had mentioned this to her.

"Oh, hello Mrs. Francis," he said anticipating another cancellation.

"Are you available Wednesday at seven?"

"Yes, seven will be fine. I'll see you then, shall I?" It was an invitation for them to meet, but she didn't respond to the suggestion.

"Sean will be with you. Goodbye."

He placed his phone back in his pocket. At least this time she'd asked if he was available.

"Chris, I know it's a long shot, but do you know anyone who's moved into the area from the north of England? A boy in a local school who plays the violin? He's a good little player." Josh hoped Chris' knowledge of the schools in the area would provide him with some information about Sean.

"Why do you ask?"

He related the story about Sean's ability and his school's failure to provide violin lessons.

"I know most of the schools round here or at least the music teachers. I'll see what I can find out for you. What's his name?"

"Sean Francis, it's his mother's surname. They live with his stepfather as well, so he might have another name, but he could only have started in September.

"I'll look into it. So, he's a good player, is he?"

"Better than most for his age. I hope I don't lose him when he goes to secondary school. He has the potential to go far."

"Just like you did."

Josh gave a bemused smile. He thought of the temptations of the time and said no more.

Josh heard a knock on his door at two minutes to seven, Wednesday evening. Sean was early. When he answered the door, Mrs. Francis' car had disappeared. He turned to follow Sean into his flat, puzzled over why she was reluctant to meet him face to face. *Elusive as ever.*

Josh had decided to introduce some traditional Irish jigs and reels and produced several photocopied tunes. Most were of an elementary level he knew his pupil would learn without a problem, but others were more advanced.

He placed two tunes in front of his pupil, and as Josh predicted, Sean played them without discrepancy.

Two minutes before the lesson was due to finish, Josh suggested it was over. He hoped it would give him the opportunity to catch sight of Mrs. Francis. The boy packed away his violin and opened the door, but she hadn't arrived.

"She hasn't come yet. May I wait in here?" As he said this, her car pulled to a halt outside the flat, and Josh escorted his pupil to the vehicle. The interior light didn't activate as he opened the passenger door, and he only saw her profile.

"Hello, Sean's getting on well on the violin. I'm very impressed with his playing. We've looked at some different types of music, some Irish tunes, tonight. I hear you're helping him at home."

"Yes, I help him a bit. I don't know where he gets it from. Come on, Sean. We've got to get back. Julian's been cooking, and dinner's ready. Thank you, Mr. Stoller."

"Oh, do you want a lesson next week? It's the half-term holiday." Josh asked.

"Yes, please." Sean said. His mother agreed.

Josh closed the passenger door and stared after the car until it rounded the bend further along the road. Mrs. Francis' monotone response had been unnatural. He assumed she'd been disguising a natural lilt for some reason and wondered what she had to hide.

Why did she say I don't know where he gets it from? She's a violinist. Why is she so evasive? I hope Chris can find a name.

Her reluctance to be seen also puzzled him.

He played some of the music he'd bought the previous week. Each tune brought back memories of his involvement with Bethan Williams. Even though he'd formed another relationship in the sixth form, it was toward Bethan he'd been drawn when the opportunity had presented itself. She'd re-entered his life in London years later, but with disastrous results. However much he'd succeeded in pushing memories of her to the back of his mind, the mention of Bethan's name had aroused his interest.

Most of Josh's pupils cancelled their lessons for the half-term holiday week. This gave him more time to practice for a gig at the weekend. The band had been booked to play at the local golf club to celebrate Halloween at the end of the week.

It would be a busy night, but with an additional financial reward, as they'd been asked to play until midnight.

Chris arrived to collect Josh for the final rehearsal before Saturday's gig. He'd found out about a talented violinist who'd recently moved to a school in the locality, but the surname wasn't Francis.

"What if I contacted the music service?" Josh asked.

"You could try, but don't mention my name. Ask the boy first if he wants to play in the set-up."

Sean arrived before time for his lesson on Wednesday, but again, by the time Josh had answered the door, Mrs. Francis had driven off. The violin was out of tune, and Sean appeared worried about it. The fine tuners had been screwed down to the limit and needed loosening. Josh adjusted these in no time and tuned the strings to concert pitch while his pupil looked on, entranced with his teacher's speed and proficiency.

"My stepfather tried to tune it."

"Oh, does he still play?"

"I've never seen him. He picked it up this afternoon and tried to."

"Any good?"

"He didn't really play anything, just looked inside it, tried to bow it, then fiddled with the tuners. He put it away after a few minutes." Sean didn't elaborate any more about his stepfather, almost as if the boy and his stepfather had a strained relationship. Josh became more intrigued regarding the ownership of the violin. To have been in possession of such a good quality instrument meant proficiency, even if he'd not played for a number of years.

Eager to find out if his pupil wanted to extend his experience, he asked, "Would you be interested in playing the violin with a group of youngsters your age?"

"Why, do you teach others?"

"No, but would you be interested in joining the schools' area orchestra?"

"My mum's been in to the school, and they've said I can't."

"I have a friend who may be able to get you in if you're interested. Check with your mum and let me know next week."

Sean had chosen to play *Lord Inchiquin,* one of the Irish tunes from the photocopies he'd been given the previous week. It had a guitar part, which Josh played to accompany his pupil. The pair played together with a high level of cohesion for a first time. Josh showed Sean a few new techniques on how to overcome tricky intervals and slides, and Sean lost track of the time. The lesson overran by a few minutes, and Josh had to remind his pupil his mother would be waiting.

He followed Sean to the car, hoping to catch sight of Mrs. Francis, but she'd pulled a hood over her head. He suspected she'd anticipated his plan to see her but failed to understand her determination to remain anonymous.

CHAPTER THIRTEEN

Saturday, 31 October, 2009

The band had prepared well for Saturday night's gig at the golf club. Josh had decided to introduce his new violin to the world of entertainment, having bought a good quality pick-up to attach to the instrument.

The musicians arrived by six-thirty to carry the equipment into the venue and set up for the sound-check before the punters arrived. Once they finished the preparations, they discussed the song list over a drink.

Josh often commented on his nervousness prior to a gig even though he'd played in some of the most prestigious venues. He claimed it gave him an edge, allowing his adrenalin to control his energy level. This night would be no different. He was on home territory and was eager to demonstrate his proficiency to the local audience, especially his boss.

To the local people, he was a shop assistant who worked for Terry Evans, but tonight he had the opportunity to be himself in front of people from the community. The other band members were amused by his mental preparations. He wrote out the song list, scribbled notes on manuscript paper, and walked across the stage several times to feel its space. This confirmed he'd give of his best once the band began to play. It was an escape from his daily routine and placed him on a higher level of concentration in which he shut himself off from reality. The invisible curtain between him and the audience allowed him to express himself without any level of embarrassment. Punters had paid to see the band. They had a reputation to uphold.

The band had been asked to begin at eight, to welcome the people as they arrived. At the agreed time, the musicians shuffled onto the small stage. They picked up their instruments and began to play, their P A at a low volume, aware they'd have to pace themselves for a long session.

More guests arrived, dressed in elaborate costumes and masked faces to celebrate the ghoulish spirits the night represented. However much they were disguised, most people recognised each other. By nine, a substantial number of revellers indicated they wanted to dance. The musicians responded and increased the tempo and volume to perform well known songs to attract people onto the dancefloor.

From time to time, people approached Dave to make requests, some not on the band's list, but most of which the musicians knew. The crowd appeared to appreciate the music, judging by its reaction to the varied repertoire, and most danced until the break at ten o'clock.

Josh went to the bar to buy a round, and as he returned with a tray of drinks, he noticed a tall bearded man talking to Chris. Josh assumed he was another anonymous reveller requesting a popular song. He placed the tray on a table at the side of the stage where Dave and Rob sat, and the three chatted about the second set.

Chris finished his conversation and joined the others.

"What did he want?" said Dave.

"He just asked if we knew a tune, *The Devil Went Down To Georgia*. Appropriate for tonight, I suppose. I told him I'd check with you."

"I have sung it. I've got the words and chords. I was going to suggest we had a go at it sometime. Do you know the violin part, Josh?"

"I played it often years ago. I think I still remember how it goes. What I can't, I'll improvise. It's got an easy chord progression."

"His partner had asked if we knew it."

Josh looked over at the man who'd approached Chris. He was talking to a lady who wore a similar mask. She appeared sullen and reluctant to join in the revelries of the night, unlike others in the room.

"Do you know who they are?" he asked.

"Not a clue, I don't recognise anyone with their masks. He asked if you knew the tune," Chris replied.

The statement aroused Josh's interest, and again, he glanced over at the couple, not wishing to attract their attention any more than necessary.

The band played the song to begin the second set. As Dave sang the lyrics, it gave Josh another opportunity to gaze over at the couple to see the woman's reaction. A smile appeared on her face. The song appeared to mean something to her. Once the impressive instrumental part began, Josh concentrated on his fingering. He took the tune to heights outside the conventional chord pattern, eager to impress, to reciprocate the woman's enthusiasm for the song.

His bandmates frequently allowed him free rein with his improvisations, especially with songs they were playing for the first time, confident he'd return to the chord structure as composed.

The audience looked on mesmerised by his virtuosity, and once the band had finished, the onlookers demonstrated their appreciation with ecstatic applause. Josh, unable to take his eyes off the woman he'd impressed, felt an affinity with her. He felt as if he'd played the instrumental part for her, but her partner looked on with no emotion.

For the remainder of the evening, she stood engrossed by the band's performance. Although her partner spoke to her, she only glanced at him, without demonstrating any interest in his comments. It was obvious to Josh her mind was elsewhere. Although tempted to approach the pair at the end of the night, Josh was deterred by the man's size and serious demeanour.

After the equipment had been packed away, Josh approached his boss, Terry Evans, who had removed his mask. He was standing at the bar with a group of men, engrossed in conversation. Josh walked over to his boss.

"The band sounded great, Josh. I think everyone enjoyed it. Some of it was a bit wild for me, but you went down very well."

"Thanks, Mr. Evans. Glad you liked it." As they spoke, the man who'd asked for the tune earlier approached them, still wearing his mask.

"Terry Evans, I assume. I want a word."

Josh, bemused by the stranger's rude interruption, said. "See you Monday, Mr. Evans," and left.

As they drove home, the man was intrigued to discover the reason for his partner's complete change of mood once the violinist had begun to play the tune he'd requested.

"You seemed interested in the violinist. Do you know him?"

"Who?" she asked.

"The violinist." He realised his partner was attempting to be evasive.

"I think he's Sean's violin teacher."

"What do you mean think? Didn't you meet him when you arranged the lessons?"

"I phoned him on the recommendation of the newsagent, when I saw the advert. He said he had a good reputation. He also told me he played in a local band."

"So you think it's him. You haven't met him yet then?"

"Of course, I see him at the end of the lesson, but it's dark when he comes out, and Sean goes in on his own. He wants to be independent. He'll be eleven in March."

"Classical player, by the sound of him."

"Oh, did you speak to him?"

"I guessed by his ability. Are you sure you don't know him?" he asked, suspecting her attraction to Josh. Whether she did or not had no consequence for the moment. He had to ensure his stepson continued with the violin lessons until Christmas time.

An oppressive silence accompanied the remainder of the journey. She wished she was somewhere else. A part of her wanted him to stop the car, to allow her to get out and walk, but with another mile to go, Sean would be worried if her partner arrived home without her. That was out of the question. Her son needed her protection. His child-minder would also suspect something was wrong.

She hadn't told Sean about her concerns regarding her partner. She wondered how she'd begun a relationship with this man, and lately, why he'd insisted on moving from Cheshire down to South Wales. She was no longer able to see her parents, who'd helped her bring up Sean.

She'd not formed a relationship with anyone after Sean was born and had never given anyone a chance. But this man, this despicable man, had charmed her. He'd almost groomed her into believing he was her saviour. How wrong she'd been. She'd moved in with him after six months and had resigned from her teaching post.

Money was no object to his family and in a more than comfortable lifestyle, her son was able to flourish, although she often wondered how their wealth had been made.

Her partner had a short fuse, and the tempers only became obvious after a few months of her moving in with him. She soon felt trapped and regretted what she'd done. She no longer had the security of her parents, and finding another post in the state sector would be difficult. She didn't want to be another statistic.

After his outbursts, he'd state he'd been wronged by a former lover who'd made a fool of him and destroyed his confidence. Mrs. Francis had been the best thing to help him get over the episode. At first, she'd been taken in by this, but his aggression became too frequent for her to be comfortable in his company. He'd never been physically abusive to her, but she often wondered if it would change. She was terrified of what he might do if she walked out. Even some of his so-called business associates suggested a less than straightforward lifestyle.

The atmosphere at home had improved after the move to South Wales, but for how long? At least Sean had formed a good relationship with Josh. She had to make sure that wasn't obvious to her partner.

Of course she'd enjoyed Josh and his band's music. She'd taken a chance asking her partner to find out if the band knew the song. It had been a favourite of hers from her university days. Josh's playing was like a breath of fresh air.

Although her partner had said he used to play the violin as a school pupil, she'd not seen any evidence of him having been a musician. She'd spotted his initials on the inside of the instrument when she'd known him and had been intrigued to find out how he'd acquired his violin. But when she'd looked at it the weekend after Sean's first lesson with Josh, the initials had been scribbled over, making them impossible to read.

CHAPTER FOURTEEN

Monday, 2 November, 2009

On Monday morning Josh demonstrated his eagerness to find out the identity of the stranger who'd approached his boss. The reaction of his female companion had aroused his interest. Although he knew he shouldn't even think about her, the enthusiasm she'd displayed in his musicianship intrigued him. It had allowed him to place Bethan in another compartment for the time being. Frustrated that he wasn't in a relationship, any attention flattered him.

"It was a superb performance on Saturday. We all enjoyed it, especially the country song about the Devil going to Georgia," Terry said.

"Thanks, Mr. Evans., I haven't played it for years. The person who approached you at the end of the night asked for it. Who was he?"

"Never met him before but he suggested putting some business his way. He deals in clothes. I told him I'd meet him in the golf club at lunch time on Wednesday. See what he's got to say anyway."

"Did he say his name or give you his card?"

"Simpson." Josh remembered serving someone called Simpson at the beginning of October. He'd been of a similar build, but the strange attitude he'd displayed was clear in his memory. "He asked who you were, so I told him you worked here. He also asked for how long, so I told him." Josh tried to remember if he'd mentioned his professional past working in music shops in London. He knew he'd not mentioned his orchestral work at any time.

"Anything more?"

"I said you worked in the music business, semi-pro stuff in your band."

"Did he ask for my name?"

"Yes, but he didn't show any interest when I told him."

Josh, intrigued by Simpson's approach to make a business offer, realised he had to forget the man's partner. That had to be a non-starter.

Several new songs were suggested in the band practice that evening. *The Devil Went Down to Georgia,* was a certainty. Simpson's partner's response had flattered Josh, but he said nothing to his friends.

As Chris drove Josh home, he interrupted the silence. "Is she playing on your mind again?"

"Who?"

"Like buses, Josh. Don't play with fire. You seemed intrigued by the woman whose partner had asked for *The Devil Went Down to Georgia* as well."

"Oh, you noticed," Josh said with some hesitation.

"Couldn't miss it. The mutual attraction was obvious. He must have realised, too." Chris looked at him and shook his head. "Don't," he said and gave a wry smile.

Josh had not mentioned a relationship since he'd joined the band. "Not something I'd intended." He remained silent for several seconds and pondered Chris' observation. "Something strange happened after the gig though. The guy approached my boss about them doing some business together. Terry told me this morning."

"Just keep a low profile," Chris said. Josh got out of the car, realising the attention he'd shown the woman had been noticed. Simpson could be a threat.

Chapter Fifteen

Wednesday, 4 November, 2009

Terry left to meet Simpson as arranged at the golf club and gave Josh both the shop and safe keys, in case the meeting ran on longer than expected. They'd arranged to meet at twelve-thirty, and Terry wished to arrive in good time to demonstrate the upper hand. He often behaved in this manner, never late and arriving ten minutes earlier than agreed. *Late* in Terry's dictionary meant uninterested. Simpson appeared to be of the same character, as Terry saw him pacing at the door as his car pulled up.

The two men met in a room, away from the bar area. Simpson claimed to be in charge of a firm that manufactured clothes and suggested Terry should consider buying school uniforms from him. He promised competitive prices to what he already paid, and his catalogue appeared impressive, but he didn't mention the location of production. With no indication of any paperwork and references, Terry stood up, replaced the top of his fountain pen, and put it back into his jacket pocket.

"I'll think about it, Mr. Simpson. You see, I've dealt with my suppliers for years. Local people might be put out of work." Terry's comment clearly annoyed Simpson, whose eyes displayed a flash of anger.

Although Terry was taken aback by Simpson's reaction, he said nothing and walked to the door to indicate the meeting was over. He was eager to get back to the shop and looked at his watch. It was almost half-past one. Josh would have worked through his lunch break.

"I could have saved you a lot of money, Mr. Evans. Maybe another time," Simpson said as Terry left the room. "You'll regret it," he added under his breath.

The two men walked in different directions across the car park, and Terry got into his car. As he drove off, he spotted Simpson speaking to someone on his phone but thought no more about it.

Terry hoped to be back at the shop by quarter to two. He'd not met a supplier as sharp or as aggressive as Simpson before, and for a peculiar reason, felt threatened by his presence.

The recent recession had hit the community, but Terry had still managed to supply the locality with good quality clothes and uniforms for the local schools at competitive prices. He'd stayed loyal to local suppliers and had never let people down just to make a quick profit. He'd run the clothes shop for nigh on twenty years. It had been a family business for four generations, since the first half of the twentieth century. There weren't many overheads, as he'd inherited the premises. Josh worked full time, and Terry's son Nathan, who attended Cardiff University, worked part-time on weekends.

Within a minute of leaving the golf club, Terry noticed a dark coloured car approaching at speed from the opposite direction. It veered over to his side of the road and forced him to swerve onto the wide verge and stop. The driver corrected his path before the threatened impact, and the car continued on its way before Terry had an opportunity to record any of its details. Overcome with fear, he pushed open his door and staggered around to the near side to investigate any possible damage. Mud had been splattered on the wheel arches and along the side of the car, but he saw no obvious damage. He didn't return to the driver's seat for several minutes, too shaken up to contemplate returning to the shop.

Anne Evans turned on the radio to listen to the news headlines at one-thirty. Before they began, her telephone rang. She turned down the volume to answer the call.

Before she had a chance to say anything, she heard,

"Hello, Mrs. Evans?"

She assumed a call centre was contacting her as she didn't recognise the voice. A very patient woman, she confirmed her identity. She hated being rude to anonymous callers, believing they too had to earn a living in a less than pleasant environment.

To her surprise the caller began, "I was driving near the golf club, and I recognised your husband's car on the verge."

Anne panicked. She expected to be told Terry had been involved in an accident. The caller continued, "He was in the driver's seat. Something wasn't right. I couldn't stop to find out, as the road was busy."

The call ended. She looked out through the window to check whether Terry had arrived but saw no sign of the car. A call to her husband's mobile phone was unsuccessful, and she dialled the local police station.

When composed enough, Terry drove home. As he entered the driveway, he saw Anne standing at the front door. She rushed to greet him as he got out of the car, and tears welled up in her eyes.

"Have you had an accident?" she said.

"How did you know?" He was alarmed she had any idea of what had happened. He held his wife by the shoulders, impatient for an answer.

"I had a phone call about half an hour ago to say you'd been involved in an accident. I tried calling you and then called the local police station. I told them you'd been at the golf club. They told me a police car would investigate. They called back. They hadn't seen anything."

"When did you say you'd had a call?"

"About half an hour ago." He looked at his watch. It was a minute to two o'clock. He'd still been at the club at half past one. He remembered checking the time.

"Are you sure it was half an hour ago?"

"Yes, I'd turned on the radio to listen to the news headlines, I tried calling you after. You must have been out of signal."

"Someone lost control of his car and veered over to my side of the road. I had to drive onto the verge. Nothing more."

"Doesn't sound like nothing to me."

Terry said no more to his wife about the time of the phone call she'd received, but she insisted on contacting the shop to tell Josh Terry wouldn't be back until the following morning. She gave no reason other than he'd come home feeling unwell. Terry Evans received a call from Simpson later, to suggest he should reconsider his decision.

At five o'clock, Josh closed the shop. His pupil arrived on time and produced an old copy of the fiddle tunes Josh had used the previous weeks.

"Where did you manage to get this, Sean?"

"My mum had a copy. I didn't know. She used to play some of this music years ago. She said she had friends who used to play in a group with her."

Josh opened the book at the front inside cover to see what he assumed was a name scribbled out, making it impossible to decipher. He turned to *Lord Inchiquin* and counted them both in. Sean had practised the piece as it was a near perfect rendition.

Before Josh had a chance to introduce a new tune, Sean

asked, "Do you know a tune called *The Devil Went Down to Georgia*? Josh gave him a puzzled look. He found two copies of the violin part and gave one to Sean to place on the music stand. Without another word, he played through the piece.

"Wow. Will you teach me how to play it?"

"Where have you heard the tune before?"

"My mum found it on YouTube. I just like it."

When his lesson finished, Sean left smiling. As Josh waited at the door, he heard his pupil exclaim, "I'm learning *The Devil* tune, Mum. Josh's a great teacher."

The car door closed, and he watched the boy and his mother disappear into the distance. He wondered about the coincidence of being asked to play the same tune from two different sources. Sean had said nothing about the schools' area orchestra, and Josh assumed his pupil wanted to concentrate on the more unusual tunes which he'd introduced.

When he arrived at work the following morning, Josh found his boss in an agitated state. Paperwork covered the floor in his office at the back of the shop. The room looked as if a burglary had taken place. Josh suspected the reason his boss hadn't returned to the shop the previous afternoon was to do with Simpson. All he could say was, "I'm glad you're better today." Terry ignored the comment but said, "I want to check all the accounts, all the records of purchases and sales we've made since April."

"Is it anything to do with Simpson?"

"Sort of. I just want to see how much we've paid Huw Rogers for the uniforms this year."

"They're probably on the shelf above your head." Josh reached over, pulled out a folder and placed it on the desk. Terry thanked him and flicked through the documents. He displayed no real interest in their contents. It was obvious to

Josh his boss wasn't happy about Simpson's interference.

Terry asked him to make a list of all school uniforms purchased since the previous spring and the mark-up on each type of clothing sold.

"I've had a good set of figures from Simpson, I'm meeting him again tomorrow afternoon, and he's bringing samples over."

"To the shop?"

"Yes, at five-fifteen, after we've closed. I'll have time to examine the quality. Can you sort out the figures from Huw Rogers' company before then?"

"What about the shop, Mr. Evans?"

"Don't worry, I'll look after it. I'll ring Huw Rogers later to see if he can drop his prices, but I doubt it."

Terry appeared to have made up his mind. Josh suspected the arrangement with Simpson wasn't an amicable one. At least, he wanted to see the standard of Simpson's clothes first. Josh could tell from Terry's body language he was tense and uncomfortable with Simpson's propositions. He suggested he should stay, but Terry insisted he should leave, aware his band had an engagement at a venue in Cardiff.

CHAPTER SIXTEEN

Friday, 6 November, 2009

The latest developments in the shop worried Josh, and he sat in silence alongside Chris as they travelled to the gig. Chris seemed to sense the tension and attempted to make small talk about the songs in their repertoire. Josh failed to match his drummer's enthusiasm.

"What are you worrying about, Josh?"

"I'm not sure. The guy who asked for *The Devil Went Down to Georgia* at the Halloween gig is trying to infiltrate my boss' business."

"What do you mean?"

"He met my boss on Wednesday and again tonight. Terry seems unhappy about it for some reason."

"You'll have to just accept it. It's his business."

"I know, but it doesn't seem straightforward."

Josh knew he had to focus on the gig, and as soon as they'd set up the equipment, he went through his quirky rituals to switch off from reality. As the gig progressed, Josh demonstrated his skills to the delight of the audience. The 70s rock standards had the audience reacting as though the songs were as fresh as they'd been at the time of their release. It gave him the opportunity to forget the shop, Simpson, and his partner.

Chris dropped Josh off at his flat at twelve-thirty after the gig. "Thanks, Chris. I feel better now," he said before he opened the passenger door. "I suppose my worries are unfounded." But he knew he was fooling himself.

As soon as he entered his flat, he turned on his phone to discover a message from Terry. His boss wanted him in work at eight. "Damn. Six hours sleep if I'm lucky." Since he'd moved from London, his sleep patterns had improved, and seven to eight hours was the norm. Terry treated Josh fairly. He never demanded more than the customary hours from him without recompense.

He went to bed at one, but lay awake for a long time, convinced Terry's request had something to do with Simpson. He was still intrigued to discover Simpson's partner's identity, especially given the two requests for a tune he'd not played since his student days in Cardiff. He hoped the devil wasn't coming down to haunt him.

CHAPTER SEVENTEEN

Saturday, 7 November, 2009

Josh turned up for work at eight as requested.

"Sorry for asking you in early, Josh. It's Simpson. I'm not sure about him. I don't like his tactics. He appears very plausible to begin with, but as soon as you question him or criticise him in any way, he becomes unpleasant."

It was as Josh had anticipated. "What's his first name, Mr. Evans?"

"Julian. Why?"

"He just reminded me of someone, but doesn't have the same first name."

Josh tidied the displays, not sure how to react to hearing the man's name. His mind raced back to the millennium year. Anger rose inside him, but he remained calm, not wishing to display his emotions. This man Simpson had to be the reason Bethan had contacted his parents. He hoped he hadn't reached the wrong conclusion.

A Julian Simpson had ruined his relationship with Bethan nine years before. Was this the same person? Those cold, penetrating eyes he'd noticed as he'd served a customer of the same name weeks before suggested the man had known him. Had he been the elusive partner of his ex-colleague and friend, Jan? Back then, he must have been aware of Josh and had seen him perform on a number of occasions. That Simpson had never socialised with the orchestra members after a concert. He'd remained anonymous, and for a very good reason, as Josh had found out later. Perhaps Josh needed to contact Bethan after all. He also needed to get in touch with Jan. She'd moved back to Manchester in the millennium year, as a result of Simpson's indiscretions.

Josh was glad now he'd not spoken about his orchestral past with Terry. The less his boss knew about him before he'd moved back to South Wales, the better. Without this knowledge, Terry wouldn't be in a position to give away too much information about his employee. To describe his experience in retail sales had been Josh's priority when they'd first met. However, he wanted to qualify his mistrust for Simpson, so he related his initial encounter with the customer of the same name.

"I served someone called Simpson a few weeks ago. It was just before we closed. He bought a shirt, paid by card. I gave the card back to him and read his name on it. I said *Thank you, Mr. Simpson*. He didn't seem to like the fact I'd addressed him by name. Have we still got the card receipts from September?"

"I keep copies for over a year in case of a dispute. When did he come in?"

"I'd taught the new pupil the night before, so it had to be a Thursday, and it was the first lesson, at the end of September. The thirtieth."

The safe contained a small amount of cash Terry had failed to bank the previous afternoon. A wad of papers and receipts lay on the top shelf.

"I must take these home, to keep them safe. The thirtieth of September, you say. How much?" Josh went through to the shop to check the shirts.

"Twenty-five, ninety-five." Terry flicked through the credit card receipts and found it in no time.

"Here it is, four fifty-eight, just before closing time."

"That's the one." Josh said. Terry made two photocopies of

the receipt and gave one to Josh for safekeeping. The other he placed in his own wallet.

Terry's son, Nathan, who worked on Saturdays to help finance his university fees, arrived at nine, eager to find out how Josh's gig had gone. The band had a good reputation in the Cardiff area, and Nathan always displayed an interest in how they'd performed.

At mid-day the shop's telephone rang. As Josh was serving a customer, Nathan answered the call.

"Josh, it's for you." By the time Josh reached the telephone, the caller had hung up. He dialled one-four- seven-one, but the number had been withheld. As he returned to the shop, he gave Nathan a puzzled look.

"Female," was Nathan's comment.

Josh wondered if Bethan had attempted to reach him but thought it unlikely. His mother wouldn't have given her details of where he worked. Had Mrs. Francis made the call? No. She had his mobile number. He remembered the conversation he'd had with Chris about the obvious mutual admiration between them

Later, Josh asked his boss about the quality of Simpson's merchandise. He wanted to find out more about the man, worried Terry Evans would be coerced into changing his supplier against his will. He sensed Terry's apprehension, and didn't want to elaborate any further regarding his suspicions.

"Not as good. I'll stick with Rogers for now. We've got a signed agreement until next July, thankfully."

The word *thankfully* made Josh feel relieved.

CHAPTER EIGHTEEN

London: Success and Disappointments.

1998

Several weeks after Josh graduated, he moved to London, his place in the orchestra guaranteed. His ambition had been realised. Although he'd been brought up and had studied in the two largest cities in South Wales, the enormity of the sprawling capital excited him. Even though he'd visited London before, it had always been under the guidance of his school or college. Fascinated by the rush, buzz, and the apparent stoicism of expressionless commuters who travelled in overcrowded carriages, he behaved like a tourist. He explored the city on both overland and tube trains to visit places of interest he'd only ever read about. His determination to take advantage of this mesmerising place was evident from the moment he attended his first rehearsal.

Josh spent the first few months in the orchestra enraptured in the euphoria of the successful creativity alongside his fellow musicians. The atmosphere was better than he'd anticipated. His enthusiasm to learn from the best endeared him to his colleagues. Jan, a fellow violinist who'd played for the orchestra for three years, took him under her wing and advised him to build up a list of pupils to supplement his income in a city ready to relieve both residents and visitors of their hard-earned money. Rehearsals, engagements, and teaching commitments ensured he had a full timetable to organise. She also helped him find a place to live on his initial visit to the city, and within a week, he'd moved into a house with four other tenants in Wimbledon, a convenient location. From there Josh could take direct tube ride to the Embankment, the closest station to the orchestra's rehearsal rooms, located in the labyrinth of streets to the east of Charing Cross.

His room, a narrow, converted attic, stretched the length of the terraced building and contained the necessary furniture for his basic comforts. Its south facing gabled window, although small, allowed him plenty of light without obstruction from surrounding buildings. Under this was his music stand, a permanent feature. Living at the top of the house allowed him the solitude to practice his violin without disturbing anyone.

He wrote to Vicky, still foremost in his thoughts, on the off chance she'd want to visit him. Her reply stated her challenges as a new teacher would demand a great deal of her time. She wished him well in his new venture. He understood this as an instruction to move on.

When free, his fellow housemates relaxed together over a few drinks in their nearest bar on Friday evenings. The first time Josh joined them, he misjudged the strength of the local beer and began to slur over his words after four pints. On the short walk home, Toni, who'd matched him drink for drink, put her arm through his to steady him. Josh assumed Toni's move as an amorous suggestion and clutched her hand.

As soon as the other housemates had gone to bed, she opened a bottle of wine and invited him to share it. Toni appeared even more attractive than he'd noticed before. His judgement affected, he wondered how the night would evolve. Although she appeared interested in his love of music as he explained the finer details of the different genres he played, the enthusiasm only existed in his head. She soon became lost as his explanations became more and more complex. Her tastes extended as far as R 'n B and Britpop.

Finally she stood and suggested they should go to bed. After draining the last drop from his glass, he stood, faced her, and stroked her upper arm.

"Look, Josh, we're all good friends here and don't need any complications. You've got it wrong. We've both had too much to drink, and I think it's doing you less good than me."

"I'm sorry. I didn't realise. I didn't mean to."

"Let's go to our own beds," she said, and walked out of the room. Josh heard her bedroom door close with a slam. He was angry with himself for assuming Toni would be prepared to sleep with him. To jeopardise a platonic relationship in which five people from different backgrounds needed to relax and escape from the rigours of everyday life in a fast-moving city would have been nonsensical. To have to look for another place to live, having just moved to Wimbledon, wasn't an option he needed.

The next morning, he found Toni and Carol in the kitchen. Before he had time to overcome his embarrassment, Toni addressed him as if nothing had happened between them.

"How's the head, Josh? We did some damage last night." She appeared to be making light of the previous evening, but her eyes displayed the opposite. He hoped she'd not discussed the incident with Carol.

"Not bad. I'll pop out and get another bottle later."

"Good idea, replenish the stocks. Never know when we all might need the odd drink."

Toni's forthright and confident manner suggested overall leadership in the school where she taught was within her sights. Nothing would stop her. Despite her easy manner, it soon became apparent the incident between them had clouded their relationship. She avoided him when they were alone together in the house. The Friday evenings spent together in the local pub provided security in numbers.

CHAPTER NINETEEN

April, 1999

Josh's workload increased in the spring with a part-time post as a lecturer at a university in South West London. Within six months, Josh was invited to play second violin in a new ensemble with four other musicians from the orchestra. Jan played the first violin, and Timothy and Winston accompanied on viola and cello. Jan's close friend, Sophie, with whom she'd moved to London from Manchester, led the group from the piano. Josh felt the most comfortable within this small group of musicians and was excited with Sophie's wish to explore the possibility of presenting several piano quintets to audiences.

They rehearsed a variety of appropriate works and became engrossed with the new challenges. The five musicians would show off their individual skills as soloists at rehearsals, and Josh decided to work on the final movement of one of J.S. Bach's Partitas, *The Chaconne*. His admiration for the composer's music and its easy adaptability for improvisation were instrumental in his choice. Owen's father had influenced his taste more than he'd realised.

The ensemble's first public engagement was at the Purcell Rooms, an intimate concert hall on the Southbank. The varied programme included two piano quintets, a string quartet, and a solo piece by each musician. The audience was mesmerised by the quality of musicianship and choice of music, given it was the ensemble's first performance. It had been rehearsed thoroughly to ensure a seamless performance, and its success was rewarded with a standing ovation.

Afterward, the enthusiasm displayed by the audience continued in the bar where the musicians were congratulated by friends and many of the orchestra's members. Josh, however, felt socially inept. He stood on the periphery of the group unable to make the small talk to allow himself to blend in with his contemporaries. All his emotions had been channelled into the performance, and he found it difficult to come down from the dizzy heights of his playing.

Jan and Sophie, his closest allies, had the natural ability to be gregarious on such occasions and fed off each other's social skills. This level of closeness between the two girls had not been so apparent to him before. He felt an outsider in this intimate atmosphere. Timothy and Winston, whose families lived in London, were engrossed in conversation with their partners and relations.

Josh's ordinary background hadn't prepared him to display the same level of confidence as many of his colleagues. He wasn't romantically involved with anyone, so was reluctant to leave, to return to Wimbledon. All his housemates would either have returned home from the pub or moved on to some planned social event. He needed the company of someone to help him unwind but felt uncomfortable attempting to break through his own wall of isolation.

Within an hour, exhausted by the evening and several glasses of wine, Jan suggested she and Sophie should leave. She'd noticed Josh's reluctance to contribute to any discussion in the bar and invited him to share a taxi to her flat in Putney. From there he'd be able to travel on with relative ease to Wimbledon.

"Thanks, but aren't you going back to Julian's?" he said, referring to her new partner. As an employee in the city, he had amassed enough money to afford to live in a property in Canary Wharf.

"He's off at seven tomorrow to go to Scotland."

"She's with me tonight," Sophie told him with a wink.

On arrival at her flat, Jan persuaded him to join them for a glass of wine. In their company, he conversed with more confidence than he'd had all evening. As they sat in the living room, the conversation continued about the concert and the audience's reaction.

Sophie, who'd achieved her aim, having presented the piano quintets, still demonstrated her delight with the ensemble's achievements. The solo items had also enhanced each musician's reputation. As a unit, their performance guaranteed further prestigious engagements.

"Do you think we should explore some other composers?" Sophie asked.

"We could try some tango music. Astor Piazzolla's a favourite of mine. Have you heard any? Yo-Yo Ma, the cellist, has an album of Piazzola's music. It's an interesting interpretation."

"Very sensual." said Jan as she looked at Sophie.

Josh continued to talk about the Argentinian composer. The two girls agreed. To highlight Winston's cello would be an interesting inclusion in their repertoire.

Their enthusiasm to plan for the future went on longer than he'd anticipated, and he realised he'd have to telephone for a cab.

"Stay here," Jan said. She went to the kitchen and returned with another bottle of white wine. "Open this for us." She gave him the bottle and corkscrew. "We've only talked about music before, never about you. Sophie and I have known each other since we were in school. I'm delighted we formed an ensemble. It's given us a chance to get closer and find out a bit more about you. To come to London on your own at twenty-one must have been a challenge. We both came down here together from Manchester."

"It's okay here. I share a pleasant house. Most of my old friends are still home, though." Josh said.

"No romantic interests?"

"No, no one now."

Jan made an excuse to leave the room, and Sophie, who sat on a settee opposite him, removed her cardigan. The top buttons of her blouse were undone, and her skirt had rolled up to show the tops of her stockings, along with more thigh than he thought she'd intended. She emptied her wine glass and held it out for him to refill.

"Fill Jan's up as well. We've got some more."

Jan returned to the room dressed in a black knee length kimono and sat next to Sophie. He felt a sensual charge in the room and wondered if his two colleagues would devour him.

"Where am I to sleep?" he asked.

"Nowhere yet. We want to find out more about you. We thought you were a shy, young, Welsh lad come to the *smoke*. You can talk the hind-legs off a donkey about your musical tastes, but what about the real Josh? We know very little about you. I'm intrigued," Sophie said.

"Another glass?" Jan emptied the bottle into Josh's glass. "I'll get another one."

She returned within the minute and gave him the bottle to open.

"I don't have a lot to tell," he said and gave a potted history about himself and his childhood in two minutes.

"Not the sort of accent I'd associate with South Wales. Another glass?" Sophie picked up the bottle and filled the three glasses. "We'll go to bed after this."

After both girls had gone to the bedroom, Josh pulled a

wrap from one of the chairs to cover him for the night and began to unbutton his shirt. Before he finished, he turned to see Sophie in the doorway of the living room, dressed only in her underwear.

"It's okay. Jan's got a big double bed." Jan stood behind her, caressing her arms in a provocative manner. She'd removed her kimono and bra. For all his sexual escapades in Cardiff, he'd not experienced what was being proposed.

Jan took his hand and led him into the bedroom. Behind him, Sophie touched his hips. Her hands moved around his waist and unbuckled his belt. Meanwhile, Jan kissed him, and finished unbuttoning his shirt, while Sophie unzipped his trousers. He responded to the stimulation and pushed Jan's panties down. She moved her attention down from his neck, and he sensed sex oozing from every pore, which ignited his passion even further. Lips, tongues, and fingers provided more stimulation to seek out their sexual desires.

Sophie waited her turn, but as she did, she prolonged Josh's pleasure to fulfil Jan's expectations.

The three naked bodies didn't experience any sleep for a few hours. Partners were exchanged and entwined in a variety of positions until exhaustion took over.

When the three awoke mid-morning, Josh lay between Jan and Sophie. He looked at Sophie, who smiled in return. Jan's face, however, displayed the opposite, prompting Josh to suspect she regretted the events of the night. She rose from the bed and left the room without a word. Josh sat up with his legs over the opposite side to Sophie, hesitant and wondering how he should react to the night's activities.

Sophie stood and put on a dressing gown. He picked up his strewn clothes from the floor to dress as Sophie sat in front of the dressing table to gaze at her reflection in the mirror and brush her hair. Even more confused, Josh wondered if the night's events would threaten the harmony in the ensemble. As Sophie appeared engrossed in her appearance, he left the room.

Jan appeared in a pensive mood in the kitchen. He suspected the alcohol fuelled evening had progressed beyond her expectations, and suggested making a pot of tea, anxious to be busy to save any silent embarrassment, but she didn't respond.

"Sorry about last night." he said after a minute of silence but realised he shouldn't say any more about their intimacy. "I'd better get back to Wimbledon. It's nearly mid-day."

Sophie joined them and poured herself a cup.

"I was just going, Sophie," Josh began.

"Fine. It was a brilliant concert. You excelled yourself. We all did."

He picked up his violin case and dress suit and made to leave. Before he reached the door, she walked over to him and kissed him on the lips, lingering with a passion, suggesting she wanted more. Jan didn't move or look at either of them. The events of the night had to be dismissed if the ensemble was to continue without embarrassment.

When Josh arrived back in Wimbledon, there was no sound in the house, and he assumed it was empty. After putting away his suit and violin, he went back downstairs. Not having eaten since the previous afternoon, he was hungry.

As he opened the kitchen door, he saw Toni alone at the table, deep in thought and cradling an empty coffee cup. Surprised to see her and unsure how to react, he grunted a greeting and approached the freezer.

She returned to her senses realising he was in the room.

"Oh hello Josh. Have you just come in? Did you have a good night last night?"

Surprised by her friendly attitude, he sat opposite her, and forgot to remove the meal from the freezer. It was the first time they'd been alone together since their misunderstanding. Unsure how the conversation would progress, he made every effort to act as if nothing had happened between them.

"We arrived back at Jan's flat after our concert and opened a couple of bottles of wine. We didn't turn in until late. I didn't realise you were here. The house was quiet."

"Jan? Your friend from the orchestra, isn't she?"

"Yes. On your own?" he asked, desperate to change the subject. He didn't want to mention anything about the previous night.

"Carol and Phil are at work, and Trevor went out early."

"Do you want another cup? Coffee? That one looks empty." She nodded in acceptance with a smile, and he stood to fill the kettle.

As soon as he'd prepared the drinks, he returned to his seat with both cups. "We've got to patch things up. Didn't get off to a good start," he said.

"I know. It was a misunderstanding. Can we go for a walk up to the common?"

Surprised by her request, he suspected she had a problem she was desperate to discuss. He could see another side to Toni's personality, a vulnerability always hidden by the confidence which had made him wary of her. He agreed to the request but was determined to keep her at a safe distance.

"I need a shower first, freshen up. It was a busy night."

"What?"

"Concert." Josh suspected she wasn't functioning in her usual manner. "Did you have a good night last night?" he asked, imitating her initial question as he'd entered the kitchen. He assumed she'd drunk more than normal. She could match him drink for drink and more on their Friday evenings in their local.

"Had a rough day yesterday, threatened by a pupil with scissors. Head suspended him." Toni seemed distant, as if she was talking to herself. He could have been anyone in the room. "Couldn't wait to get home. We had loads of forms to fill in." She got up and moved items from one place to another. As she did so, she continued to speak. "Night out only masked it. Could do with fresh air. I'll see you in ten minutes."

After he'd showered, he joined her in the hallway. Within half an hour, they'd walked up Wimbledon Hill, through the old village toward the Common and the two popular pubs located side by side.

His mind elsewhere, Josh only half listened to Toni. She talked in great detail about her work and the incident at school. Finally she turned to look at him. "What did you get up to last night? You look knackered."

"Late night, that's all. The concert went well, and we had a few drinks at the bar. By the time we got back to Jan's flat, it was too late to get a tube here, so I stayed. We shared a bottle and talked about plans for more concerts."

Reluctant to discuss the ensemble's dynamics any further, he deflected the conversation back to Toni's work. "Do you normally have problems with discipline in school? It must be tough. I can remember some boys and girls at school who'd give the teacher a hard time, but it was when we were much older. I was lucky. I had my music and could focus on most other things as well."

"We don't, but this kid just kicked off."

After Josh bought drinks, they both studied the menu. Toni continued to talk about her work between discussing the menu's choices as she drank her wine.

Once they'd ordered lunch, they began to relax. Pleased the strained relationship between them had been forgotten, Josh turned the conversation to include their university experiences before moving to London.

Two hours later, after Toni had drunk three large glasses of wine, they left and walked to the main road. Josh, more sober than his companion, after resisting the temptation to match Toni drink for drink, took her arm to steady her. She didn't complain. He hoped she didn't assume this was a repeat of the advance he'd attempted before and took as long as possible to lead her home, stopping at various shops to gaze in through the windows.

No one else appeared to be in the house when they arrived, and Josh suggested preparing coffee.

"I have to lie down," she said and left him to assume she wanted him to take her coffee to her room. He found her lying on top of her bed, her eyes closed, and not wishing to disturb her, he placed the coffee on the bedside as he turned to leave, he heard her say, "Don't go. Sit with me. Thanks for keeping me company today. I've made a bit of an arse of myself. I didn't think school would get to me."

"We all get our off-days. I could tell you some tales."

"I drank too much last night, and now today —" Without warning, she stood and ran from the room. Josh heard the sound of her vomiting in the toilet and the flush being operated.

As he stood in the hallway, unsure how to react, she left the bathroom and wiped her face. She stumbled to him, and he led her back to her room, concerned she might fall. Once there, she began to undress.

"I'd better go," he said.

"No, Josh, please help me get my blouse off."

She seemed incapable of unbuttoning her clothes, and he held her to prevent her from falling. Within seconds, she'd unzipped her skirt and pulled her blouse over her head. She stood in front of him in her underwear with a stupid smile of inebriation.

The sight of her body tempted him to take advantage. Sober enough to realise she wasn't in a position to agree to sex, he suspected it was a situation into which he was being drawn. They'd both regret what could happen, and he snapped out of his train of thought, insisting she should get into bed alone if only to absolve himself from any accusation of taking advantage of the situation. He'd found himself in many a bed, but he'd never initiated sex without mutual consent and in relative sobriety.

After he'd covered her, she drifted off into a sleep of recovery. Before leaving, he scanned the room and noticed a half empty vodka bottle on her dressing table. He suspected she'd drunk some before they'd gone out, as she'd only had three glasses of wine with him, less than she drank on a Friday.

Twenty minutes later, as he lay on his bed, having drifted off to sleep, he heard his door opening. He looked up to see Trevor walk toward him, obviously angry.

"What have you and Toni been up to, you bastard?"

"What are you on about?" Josh sat up as his enraged housemate stood over him with clenched fists. He thought Trevor was about to hit him, and raised his arms in front of his face, but the threat didn't develop any further.

"I've just been to her room to ask her where she'd been. She said you'd been with her."

"Yes, she had too much to drink, and I put her to bed."

"Did you try to have sex with her?"

"No, I bloody didn't. What do you take me for? None of your business what we do anyway."

The last spontaneous remark angered Trevor even more. "It's got everything to do with me."

The comment had betrayed his feelings toward Toni, and he rushed out of the bedroom. His rapid footsteps descended the stairs and doors slammed. Josh had no idea Trevor had aspirations for a relationship with Toni.

Josh gave Trevor time to calm down before he went to the kitchen. Here he found Phil sitting with Trevor. The look Phil gave Josh begged an answer to Trevor's agitated state. Although Josh attempted to apologise, Trevor stormed out and went to his room.

"What's up?" said Phil.

"Toni and I went out for a drink. She had too much. I put her to bed. He thinks something's going on between us."

"I didn't think you two got on."

"She had a work problem. It was just me here, and she wanted to talk. I didn't know he fancied her."

"More like a little puppy afraid to make a move."

"Never said anything before."

"You've not noticed, obviously."

"I didn't realise. I'd better go and see if she's all right."

"Careful, her mood swings can be —"

"I know."

Josh went to Toni's room and knocked on her door. He heard her voice, opened the door and saw her alone, still in bed.

"You've spoken to Trevor," he said.

"Yes, look Josh about this afternoon, it mustn't happen again."

"We had a few drinks and a chat. Nothing else."

"Are you sure? I don't remember much after we walked back from the Common."

"You threw up. I put you to bed, and you slept."

"I've got nothing on underneath the duvet, I'm naked. Did you take all my clothes off?"

"You were in your bra and knickers when I left. You must have taken them off yourself. Do you want another coffee? I'll get one for you."

Phil was still in the kitchen, and as the water was boiling, Josh related the conversation he'd had with Toni.

"She thinks you took advantage of her while she was unconscious."

"She was pissed. Must have just topped herself up from last night. She's got a half-empty vodka bottle in her room. Did you go out with them?"

"Yes, I got home late and met them up the pub. She was quiet but didn't appear to have drunk more than normal."

"Did she say anything about her work problem?"

"Nothing." Phil looked surprised. "Strange, she never talks about her work with anyone. She makes out she's totally in control. I wouldn't have thought she'd have any problems."

"I'll take her coffee up and see what she says now."

"Is it sensible?"

"More so than if I didn't."

Josh found Toni sitting at the side of the bed in her dressing gown. He looked over at the vodka bottle which appeared untouched from earlier and sat on the end of the bed, an arm's length away from her.

"What happened this afternoon?" she asked. He related the events from the time he'd returned at mid-day, the visit to the Common, and the reason for him having to put her to bed.

"Did we do anything else?"

"No, we didn't. Honestly."

"Did you want to?"

"It wouldn't have been fair."

"I thought you fancied me, Josh?"

"Drink your coffee and go back to sleep. I'll stay with you while you finish it."

At another time and in another place, he would have been happy to comply. He'd fancied his chances before, but the signals she displayed left him wary.

Since he'd moved to London, he'd brought several girls back to his room for the night, but no one with whom he'd wanted to form any form of relationship. Over the last twenty-four hours, he'd received attention from one of his housemates and two of his colleagues. He needed some time on his own and walked to his local for a drink. Although Jan lived only a short distance away, he was reluctant to visit her. Monday would be a better time to resume contact.

The Following Monday's buzz of excitement filled the rehearsal room as a result of Friday night's success. Josh approached Timothy and Winston to discuss the ensemble's next venture. Jan was nowhere to be seen. She'd not arrived, and Sophie was in discussion with Clive, the conductor. Winston listened with interest to the suggestion of an arrangement of Astor Piazzolla's music for the quintet. To use his cello to play the melody would be a departure from his usual role in the orchestra. Timothy said little, but appeared to be in agreement.

Sophie approached the three to embrace them. Winston confirmed playing interpretations of the Argentinian's music would be a welcome challenge.

As Timothy and Winston resumed their places, Sophie whispered in Josh's ear, "You were bloody marvellous, Josh. You make the violin sound angelic, like." Flattered by her comment, Josh took his seat and turned his music to the correct page. He looked around again, but still failed to see Jan. He hoped she wasn't too embarrassed to attend after Friday night's threesome.

As he picked up his violin, she walked into the room and apologised for her late arrival. Although she sat near Josh, she didn't acknowledge him. Clive stopped any chatter and introduced a new piece of music, Louis Gottschalk's *The Union*.

They played through the first melody, stopping periodically to ensure the dynamics were correct, until the break.

To his relief, Jan approached him and pulled him to one side. "Can we meet alone for lunch?"

He assumed she felt the need to resume their friendship, without complications. "Don't tell the others. We can talk about the ensemble at another time."

As soon as the break was over, the orchestra resumed playing. Clive, the conductor, sang the words of *Yankee Doodle,* at the appropriate time, and the musicians all smiled. His dry sense of humour appealed the orchestra members. He had the ability to draw the best from them. Josh was a convert to music from the Americas, both North and South, and was pleased with the choice.

The two violinists pushed through the crowds of tourists to find a café with vacant seats. Josh sensed her impatience and suspected she wanted to discuss Friday night. He waited in anticipation as she ordered two coffees and joined him.

"Julian's not back. I'd arranged to meet him late yesterday afternoon at the station near his flat. I tried to phone him on his mobile, but I couldn't get an answer."

Josh sensed guilt for the events of the weekend were consuming her. "Eventually, I got through late last night. He couldn't come back as planned, was held up with something important, and won't be back until today."

Josh was relieved she wanted to discuss her relationship with Julian. He could consign the events of Friday night to the back of his mind. "These city types are always busy with the, next deal to be made," he said, attempting to make light of the situation.

"No, I heard another voice, a female one in the background."

"It could have been one of his colleagues. It was probably someone having a drink with him after their conference finished. He wouldn't have phoned you in front of a bit on the side. Go over to see him. It won't take long. Telephone him at the end of the rehearsal."

Jan telephoned Julian at four o'clock. After the call had finished, she turned to Josh. "He's asked me to meet him at the Queen Eleanor Cross, outside Charing Cross Station. Will you come with me? What if he doesn't turn up?"

Josh agreed on the condition they should arrive in good time. "You don't want him to think I'm another romantic interest." He didn't want to place any seeds of doubt in Julian's mind. The incident the previous Friday had to be forgotten. He confirmed he wouldn't divulge the details to anyone.

They arrived quarter of an hour before the agreed time, and Josh waited at a safe distance to make sure he wouldn't be seen by Julian. Within five minutes, a man who towered over Jan approached her. He appeared from nowhere and Josh could only see his back. Jan stretched up to kiss Julian, and Josh waited for a signal to leave. He saw Julian put his arm around Jan's shoulder to lead her to the street. Before they disappeared, she turned to look toward Josh and smiled. Julian's display of affection had eradicated her apprehension.

The events of the weekend raced through Josh's mind as he returned to Wimbledon. He wondered how genuine Jan's affections were for Julian. He was alone emotionally and, in reflection, believed the sex between him and Jan had been intense, more so than just an erotic adventure, but he had to forget any emotional connection to her. To wait in the background for another person wasn't a situation he wanted to find himself in again. He didn't want to lose control of his emotions as he had in Cardiff with Vicky.

When he arrived at the house, he went straight to his room and removed his violin from its case. The opening phrases of the music they'd received at the rehearsal needed extensive practice before they next met. He pencil-marked these and repeated them several times, completing them without fault before he put his violin away.

He found Toni, alone in the kitchen, stirring a meal on the hob. "Something smells good," he said to break the ice. "How was work today? Any better?"

"Fine, thanks. "

She said no more, but he sensed her discomfort. "This isn't doing either of us any good. Whatever you think about me, that's fine. We don't have to be friends, but we can at least get on, can't we?" He looked at her, hoping to appeal to her better nature.

"Did you strip me?"

"No, I didn't. You were sick. You began to take your clothes off, but I stopped you. I put you to bed. Don't you believe me?"

"I don't know."

"I didn't try anything. We'd been drinking." He sat down to gain his composure and continued. "I wouldn't take advantage of you. We'd both had to be willing and aware of what was happening. I had a girlfriend once, and a so-called friend took advantage of her when she was stoned."

He related the episode between Bethan and Tom Parker.

"What about Friday night with your friends?"

"Oh, we just got back too late to get a tube home, had to stay over." They continued to prepare their food in silence until Toni said.

"Hurt you, did she? We all have something we regret happened. Life isn't easy sometimes."

He said no more about Bethan and how he'd treated her in Cardiff. He hoped the conversation had silenced Toni's suspicions regarding Saturday afternoon's events.

Josh tumbled from one short relationship to another. Although he met girls who'd attracted him, the relationships never developed into any more than casual, these lasted a few weeks at most. His work schedule, rehearsals, and teaching commitments meant little time to devote to another person, but he missed the regularity of an emotional relationship.

"I thought you were different, but you're too different. You're not boyfriend material," Toni said one afternoon as they sat in the kitchen. "You're drifting from girlfriend to girlfriend"

"Not many have kept my interest."

"Drifting through life, Josh?"

"I'm twenty-three, I don't want — "

"I don't believe you. What about the girl from home you told me about?"

"It was different, but I find it difficult to trust anyone. We met up again in Cardiff, but it didn't work out."

"All these have been substitutes."

"Not really. Anyway, I met someone else, but she wasn't available."

"Not worth fighting for?"

"I didn't feel I could win."

"Giving up shouldn't be an option if you love someone. You obviously did, because it's what you really want."

Vicky still dominated his thoughts. Every girl he'd met afterward, he'd compared to her. Occasionally, he believed he hadn't tried hard enough. He still had an address for her, but what would be the point of writing again? He'd read and reread her reply many times. It had been the final communication. He'd heard no more even though he'd written again to her. Bethan, on the other hand, was part of his past. He was certain she would never consider him again. The chances would have been remote, anyway. He assumed she'd moved back to Swansea to teach.

"You need someone you can care for, but living in the past isn't good for you. You'll have to bury it before you can move on." Toni added.

"You're probably right." It was the only answer he had for her.

"If you were older, I might have fancied you." She stood, placed her hand on his shoulder, and left him.

Surprised by her candid comments, he stared after her as she walked through the doorway. *What if?* He'd fancied her, and she'd fancied him, but at different times. A relationship with Toni would have caused too many problems in the house.

His multiple commitments left him exhausted, and South Wales beckoned from time to time. To escape the London rush and to go home to Swansea often appealed to him. He could enjoy the tranquillity of the surrounding countryside.

The three-hour journey by train took him through familiar territory and the memories of his formative years. As he searched for a seat, he would glance at peoples' faces for a split second, no more, for fear in becoming involved in conversation of which he had no interest. Some people he would recognise but was reluctant to acknowledge them with either a smile or a greeting. To ignore them was preferable.

On one occasion he spotted Susan Ellis, but turned away before their eyes could meet. He hadn't realised she lived in the city. London attracted many young ambitious people, and he hoped it was big enough for him not to encounter her again.

CHAPTER TWENTY

Autumn 1999

Another time he boarded a crowded train at Paddington to take him home and had difficulty finding an empty seat. After he'd walked through several carriages, he spotted one in a group of four. He placed his violin on the luggage rack above and sat with his rucksack on his lap.

A young female passenger had already taken the inside seat next to him and was looking through the window. She ignored his presence, and he assumed she had no interest in making conversation.

After the stream of passengers had passed through the carriage, he placed the rucksack on the luggage rack at the end of the corridor. As he returned to his seat, he could see the face of the girl on the seat next to him — Bethan. The guilt he still felt for abandoning her when she needed him most made him reluctant to display the jocular façade he used when flirting, but he knew he'd have to acknowledge her. Three hours together ignoring her would have been both anti-social and immature. He assumed she'd recognised him. He hadn't changed his appearance.

"Excuse me, Bethan, isn't it?"

She turned to look at him and with a look of surprise, she responded. "Josh, oh, hello. I didn't realise it was you. Where are you going?"

"Home for the weekend. You?"

"The same. Do you live in London now?"

"I live in Wimbledon."

"Oh, I live in Wandsworth. That's not far"

They continued to talk from time to time. It would have been impolite not to do so, but neither made any mention of the past. Once they arrived at Swansea, they went their separate ways. They claimed they'd been pleased to have met again.

Josh mentioned he'd met an old friend on the train to his parents but didn't elaborate any further. He lay awake that night, pleased he'd met Bethan again, and the journey had been amicable.

The following day, he searched his room for an old address book in which he remembered he'd written her home phone number. He found it but failed to pluck up the courage to phone. The episodes from their past had not encouraged a fresh start, but having met her on the train, the old attraction began to resurface.

The short escape from London hadn't rejuvenated Josh as he'd hoped. An intense rehearsal in preparation for a concert the following Friday lasted for most of Monday, but Bethan had been on his mind all day. He telephoned her parents that evening with hope they'd give him her mobile phone number. They were reluctant to give him her details, but promised to give her his. No news by the weekend would confirm she didn't want to renew the friendship, yet he remained optimistic.

After Friday night's performance the musicians congregated in the bar with a few members of the audience. As Josh stood at the bar to order a drink, he heard a familiar voice.

"I'll have a white wine if you're buying, Josh." He turned and saw Bethan at his side.

"How did you know I was playing?"

"My mum said you'd phoned, and you'd mentioned the

name of the orchestra, so I checked Time Out on the off-chance, and now I'm here." They found seats and spent the next half-hour engrossed in conversation.

Sophie smiled at him across the room, and he called her over to introduce her to Bethan. She declined Josh's offer to buy her a drink and spent no more than a few minutes in their company.

"One of your friends? Seems pleasant," Bethan said.

Josh explained her role in the orchestra but said no more. He wanted to find out more about his re-acquainted love interest.

They shared a taxi home, and she kissed him, leaving him to continue to Wimbledon. Josh had her contact details. He said he'd phone. She agreed.

He spent the next day practising a variety of pieces for future concerts. But by three in the afternoon he felt ready and contacted Bethan. They agreed to and spent the night together. The world seemed right once more.

Surprised Bethan had made the first move to renew their friendship, Josh was wary. He feared he would be hurt once again, but she was attentive without distraction and didn't discuss their past. When he didn't have an engagement at the weekend, they'd travel home to Swansea. On journeys home, the two visited the Swansea Valley waterfalls to take advantage of the natural solitude denied them in a busy London. The affection between them appeared to bring out the best in each other.

CHAPTER TWENTY-ONE

The Millennium Year — 2000

As the year progressed, the initial attraction between the two began to wane. Bethan realised Josh's love of music was his priority, not her. He made excuses he had to attend extra rehearsals on occasions when she felt she needed his attention. Yet again Josh regarded his violin as problematic and made excuses its construction was not of the best.

Bethan failed to understand this and would take every opportunity to play it. Impressed with its tone, she remembered how she'd coveted it in the past. She believed most professional musicians' desire of instruments with a superior quality to their peers' was to satisfy their egos.

One Saturday in April, she accompanied Josh to the West End of London. He carried his *Hoing* over his shoulder, and she realised he was going to exchange it. After visiting several specialist music shops, she was annoyed to see him choose a more expensive violin, one by *Andre Coinus*, a French luthier who'd won a prestigious prize in Paris for his skills. Josh's savings covered the additional cost, but Bethan wasn't impressed. She'd hoped he would have treated her to a romantic weekend away on the south coast. Brighton held an attraction, but he appeared oblivious to her needs.

CHAPTER TWENTY-TWO

Friday, 5 May, 2000

The orchestra had an engagement at the South Bank concert hall. Enthused with his new instrument, Josh wanted Bethan's approval and bought her a ticket. Although reluctant to attend, her mood changed soon after she took her seat.

She spotted an attractive man passing people in her row and making his way towards her. She stood to let him pas,s but he stopped to look at the number of the empty seat next to hers. He looked at his ticket to confirm the numbers corresponded and sat, acknowledging her. She hoped he was willing to converse with and wasn't disappointed.

He commented about the venue and the programme for the evening. He wanted to know how often she attended such concerts and as the conversation intensified, he turned to face her, his hand close to hers on the arm of his seat. She felt flattered. This stranger appeared keen to get to know her.

The auditorium lights dimmed, and their conversation had to stop, but she failed to concentrate on the performance. The interval couldn't come soon enough when she could continue to socialise with her new acquaintance.

He asked her to accompany him to the bar, where he continued to charm her. Attentive to a fault, his body language suggested he wished to go beyond the formalities of a friendly introduction, and he placed his arm on the back of her chair. She responded and touched his jacket sleeve several times as they continued to speak. As her interest in him appeared to have increased, he told her he'd once played the violin, but had stopped after he'd left school. It crossed her mind to let him know about Josh's old violin, but she thought better of it for the moment. It would give away too much information about herself. As he appeared an attractive prospect, she didn't want to mention her relationship with Josh.

"You'll have to give me your number." he said.

She agreed with no thought of the consequences, and they exchanged their contact details.

As soon as he told her his name was Julian, he waited for a response, but Bethan didn't react. His true identity appeared safe for the time being.

As they returned to their seats, she asked why he'd come alone.

"I'd arranged to meet friends, but they haven't turned up," he said as he looked at two empty seats in the row behind theirs. She turned to follow his direction of sight, asking, "You couldn't get them together."

"No. You're here alone as well, I see."

"I often attend musical events. They inspire me to choose pieces of music I can play to my pupils."

After the concert had finished, he made an excuse to leave. She was relieved she didn't have to introduce him to Josh.

"Do you mind if I call you in the week? Perhaps we can meet up. It's been lovely talking to you. May I call you a cab?" he asked.

"No, it's fine. I'm meeting a friend in town, but first I have to go to the loo."

He touched her arm to demonstrate his interest in her before he left.

Bethan watched him go and wondered if a choice had to be made in the near future. Josh had preferred to spend his money on a new instrument rather than treat her to a weekend away. She was still annoyed. Maybe this new man would be more attentive. Temptation had presented itself.

She walked towards the bar to meet Josh, her mind elsewhere, and hoped Jan had stayed behind so she wouldn't have to focus all her attention on him, but she'd left the venue as well.

Josh was alone at the bar. He'd waited for her to join him before he bought a drink, no doubt expecting a positive comment about his new violin, but she was indifferent to his enthusiasm. She closed her body away from him, leaving him to initiate conversation to her distant, monosyllabic responses.

After two drinks, they left to go back to her flat by cab, where she made an excuse of feeling tired. She wanted to be alone, and went to bed, while Josh sat up for an hour to unwind before he joined her in the darkness. She lay quietly, and didn't acknowledge him, a possible meeting with her new interest on her mind.

Julian phoned Bethan the following Tuesday, and they arranged to meet late Wednesday afternoon in South Kensington. With the ensemble's rehearsal the same evening, the chance of discovery would be unlikely. The banter between them flowed as dinner progressed, but soon the conversation moved to another level.

"Look, I hope you don't think I'm being presumptuous but what are you doing this weekend? Do you fancy going down to Brighton?" he asked.

"I'd love to. I've never been there," she said without hesitation.

"We'll go down in the morning and spend some time on the front. See the sights. You'll love it."

He arranged to collect her at ten, but she didn't want to reveal her address until after the week-and agreed to meet him at the corner of her street. He refused a contribution for the meal and paid the bill, "You can buy me fish and chips on

Saturday."

As they walked towards the tube station, she pushed her hand into his, and he smiled at her from his tall frame. This attractive, dark-haired man, the opposite of Josh, appeared generous to a fault. Where would this lead? She had a good idea, but Saturday had to arrive first. Before they descended their respective staircases, he held both her hands and kissed her.

"Saturday." he said.

She took the tube to take her to East Putney from where she could catch a bus to her flat. The tube map displayed above the opposite side of the compartment attracted her attention, and she wondered where he lived.

Without any warning, Josh appeared at her side. His unexpected presence shook her into the reality of her situation.

"Hi, Bethan. Where have you been?"

Surprised to see him, she had to think of a plausible reply. "I've been to a course in the museum. It ran on a bit. You gave me a fright then." She directed the conversation back to his activity. "Rehearsing?"

"Yes, finished about an hour ago and went for a quick drink. Now, everyone's gone home. I'll call round over the weekend."

"I'll let you know." Before Josh had a chance to question this, the train arrived at her stop. She stood to leave, relieved she didn't have to make further conversation. Her wish to visit Brighton would be fulfilled. But at what cost?

On Friday evening, Josh made a detour via her flat on his way home, but she wanted to be elsewhere.

"I came round to see if we could go out tonight."

"Sorry, Josh, I've got to get on with work. It'll probably take all weekend," she said as she removed some papers from her bag.

"I've not seen you all week. I'm rehearsing tomorrow afternoon and on Sunday. You could stay with me tonight, get up early, and spend tomorrow working when I'm up in town."

"I've arranged to go into school tomorrow."

"What? Over the weekend? Can't it wait till Monday?"

Desperate for him to leave, as she wanted to buy some new clothes for the weekend, she became frustrated.

"No, Josh, it can't." She raised her voice. "Can you go? If you're going to pester me you may as well, please."

She'd never made a great deal of an effort with her appearance for Josh.

He, in his usual casual clothes, didn't make any effort for her. His formal wear stretched to two dress suits he reserved for orchestra and ensemble performances. Otherwise, he was happy in jeans, T-shirts, fleece tops, and a leather bomber jacket.

"Tomorrow night?" he asked.

"I'll ring you." She disappeared into her room without another word or any physical contact of affection.

Within an hour she heard her phone ring ,and his name appeared on the display panel. She ignored the call as she was now in a department store buying some clothes she believed would draw attention to her attractiveness. As she approached the counter, happy with her choice, she bumped into one of her male flatmates. He raised his eyebrows when he noticed the underwear in her hand, and she smiled red-faced.

As soon as she returned to her flat, she disappeared to her room to pack a few items into a large overnight bag. *What will Julian think if I turn up for her date, obvious I'm prepared to stay with him overnight?* It didn't matter — she'd convinced herself she had nothing to lose.

She tried on all the clothes she'd bought and admired

herself in her mirror. *God, I didn't think I looked that good. If it's what I want to happen, this lot will seal it.*

After she'd undressed and put on her utilitarian nightdress, she pushed the underwear and a few other items into her bag. Just in case.

Josh sat in his room deep in thought. Bethan's attitude towards him was a puzzle. A knock sounded on his door, and Carol's voice interrupted his thoughts. He opened it if only to distract him from his worry.

"No Bethan tonight? A first," she said realising he was alone.

"No, busy, working."

"Fancy going for a drink? It's just Toni and me," she said.

"No thanks, I've got to practise." He didn't want the company of anyone else. He had too much on his mind.

Frustrated by Bethan's off-hand attitude, he played his violin for over an hour, the only substitute to take his mind off his girlfriend's distant mood. He also had demands upon his time.

The orchestra was due to perform at the Royal Festival Hall the following Tuesday and the ensemble three days later. A busy weekend of rehearsals demanded the need to focus. Bethan's indifference towards him had to be forgotten. He hoped to see her on Saturday night and part of Sunday. Spending time with her would help him unwind.

CHAPTER TWENTY-THREE

Saturday, 13 May, 2000

Julian drove around Wandsworth for ten minutes. He wanted to familiarise himself with the district in which Bethan lived for future reference. Knowledge of her link to the orchestra had aroused his interest in her, and he wanted to make an impression. Her South Wales accent confirmed she was the girl he wanted to meet, not because it appealed to him, but because could use her to his advantage.

He'd left his partner in bed and had set off with a few extra clothes in the small leather holdall he took to meetings. As far as she was aware, he had a meeting in Windsor and would possibly stay overnight.

He pulled the car over to allow Bethan to jump in beside him and place her bag on the small seat behind. He'd lowered the roof, and the sun smiled down on them.

"You've brought a big bag for a day out in Brighton," he said.

"I've got a thick sweater. I'm from Swansea. It's always cold by the sea."

He laughed and drove off, assuming he would gain her trust without a great effort. Since they'd met, she'd behaved as if she'd agree to any thing he suggested.

After they'd reached the motorway, he accelerated to take them towards their destination on the south coast and closed the roof so they could speak, keen to make conversation while she soaked in the atmosphere. He could tell this was a new experience for her. Taking advantage would be easy.

"Where exactly do you live in London?" Bethan asked.

"Over in the East End, near the City. Do you know it?"

"I just stay around the South West. Sometimes I go to Wimbledon."

"That's a nice place. Have you got friends there?"

"No." she said.

He knew she was lying.

"What about Wales?" He was perfectly aware of her roots. "Do you go home often?"

"Yes, now and again, at weekends."

They sat in the sunshine outside an overpriced café in the popular tourist district of Brighton and continued to talk without embarrassing silences. It was a better environment compared to the rattle, hum, and fumes in the choking atmosphere of a London pavement bar. As they ate a light lunch of chicken salad accompanied with two bottles of ice cool lager, he didn't take his eyes off her.

She felt flattered by his attention.

Well used to charming people around him, he sensed he could achieve his objective sooner than he'd anticipated. His business ventures depended on his subtle powers of persuasion.

As evening approached, she reminded him of the meal she'd promised to buy. "Shall we grab some food before we go back? Fish and chips?" She'd spotted a fish restaurant on the opposite side of the road. It wasn't a standard fish and chip shop but a restaurant with an extensive menu of exotic sea-fare.

As they studied the menu, Julian suggested a small glass of wine each, but Bethan stretched her hand over to his and said,

"A bottle would be better."

"I won't be able to drive back."

"Do you need to?"

He looked at her, feigning surprise. Beneath his innocent façade, he realised his speculation would materialise quicker than he'd anticipated. "Not if you're willing."

"I don't want today to end. I've had a fantastic time here."

Between courses, she excused herself to go to the toilet. Once out of the way, he took a card from his wallet and phoned the number displayed. The call took a matter of seconds, and he finished before she returned. After drinking their bottle of wine, she paid the bill as arranged. They walked along the street, and Julian placed his arm around her shoulder.

"Where are you taking me?" she asked as she looked up at him.

"I know a pleasant hotel here where I do business from time to time. I haven't stayed for a while. Do you fancy having a look at it with me?"

Once they'd walked in through the front entrance, he pointed to a comfortable leather chair for her to sit and wait as he approached the desk.

"Hello, the name's Simpson, I telephoned earlier to confirm my time of arrival. Do we have the room I'd booked?"

"Yes, on the second floor, two hundred and four Mr. Simpson, your usual, as you requested on Wednesday."

"I have to get my bag from the car. I'll collect the key and deal with the payment when I come back." He signalled for Bethan to join him at the front door. On their return, he directed her towards the lift away from the view of the reception desk while he collected the room key.

"May we take your card number, Mr. Simpson, just in case you wish to purchase anything at the bar?"

"I'll pay in cash this time." He placed two hundred pounds on the counter. "It should cover everything, including forty for you." The receptionist smiled at him. She knew when to be discreet.

The lift took them to the second floor, and as they stepped out, he looked down at the key in his hand to give her time to find the room number on the indicator board. How many times had he used it?

Happy for her to find the room, so as not to arouse suspicion he said, "Oh, well done. I mistook the arrow directions as we came out of the lift."

As soon as they entered the room, Julian picked up the telephone. "I'll just call up something."

"I don't want any more to eat. The fish hit the right spot."

"Don't worry, you'll like it," he said.

That same morning Josh and Jan made their way to the rehearsal rooms. Once the orchestra rehearsal had finished, the five ensemble players stayed on to ensure their own programme for Friday's concert was seamless.

Afterwards, Josh attempted to contact Bethan.

"Trying Bethan? You'll see her tonight, though." Sophie said.

"Yes, but no answer."

"Call in on your way home,"

When he arrived, he found an empty house, so he made his way back to Wimbledon. Carol and Toni were in their kitchen and noticed his agitated state.

"Anything wrong?" said Carol.

"No, nothing."

Josh, a solitary character, found it difficult to share his emotions. Apart from Bethan, Jan and Sophie, he had no real friends in London. Even his housemates lived their own lives. They only met up for drinks on Fridays, when convenient. Assuming his closest friend, Jan, was with Julian, he was reluctant to telephone her.

"Carol and I are off to the pub. Do you want to come?" Toni said.

After one drink and little contribution to the conversation, Josh returned to the house by ten. Impatient with his inability to make contact with Bethan, he opened the only bottle of red wine he could find in the kitchen. It took him less than an hour to finish it as he sat in front of the television. He finished his last glass as Phil and Trevor returned from the pub, hoping to have a nightcap. They were annoyed with him for having denied them their hoped-for last drink.

The next morning, regretting he'd finished the whole bottle, he walked to the nearest supermarket to replace it. For the remainder of the morning, he waited for Bethan to phone him. Frustrated she'd not rung, he texted her again without success.

When he arrived at the rehearsal room, Jan didn't appear too concerned by his failure to reach Bethan. She'd spent the night alone as well. "The network must have been down. I couldn't get hold of Julian at first. He did text me later to say he'd been held up and would have to stay over in the conference hotel. I suppose he's busy, has to go away a lot. He called this morning to say he was on the way home. Should be back with a meal ready by the time I arrive. He loves to cook. Lucky me."

After Julian and Bethan had finished their room service breakfast, they dressed and packed.

"Let me pay half?" Bethan said.

"It's okay. They've got my card number. Here are the car keys. Give me two minutes while I sort things out. You can get lunch."

When she reached the car park, she turned on her phone,

assuming she wouldn't be disturbed for several minutes, and saw Josh had made repeated attempts to make contact. Julian joined her sooner than she expected, and she placed her phone in her bag to save the embarrassment of being seen checking for calls.

"What time will we get back?" she asked as he started the engine. Guilt had begun to kick in. She hoped Josh wouldn't attempt to call her on the journey back to London, but she couldn't think of a way to place her hand into her bag to turn off the phone without making it obvious she was attempting to conceal something.

Julian sensed her worry but didn't care. He just needed to shower her with his convincing charm for a few more weeks, and upon the evidence shown it appeared to be easy. He expected short periods of guilt, but it would be of no consequence by the beginning of June. Her willingness to comply with his wishes would pay dividends.

"Plenty of time. We don't have to get back until later this afternoon. Is that okay?" he asked.

"Yes, all well," she said, and looked out through the passenger window as they travelled along Brighton's streets. She wondered if her infidelity had been carried out as an act of revenge for Josh's insensitivity, without any thought of the consequences.

"Lovely property around here," Julian said to break the silence.

"Yes, just admiring them." She said little else as they left the city.

As they joined the motorway, he heard a text alert on her phone. "Are you going to answer it?" he said. She pulled the phone from her bag and said,

"It's my mother, she always calls on Sunday morning." She

returned the phone to her bag, but not before Julian noticed her turning off her phone.

They reached the outskirts of London at twelve thirty, and he pulled into a garage to buy fuel. As he stood in the queue to pay, he saw her with her head down focussing on her lap. It was obvious to she was searching for her phone. Having seen her turning off her phone, he knew no-one else could contact her. He didn't care if it was her boyfriend. He knew about Josh, but it was of no consequence to him. He needed her and didn't want any confrontation for another few weeks.

When he returned to the car, he presented her with a bag of sandwiches and a cold drink. "We'll go over to Richmond Park for a snack. Do you know it?"

"Oh, I thought I was getting lunch," she said.

But he'd promised to cook a dinner for his partner and didn't want another meal at mid-day.

Two hours later, they arrived in Wandsworth, at the street corner from where Julian had collected her. By now he'd succeeded in impressing her enough for her to want to continue the relationship.

"I'll ring you," he said. "I'd like to see you again." She kissed him as she got out of his car, confident she'd made the right choice. "Next Friday evening?"

"Where shall we go?" she asked.

"Don't worry. It's all arranged." To ensure Jan wouldn't be suspicious, he had to get back to his flat before she returned from the rehearsal. The meal wouldn't be an elaborate one— a stir-fry. It was an easy task. He had plenty of ingredients in the flat. It would be ready when she returned. Similar excursions had provided him with the expertise to ensure suitable preparations had been made.

Josh returned to an empty house after the rehearsal had finished. He went to his room and placed his violin in the corner. His music stand stood in front of him, but he ignored the necessity to revisit what had been agreed in the rehearsal. He had too much on his mind to contemplate practising for the performances. He didn't even want to join his housemates, who he'd heard laughing in the kitchen as he'd passed. He wasn't in a mood to be frivolous.

Bethan phoned during the evening and apologised for not contacting him. She claimed she'd only spotted his calls after realising her telephone battery was flat. When he told her he'd called round the previous evening, she gave the excuse she'd gone for a walk to clear her head and had forgotten the time. Although reluctant to believe her, he was unable to contradict her statement. After some hesitation, she agreed to see him the following evening. He sensed he would not be welcome.

CHAPTER TWENTY-FOUR

Monday, 15 May, 2000

When Josh went to meet Bethan at her flat, he was met with a reluctance to embrace him. He attempted to demonstrate his affection for her, but the response he received was anything but cordial. She pushed him away. His insecurity began to show. He attempted to hold her a second time, but again, her response was the same. He realised he wasn't welcome when she said, "Please, just piss off, Josh. I've got a lot to do tonight." She'd never spoken to him in that manner before.

"I'll call you tomorrow evening after our rehearsal's over. I've got a concert again on Friday, the ensemble, in the Wigmore Hall. I've got a ticket for you," he said more in hope than expectation.

"I want to go down to Swansea this weekend."

"But we went down together just a few weeks ago."

"It's my dad's birthday, and I want to see him."

The comment surprised him, as she'd not mentioned the anniversary before.

"I'll get the money back. I'll sell it on. Maybe Jan's partner, Julian, can come. I'll ask her. I might get a chance to meet him at last. They always whisk each other away at the end of concerts. They've got a flat in Canary Wharf. I think she's happy with them living together. Makes sense to share, when you want to be together, doesn't it?"

"Oh, do they live together? I didn't realise," she said,

sounding uninterested.

Josh suggested meeting her on Wednesday, but she claimed she had too much work.

Once Josh had left her, Bethan sat on her bed to contemplate her predicament. The suspicion the man with whom she'd spent a weekend could be Jan's boyfriend made her realise he already had a partner, and one closer than she could have imagined. Of course, tickets bought by performers for friends had to be close together. Julián had disappeared after the concert the previous weekend, as had Jan. Bethan wondered if it was Julian's intention to break off his relationship with Jan to begin one with her.

The ensemble members were pleased with their performance Friday evening and relaxed over some drinks afterwards. Jan went to stay at Sophie's, as her partner was away, but with Bethan also away, Josh spent the entire weekend alone.

After he'd completed his university tutorial on Monday, he went to see Bethan. She greeted him in the same manner as she had the previous week. As they sat in the kitchen, Josh attempted to make conversation, but her reluctance to engage with him was obvious. Uncomfortable with her indifference, he suggested they could go to her room. Reluctantly, she agreed.

"What's the matter?" he said. "You've been evading my calls, almost as if you want to be somewhere else."

"It's Monday. I've had a busy day, and I need to get to bed."

"I could stay with you?"

"No, Josh, I'd rather you went." Her telephone rang, and she looked at the display screen. "Oh, shit."

"Problem?"

"No, work. Now can you go, Josh? I'm tired, and I need to talk to this person, then I need my sleep."

He attempted to kiss her, but she shrank away from him.

"Please go, Josh"

"See you at the weekend?"

"I'll see. It's half-term, and I may go to Swansea again to unwind for a few days."

He left the room, deflated. As she answered the phone, he heard her say, "Hang on a minute. I'll be with you now." Josh pulled the door but left it and overheard her speak to the caller with a complete change of tone. After several seconds, he moved away convinced she was lying.

On his way back to Wimbledon, preoccupied by Bethan's attitude and oblivious to all around him, he missed his stop and called in at his local pub. After an hour, his head in turmoil, he telephoned Bethan but couldn't get through. She was unavailable, in conversation with someone else, he was sure. It was nine o'clock. She'd stated she was tired, yet she was still awake. He tried her again in five minutes time. Her telephone rang, but she didn't answer. He drank another three pints of strong beer and staggered home at ten- thirty.

Josh resurfaced at eleven o'clock the following day and panicked. The rehearsal, due to start at twelve, meant he'd be late. When he arrived at twelve-thirty, Clive displayed his anger. He was only able to join the others after he'd tuned his violin, and several errors became obvious and weren't overlooked. A new challenging piece of music had been presented to the orchestra, and he was unable to sight read the continuous chromatic phrases as effectively as Clive had come to expect of him. Jan guessed the reason after smelling his breath.

"Good God. How much did you drink last night?"

"I don't know. Must have been six or seven pints, perhaps

more."

"Why, Josh? You knew we were starting on a new piece. Schoenberg's bloody difficult, impossible when you're half-pissed. I'll see you at the end. We'll go for a drink, a soft one for you."

As they both sat in a bar nearby, she asked, "You weren't on form at all today. What's the matter?" He told her of his concerns regarding Bethan. She was away for a third week-end in a row.

"I thought you were quiet last week. You can't go on worrying like this. Drinking heavily isn't the answer. You're no good to the orchestra or the ensemble, or more importantly, to yourself. Maybe have a break from her. Don't phone. If she wants you, she'll contact you."

Josh took her advice at first, but by Thursday evening, he could wait no longer and telephoned Bethan, but without success. He was resigned to the fact she'd lost interested in him, but couldn't understand why.

Friday afternoon's rehearsal finished at six o'clock and he went for a drink with his four ensemble colleagues. He wasn't eager to go back to Wimbledon. He knew he'd drink too much.

Winston and Timothy left, and Jan realised the weekend would be a make or break for Josh's She asked him what he had planned

"Nothing really. I'll probably practise the new pieces for the orchestra."

Sophie, also aware of Josh's concerns, said, "Come over to-morrow, both of you, to run through a few phrases. I've got my electric piano set up." Jan had already arranged to stay with Sophie, as Julian's work demanded another weekend away, and joining his two friends was a welcome suggestion.

CHAPTER TWENTY-FIVE

Saturday, 27 May, 2000

Josh didn't sleep well. He contemplated telephoning Bethan that but wondered what to say. After failing to make contact, he decided to contact her parents to check up on her. To phone her parents from his mobile was pointless. They'd recognise his number, so he had to find a phone kiosk.

As he walked through the station entrance on the way to Sophie's, he saw one and rang the number. Did he really want to confirm whether Bethan was home or not? He had to, he needed to know if he was wasting his time with her.

Bethan's mother answered, and he gathered his senses to be a colleague of hers he'd met. "Good morning, may I speak to Bethan Williams?" He hoped he'd disguised his voice enough not to give himself away.

"No, sorry she's not here. Who's calling?" Although thrown by this revelation, even though he suspected Bethan had lied, he continued.

"Oh, it's a colleague of hers, Richard."

"No, Richard, we've not seen her for a good few weeks."

"Oh, she said she might be going home this weekend, I'll catch up with her sometime next week."

"I'll call her to say you phoned. You must have her mobile number though?"

"No, no, it's fine. I couldn't get through to her, and as she said she might have been going home over the holiday, I thought I'd try your number as she'd given it to me."

Josh rang off in a hurry. The emptiness in the pit of his stomach shook him to the core. The girl to whom he'd felt a natural attraction, as if by destiny, had finally lost his trust in that phone call. As he mulled over the confirmation, the reasons behind her recent behaviour became clear.

He stood in the phone box for five minutes picking up and replacing the receiver in a state of confusion. Did he want to phone her from the call box phone? It wouldn't give his identity. Was it best to leave well alone until he'd calmed down? What if her parents phoned her to tell her a colleague had wanted to speak to her? It didn't matter now.

Once he reached Sophie's flat, he took out his violin and music. "Let's get on with it," he said without any pleasantries.

Jan and Sophie looked at each other but made no comment.

He placed his violin under his chin and closed his eyes. After several deep breaths, he drew the bow across the strings. The fingers of his left hand leapt and fell in succession as he played a series of chromatic scales. He stopped, opened his eyes and indicated when to begin. He took the music to unwritten heights and depths, displaying extremes of improvisation, leaving his friends unable to accompany him. His entire emotions were manifested in his playing.

After a minute, he realised nobody was accompanying him and stopped. He hunched his shoulders. He felt alone.

"Just play the dots Schoenberg wrote, please," Jan said. Tears formed under his eyes, and she put down her violin. She took his from him, placed it on Sophie's piano, and wrapped her arms around him. Her action triggered an outpouring of emotion, and he proceeded to tell them about his complete history with Bethan. They listened but said nothing. Sophie produced three coffees after which he became calmer.

"Stay here tonight," she suggested.

After half an hour, they began rehearsing under Sophie's guidance and continued perfecting their individual parts as written. After a profitable rehearsal that continued until the evening, they consumed take-away meals and two bottles of wine. Josh spent the night on the sofa after agreeing to continue rehearsing the following day. Although he'd resigned himself to the fact he'd been deceived, he knew it was necessary to contact Bethan at some point to terminate the relationship.

CHAPTER TWENTY-SIX

Sunday, May 28, 2000

Happy with what they'd achieved by mid-day, Josh decided to return to Wimbledon. Before he left, Jan phoned Julian. This prompted him to attempt contacting Bethan. He had to meet her. Whatever had happened between them had to be resolved, and their relationship probably terminated.

Julian answered Jan's call at the same time as Bethan's phone rang. Its ring tone, the well-known Bach's Second Violin Concerto, sounded in the background.

"Oh, is someone playing some music in the hotel?" Jan asked.

"No," he said, as he walked away from Bethan

"I'm just signing out. Someone just walked past. It must have been their phone." As soon as he'd said it, he realised he could have given himself away, but Jan appeared to ignore the answer.

"Can you come to pick me up from Sophie's? It's on your way back from Windsor. Here's the address. How long will it take you to get to me?"

"About an hour, maybe more." Julian, fearing Bethan's voice could be overheard as she answered her phone, walked away from her.

"Shouldn't take long, surely." said Jan.

"Traffic's bad. I'll be with you as soon as I can."

Bethan answered her phone, to Josh's surprise.

"Are you back?" he said.

"Yes, I caught the early train. I've got work to do."

"Oh, I need to see you."

"What's the matter?" Bethan asked.

"I can't tell you on the phone."

"Yes, I suppose we should meet," she said. She turned away from Julian and wandered along the reception hallway attempting to look nonchalant, holding the phone to her ear even though the call had finished. She feigned ending the call and turned to face Julian. "I need to sort out something in work," and placed her phone into her handbag. The less he knew the better. What she had with Julian was no more than a fling she wanted to enjoy, for however long she could. She didn't care any longer. Her relationship with Josh had run its natural course. "Can we get back to London, please?" She had to get back. She had to be honest with Josh.

"You teachers are busy, aren't you?" he said. He didn't challenge the obvious lie. All he had in mind was her link to Swansea.

"We've got an inspection in work in a few weeks, every-one's concerned. We've got to get it right," she said.

Bethan insisted Julian dropped her off by the station in Wimbledon with the excuse she needed to see someone from work. She kissed him on the cheek and walked away.

Josh appeared surprised by Bethan's appearance.

"Where've you been? You don't look as if you've just got off a train, but you said you'd been home when I phoned you. Got changed to come to see me, did you? Bollocks. You've been lying to me for weeks, haven't you?"

"But, Josh."

"Who is he, Bethan? Don't think I haven't worked it out. You've been seeing someone else, haven't you? Why are you dressed so smartly?"

"No, Josh." She appeared upset by the accusation. "There's a fund raiser at school." It was the first excuse she could think of. Her appearance didn't look appropriate for a school event either.

Josh glared at her to add to her discomfort, and she made an excuse to leave, feigning being upset by his suggestions to cover up her guilt. When it had come to it, she'd been unable to end the relationship. She left the house and passed Carol on the way out without a word.

"Not good, Josh!" Carol exclaimed as she entered the kitchen.

He attempted to explain the events of the previous few weeks and how Bethan had lied to cover her tracks.

"Surely she has a genuine explanation," Carol said.

"Don't you think I've been looking for one? I thought I loved Bethan, and she me. We've known each other since we were sixteen. We've been through a lot. Some things we both regret, but lies and false excuses, going behind my back."

Tears gathered, and he stood at the window away from his house-mate's gaze.

Bethan realised she'd left her overnight bag in the boot of Julian's car as she walked towards the bus-stop. She opened her handbag to check if her contraceptive pills were there. Fortunately, she spotted them and breathed a sigh of relief.

For a few months, even before she met Julian, she'd questioned her real emotions for Josh. Had they ever been as genuine as she'd believed? For a second time she'd chosen another person behind his back but needed time to escape the dilemma of a rash decision. Although she'd planned to confirm the break-up to Josh, his approach had thrown her.

She could do without the turmoil of the imminent inspection at work. Tuesday and Wednesday had to be spent in preparation, but a few days home in Swansea would be welcome. She could see her family and her friends and sort out her priorities.

Julian drove to Streatham to collect Jan. The journey from Brighton to Wimbledon had taken two hours due to heavy Bank Holiday traffic. Half an hour after leaving Bethan, he arrived at Sophie's flat in Streatham, where he saw Jan pacing along the pavement. As he pulled up beside her, he couldn't miss her annoyance.

"Where the hell have you been? Two and a half hours, where were you? An hour you said."

"It's the bank-holiday weekend. I was stopped."

"What do you mean stopped?"

"Speeding."

She got into the car, and Julian drove off. She sensed his excuse was a lie. "What's the smell in here? It's perfume. Who've you been with?" she demanded.

"A bloody meeting with a property developer, a female. Okay?"

"Just get me home, will you?" She knew being stopped for speeding wouldn't have taken two hours. Suspicion crept in, but she said no more. The journey to their flat was one of uncomfortable silence.

As soon as they arrived at their flat, she stormed out of the car. She marched inside with her violin and overnight bag over her shoulders. When Julian opened the boot to remove his bag, he saw Bethan's next to his. He'd dispose of it when he had a chance. A phone call had to be made before he joined

Jan. As he finished the call, she walked towards him carrying a hold-all, with her violin over her shoulder, she passed him before stopping.

She turned to face him and said, "I need some more rehearsal time with Sophie. I'll see you later in the week."

With her out of the way, he could contact Bethan the following day. However, another more important call had to be made first.

CHAPTER TWENTY-SEVEN

Monday, 29 May, 2000

Bethan awoke and drifted back to sleep all night. The previous day had finished in a less than satisfactory manner. Josh had seen through her lies, but she'd not had the courage to terminate the relationship. The more she thought about the consequences of her recent infidelity, the more she realised she couldn't tell Josh the truth without Julian agreeing to terminate his relationship with Jan.

She phoned Julian at nine o'clock.

"Bethan, I want to see you. Meet me in town today, this afternoon," he said before she had a chance to speak.

Surprised by his insistence, she read it as enthusiasm to see her again, and asked, "Where?"

"Outside Charing Cross station, by the Queen Eleanor Cross, at three."

"Can you bring my bag? I left it in the boot of your car."

His request brightened up her morning. She could forget the acrimony between her and Josh. She assumed Julian would be willing to terminate his relationship with Jan within days.

With half an hour to spare, she looked around Trafalgar Square and the buildings surrounding the landmark before meeting Julian. She lost track of time and arrived at the planned meeting place five minutes late.

"You're late. Let's go for a drink" He said little else as they made their way to a small nearby bar. Before he ordered their drinks, he gave her the bag she'd left in his car.

"Oh, take this as well," he said as he gave her a large, padded envelope to hold, and she found a seat by a window.

As she gazed out at the busy street, she hoped Julian's mood would improve before he brought the drinks over. She turned her attention to the other people in the bar. Some couples appeared to enjoy each other's company, others sat in silence, fingering their glasses, because conversations, if any, appeared to have dried up. Their gazes fixed on the walls and tables as people searched for topics on which they could focus, to relieve the boredom of each other's company.

The atmosphere helped to make Bethan feel anonymous. The inanimate faces prompted her to suspect the direction her relationship with Josh would become after his limited conversations about music had dried up.

She made sure Julian's attention was focussed on being served before she examined the envelope he'd given her. It appeared official and related to his work. The inquisitive part of her character prompted her to read the name and address which she assumed was an accountancy firm located in Manchester. Upon turning it over, she saw a return address she believed was the one where he worked in the business centre of London.

Julian noticed her examining the envelope and felt even more confident she could be manipulated to do his bidding. Satisfied she'd been taken in, he returned with the drinks and smiled. Her lateness could be forgotten.

Aware of her post as a music teacher and her skills as a musician, he wanted to know her background in South Wales. After several innocuous questions regarding her past, he arrived at his goal, finding out which other musicians she'd come across in the Swansea area, specifically cellists

"I knew one, but not too well. I think he was called Tom. Went to an independent school, so I only came across him in an orchestra in which I used to play," she said. She was unaware Julian's plan was gathering momentum. He hoped she wouldn't object to meeting Parker. The mention of the cellist's name was all Julian had in mind.

"Oh, you've come across him," he said.

"I haven't seen him for years, since I played in the school's orchestra as a teenager, but I don't remember much about him, only what I've just said. Why do you want to know?"

"Oh, it's just we want to set up a project through the firm of accountants he works with. We've been given his name as a link. It's a small world, really. I've spoken to him on a few occasions. He seems a decent enough chap. We've got similar interests. He told me he used to play in an orchestra in the Swansea area. I just wondered if you'd ever come across him, knew a bit more about him."

Bethan wanted to turn the subject away from Parker and the unpleasant memory of the marijuana fuelled night with Tom Parker years before. "You said you used to play the violin too. But you don't have one now?"

"Not any longer. I stopped. Don't have the time, sold my instrument years ago. I've been meaning to replace it but was always distracted and put it to the back of my mind, until I met you." The comment confirmed she'd made an impression.

"I know of a good second-hand one in a shop close-by. It would be worth getting if you want a replacement. I always look out for violins. I saw someone part with it, exchanging it for a more expensive one."

"Who?"

"Didn't know him, but it's a good one. I tried it out after

he'd gone."

Julian knew Bethan was lying about something but feigned interest. Where it could be found was secondary in his mind, but he agreed to look at it another time. Bemused by her comment, he knew he'd have to humour her to ensure his plan would be successful. A large sum of money could be made from his connection to Tom Parker, A small sacrifice to maintain her co-operation would cost little in comparison.

As they rose to leave, Julian picked up the other package he'd brought.

"Work things?" she asked.

"Yes, I wanted to post it but forgot the post office doesn't open on bank holidays. I'll get it off tomorrow." He'd achieved what he wanted. "What about meeting later this week?"

She agreed, and they arranged to meet by Charing Cross on Wednesday for some dinner and a stay over before she went home the following morning. Convinced his plan would fall into place, Julian phoned Tom Parker later, the second call he'd made to his Swansea link in two days.

The following day Jan phoned Josh, aware he was at a loose end. She suggested the three musicians should have another rehearsal at Sophie's flat before the orchestra's next rehearsal on Thursday. She gave the excuse she wanted to ensure their entrances were timed to perfection. She'd already stayed over for two nights, and both she and Sophie were concerned with Josh's overconsumption of alcohol.

When he arrived, he gave the impression he'd accepted the inevitable regarding Bethan. The three rehearsed into the evening, satisfied they were ready to demonstrate their command of the music at the orchestra's rehearsal on Thursday. Josh stayed the night on the settee yet again.

CHAPTER TWENTY-EIGHT

Wednesday, 31 May, 2000

Julian phoned Jan to ask when she'd be returning to their flat. He explained he'd have to work late and would not see her until Thursday. She apologised for storming out and told him she needed to stay at Sophie's to practise in preparation for Thursday's rehearsal. As she placed the phone into her bag, she muttered, "If he's cheating, I'll make sure he'll regret having met me." Would he have lied about the perfumed smell in the car? Although the same as hers, it had been weeks since she'd last travelled in it.

Jan suspected too many inconsistencies in the excuses he'd given for his lateness on Sunday, but if the relationship was over, she didn't want to waste any more time listening to the bogus reasons for his activities. But she'd have to have a safe place to stay. Sophie's flat was too small for them both, and he knew the address. Until then she'd not considered that his reluctance to socialise with her colleagues had any bearing on their relationship. She'd complied with his insistence to leave the concert hall after every performance he'd attended, without question. He'd always taken her for a meal to an exclusive club afterwards. but she'd begun to wonder if he'd had an ulterior motive.

Jan wanted to buy new violin strings and planned to stop off in the West End before making her way to Canary Wharf. She assumed she'd have an opportunity to find some evidence of what she suspected before his return on Thursday.

Bethan made her way to Charing Cross as arranged and arrived five minutes early. As Julian made his way to meet her, he saw Jan walk towards the station. He tried to telephone Bethan to say he'd been delayed, but the connection took longer than he'd anticipated. Bethan's telephone rang as Jan walked past her.

Jan never paid much attention to the streams of passers-by she encountered on the busy walkways, but the ringtone caught her attention. She recognised J S Bach's violin concerto, the one she was sure she'd heard when she'd phoned Julian the previous weekend. She turned to see from which direction it had come and saw a smiling Bethan about to press the answer button on her phone. Jan reached the entrance to the main-line station and took out her phone to appear inconspicuous but continued to watch Josh's partner.

Julian instructed Bethan to walk along the side-street towards the Embankment tube station and buy a Zone A day ticket to take a tube train to Westminster, one stop westbound.

"I'll meet you outside the station, opposite Big Ben. I want to avoid someone from work, as I left early," he said. He hadn't expected to see Jan. His plan had been thwarted. Meeting Bethan that afternoon was essential. The final part of his plan had to be completed the following day.

Jan put away her telephone to make her way along the same route as Bethan's. This almost caused him to panic. His only option was to walk along Whitehall towards

Westminster, with both his overnight bag and the package he'd brought. This added to his frustration.

Both Bethan and Jan boarded the same crowded compartment, but Jan made sure she kept a reasonable distance from her quarry, not to be spotted. At Westminster station, she saw Bethan leave the train and followed, but lost sight of her in the crowd and ended up on the opposite side of the road by the Parliament building. As Jan looked across to the other side of the road, she saw Bethan at the other entrance, and hoped her mistake had worked in her favour. She assumed Bethan had been instructed to change the location where she should wait for someone, a person she could tell Josh about, if he was still interested.

Not wishing to appear conspicuous, Jan leaned over the wall to face the clock tower. She continued to turn to watch Bethan's actions, but saw no indication she'd been told to move to another location.

After fifteen minutes, Bethan took her phone from her bag to answer a call. Several seconds later she placed the telephone back in her bag and made her way back to the trains. Jan ran down the staircase to take her underneath the road, hoping to catch sight of her quarry, but failed to see the direction she'd taken. She had to admit defeat.

Julian had spotted Jan on his approach to Westminster and instructed Bethan to return to the Embankment by tube. He accessed the station via another entrance, and they both arrived within minutes. They pushed their way past a number of people to reach the exit, where Bethan demonstrated her annoyance, but she would be useful for the next twenty-four hours. He felt obliged to apologise and thanked her for agreeing to his instruction.

As they made their way towards the hotel, Bethan stopped outside a music shop. She persuaded Julian to accompany her in. Although he had no interest in the shop or what he knew she'd suggest, it was a necessary distraction to keep her happy and waste time, to ensure his plan would work.

"This is where the violin is," she said as she approached the counter. Julian didn't attempt to stop her. Agreeing to purchase the violin would be a small price to pay for the lucrative return on what he had in mind.

The assistant found the bow, and Bethan proceeded to play several scales. It didn't need tuning. The standard she displayed impressed the assistant. She now hoped he didn't remember her from the time Josh had exchanged it.

"It's a good one. We're selling it for six hundred, as it's got a scratch on the back. We have a repairer who can sort it out if you want."

"You try it. You said you were interested in starting again," Bethan said as she gave him the instrument. He attempted to play a major scale. Although he failed to demonstrate the correct fingering positions, he hadn't lost his bowing skills.

"I'm rusty, haven't played for years. Go and find me a tutor book." As Bethan went to look, he took the violin to the counter and said, "Where did you get this?" He looked inside and saw the initials J S written on the label. "What was his name?"

"Sorry, sir, but we're not allowed to divulge information about other—"

"Do you want to sell this or not?" Julian interrupted. "Was he local? Do you know his name?" The assistant claimed ignorance.

"No, I didn't deal with him."

"I tell you what." He lowered his voice to ensure it was

inaudible to Bethan, "I'll give you four hundred. Two today and I'll collect it tomorrow with the remainder. It's been here a few weeks, so you'll be pleased to get rid of it. You understand what I mean, don't you? Maybe your other assistant will be here to help me. It's good to do business with honest people."

Julian pushed out his hand to take hold of the unsuspecting assistant's hand and held it in a vice-tight grip for several seconds. He saw the pain etched on the man's face and said, "Oh, sorry. I'm quite enthusiastic about this instrument. Please, forgive me." The icy stare didn't leave his face throughout the conversation. It was obvious to Julian the assistant felt threatened. It was one of his ways to secure agreements in his particular world.

He saw Bethan approach him holding a tutor book and withdrew his hand. "We've made a deal. I'll collect them both tomorrow. Let's go." He took her arm to lead her from the shop before she could engage with the assistant.

Bethan had coveted the instrument for a long time, wishing it had been hers. That was now a possibility. The thought of a Hoing violin within her grasp, excited her, and she wanted to thank Julian in a manner he'd appreciate. Once in the hotel room, she set out to arouse him. His response assured, she sat astride him, demanding his attention. The perspiration mixed with the lustful juices of the moment, resulted in them both showering. Here they continued their pleasure-seeking in a manner she'd not experienced at any time with Josh. Afterwards, they dressed into the only change of clothes they'd brought. They'd not been prepared for either the sweaty race in the West End or the spontaneous act of passion.

While they ate in a restaurant near Piccadilly, Bethan initiated the conversation around their compatibility in bed. Julian pretended to listen, but with far more on his mind, he turned the conversation to discuss her weekend in Swansea.

The plan he'd begun to formulate weeks before had no consideration for her well-being. She was a gullible link in an activity he'd planned with Tom Parker.

On their return to the hotel room, he pointed to the parcel he'd been carrying earlier. "Do you remember we were talking about Tom Parker? This was meant to be posted to him this afternoon by special delivery, as it's needed tomorrow. Unfortunately, with what happened, I didn't succeed. Will you take it down with you on the train? I can phone to get someone to collect it from you at the station. It's important it gets to the accountant tomorrow."

"Course, I can, who'll meet me?"

"I don't know. I'll phone their office in the morning so they can arrange for someone to meet you. "Bethan agreed to his requests without question.

Frustrated by her failure to discover Bethan's new love interest, Jan made her way back to Canary Wharf, but found it difficult to relax once inside her flat. Suspicions regarding Bethan's ringtone played on her mind and she contemplated phoning Julian to find out where he was but thought the better of it. She'd had no reason to disbelieve him before but was no longer sure.

During their relationship he'd done nothing obvious to arouse suspicions of another life. As far as she was concerned, he worked as an accountant in a respectable city firm for which his responsibilities took him to different parts of the country and the Netherlands. The latter occurred every two months to ensure company activities were registered to adhere to European laws. He'd always seemed to have an innocent reason for these weekends away.

Unable to contain her curiosity, she searched the cupboards and drawers in which he kept his belongings, but failed to find anything to arouse her suspicion. After she'd replaced everything, she returned to the living room frustrated by her lack of success. Their relationship would change. She could sense it.

At eight o'clock, desperate to discuss what she suspected regarding Bethan, she phoned Sophie. The coincidence of hearing the ringtone again played on her mind all evening, but Sophie failed to enlighten her. Hoping Josh would be able to confirm her suspicion, she phoned him.

"Yes, Bethan's got it. I fixed it up for her some weeks ago," he said. "Why do you ask?"

"Oh, nothing. I didn't realise you could place a chosen ringtone onto your phone. I was looking at my phone for something to do and was given a choice of for me to select. That's all."

"Yes, it's easy. All you've got to do is choose from the list on your phone. You'll soon be able to download any tune or song you want from the internet. Technology's moving too fast for me."

"Does every phone have the same selection?"

"It depends on the make, I suppose

"Oh, fine. See you tomorrow."

By nine- thirty, Jan was tired and needed to settle down to some sleep, but her mobile phone rang. Julian wanted to know her whereabouts. Fortunately, she remembered she'd told him she'd be at Sophie's flat and lied, and told him she was still there, practising with her friend, and would stay the night.

Why would he phone so late to find out where I am? He's not done so before. He'd phone in the morning, but never late at night. If he's seeing Bethan, I have to give credence to my reason for having been in town. He must have seen me.

"I went into town this afternoon to get some new strings and had a look around before coming back for more practice before the rehearsal tomorrow."

"So, you're with Sophie tonight?"

"We've been busy sorting out what's needed for tomorrow." He confirmed he'd see her the following evening and ended the call.

At ten-fifteen Jan heard her door-bell ring. Julian had mentioned a colleague of his lived in the same complex of flats, and they'd often travelled to and from work together. Although she'd not met this person, she wondered if he wanted Julian for some reason. Reluctant to answer the door at this late hour, she switched on the close circuit video communication link. Two well-built men, faces concealed with hoods, appeared on the screen. They looked around as if watching for anyone who might question their presence before pressing the doorbell a second time.

They walked away after no success, but Jan continued to stare at the video link, anticipating their return. After five minutes she turned off the screen. She was reluctant to call either Josh or Sophie to voice her concerns. Sophie, an early riser, would invariably be in bed by ten. The morning would be a better time. She planned to check if any strangers had gained access to the complex with the security guard in the morning.

Unable to relax, she looked in the spare bedroom where a filing cabinet stood between the bed and the window. The top drawer was locked. She opened one of the dressing table drawers to look for a key and found one under several sheets of paper. As she turned the key in the lock of the top drawer, it opened. She pulled out several files with what she believed were customers' names written on the front and placed them on the bed. As she opened each, she saw what she thought were invoices, each containing a heading in the company name of the firm she thought employed Julian. Underneath the headings were names and addresses of people who lived in different parts of the country, and several in the Netherlands.

On these were large five and six figure sums, but nothing specific apart from "Goods Purchased" and "Goods Sold" typed next to the amounts of money. Reluctant to examine the others, she returned all the files to the drawer and closed it. After she'd replaced the key, she went to bed, none the wiser about his activities. It was after eleven, and she needed to sleep.

CHAPTER TWENTY-NINE

Thursday, 1 June, 2000

Once the two intruders closed the door behind them, they crept along the narrow hallway. Careful not to disturb any object that might have protruded into their path, they reached another door that led to the living room. The first turned the handle and pushed the door open, half-expecting to find someone asleep on the settee, but they saw no sign of anyone. It would make their task easier. In the faint shadows, they made out the remaining furniture and an empty table with two chairs underneath. At its side stood Sophie's electric piano. They scanned the room and saw two closed doors. The one on their right with solid panels, they assumed led to the bedroom. The illuminated glass panels on the other in front of them indicated the kitchen where they'd find what they were looking for.

Before opening the door, they stood still for a short time, listening for any sound from the bedroom, but heard nothing. They'd not disturbed anyone.

Once inside the kitchen they closed the door behind them and pulled down its roller blinds. The streetlight outside allowed them to locate the appliances, and above the sink they saw the gas-fired water heater as they'd expected. They put on their head-torches. One of them removed the screws from the front panel. They placed it onto the work surface and located what they needed to adjust. Nodding at each other in agreement, they put on their protection masks and within thirty seconds, they'd completed their task.

They cleared all evidence of their presence and returned to the living room with the kitchen door left open. As they made their way back towards the entrance, they stopped to listen for any sound from the bedroom. Satisfied they'd not disturbed anyone, they left, removing their masks after they'd closed the main door. Once inside their vehicle, parked fifty metres away, they removed their latex gloves and shoe covers.

"Easier than we thought," said the passenger.

"Reliable information. We'll know more tomorrow when I get a call." said the driver. He turned on the engine and checked his mirrors for traffic before pushing the gear stick into position. As he approached the T-junction at the end of the road, he turned on his headlights.

Sophie slept on, unaware she'd been targeted. As night progressed, she sank into a deeper, sinister state of unconsciousness, too deep to hear her friend's attempts to phone her in the morning.

Jan's attempt to phone Sophie failed. For several seconds, she accepted she'd have to wait until the rehearsal to share her worries, but her friend always answered her phone. An early riser meant she'd be awake and would have called back if unable to reach her phone in time. Sophie would never ignore Jan. 'I even take my mobile to the toilet', she would often say, the mobile phone still a novelty to her. Jan's failure to get through prompted her to call Josh to express her concern. He also failed in his attempt to reach Sophie.

"We need to get over to her place. Something's not right," he said when returning her call. "See you at Streatham station."

London's crowded transport system left them both frustrated. In their anxiety, the wait at each stop seemed to take longer than normal. They both arrived at the station within minutes of each other, having attempted to make contact with Sophie countless times. As they hurried towards her flat, they were forced to push against the tide of impatient faceless commuters on their way to work, often on the road, and avoiding an ambulance as it raced by, its sirens blaring.

They arrived to find a cordoned-off building with police and a fire crew in control of an emergency.

"What's happened?" Jan asked a policeman, who stood behind the blue taped barrier, hoping her fears were incorrect. "My friend lives here. What's wrong?"

His serious face prompted them to believe they were dealing with a possible fatality.

"The emergency services were called earlier by a neighbour complaining of a severe headache. He suspected a gas leak and broke into a young lady's flat. He found her unconscious. They've both been taken to hospital."

"Which floor?

"The first, but we've evacuated the whole building." They saw dazed residents on the pavement outside the taped area, but there was no sign of Sophie.

"It looks as if it's our friend Sophie," Josh said. "Where have they taken her?"

"St George's in Tooting. Do you have any contact details for her next of kin?"

"God! She's not dead, is she?" exclaimed Jan.

"I'm sorry Miss, but we can't say any more for now"

"I haven't got her mother's mobile number, but it should be on her phone. It must be in her flat. She lives in Manchester." She gave him Sophie's address and house number as Josh looked along the street for some means of transport to get them to the hospital.

After a minute, he succeeded in flagging down a vacant taxi, and they made their way to Tooting. Jan gripped his hand as the driver negotiated the traffic on the overcrowded road.

The A and E department contained some patients in silence, waiting to be seen. Others held on to impatient children, some in tears. Jan accosted each doctor she saw, eager for news of Sophie, while Josh stared into the empty void of his week.

After an hour, a female police officer arrived to interview them. Sophie's mother had been notified by her local force.

"Before you go, can you explain how our friend was gassed?" said Josh.

"We believe it was carbon monoxide, from the water heater in the kitchen, the only source in the flat."

"She's only recently moved in. Shouldn't it have been tested before?"

"It's something we're investigating, sir. When did she move in?"

"About a month ago. We stayed with her earlier this week but didn't notice anything."

After jotting down this information, the officer left, and the two attempted to make sense of what they'd been told.

"I don't understand, have you felt any effects?" Jan asked.

"No, nothing. You?" Josh shook his head and looked towards the floor deep in thought. After several seconds he asked,

"Why did you phone Sophie this morning when we had a rehearsal later?"

"I had strange visitors at my flat late last night."

"Who?"

"I don't know."

"What did Julian say when he came home?"

"He didn't."

"You were on your own all night? Who do you think they were?"

"I don't know. I only checked to see who'd called, on the security screen, because it was so late. I didn't speak to them. I don't think they should have been in the complex. It's supposed to be secure."

"What did they look like?"

"I couldn't tell. Their heads were covered."

"Didn't you let him know?"

"No. He'd phoned earlier to say he had to work overnight and to see if I was home or not. I told him Sophie and I were rehearsing at her flat, so I couldn't. I didn't want to disturb either of you, so I tried her this morning. She's always up early."

Jan had great difficulty controlling her emotions and needed a considerable amount of comforting from Josh.

"Is something wrong between you and him?" he asked.

"No." She didn't want to reveal what she suspected.

"You'll have to tell him you were home, otherwise he'll think you were with someone else." he said.

What Josh suggested hadn't crossed Jan's mind, but it didn't matter anymore. She took out her phone and phoned Julian's mobile, but failed to get an answer. She tried his office. She'd never needed to call him at work before, but the number he'd given her appeared unavailable.

"I can't get hold of him," she said. Josh didn't pursue the matter any further.

"I'll phone Clive, tell him what's happened, why we won't be at the rehearsal, he'll understand," he said. Their musical director was devastated by the news.

Sophie's mother Anne arrived at mid-day and went to her daughter's bedside, accompanied by Jan. A doctor spoke to Anne as Jan looked on, devastated at her friend's condition.

"We've not had a cerebral response to any stimuli since

she'd been admitted." A life-support machine assisted her breathing, but Sophie showed no other sign of life. Anne Carter sat at her daughter's side and held her lifeless hand. Tears ran down her cheeks, and Jan stood at her shoulder, unable to speak.

The doctors turned off the life support machine mid-afternoon and the three stood together with the aura of death surrounding them, unable to comprehend what had happened. The tension and physical pain in equal measure expressed by Jan and Anne were uncomfortable to Josh, who was unable to help, unable to console. He'd never experienced the death of anyone close before. Both sets of grandparents were alive, but he had little contact with them. As an only child, he'd always been alone without natural empathy, but he knew he had to express his sympathy towards both women. Outcomes as a result of the tragedy raced through his mind, but those he had to keep to himself.

He returned to Wimbledon unable to understand why the water heater had become faulty without warning. As he sat on the bus lost in his thoughts, the earlier events of the week paled into insignificance compared to the tragedy which had engulfed his friend's family.

Sophie's mother needed Jan's support. Jan insisted on travelling back to Manchester with Anne, but she had to collect some of her clothes from her flat. Once she'd packed a holdall, she threw her violin over her shoulder, unwilling to leave it behind.

Julian arrived home with a large box under his arm as they were about to leave. Seeing both women, he appeared confused.

"I tried calling you this morning, Sophie's been gassed. She died this afternoon. This is her mum. We're going back to Manchester to sort out things. I don't know how long I'll be. Where were you? I tried to ring."

"Oh, I'm so sorry. How did it happen? When?" He stood facing the two, unable to say any more. "I must have been out of signal. Let me know when you'll be back."

"Next week possibly. It'll be sometime after the funeral." She said no more and left him staring after them. Distracted in her grief, Jan forgot to approach the security guard regarding the previous night's visitors.

Once inside the flat, Julian checked his phone. He saw a missed call from Jan. He realised she hadn't wanted him to know she'd been at their flat and wondered if she'd been snooping around in his business affairs. He unlocked some of the drawers in the filing cabinet containing confidential records he didn't want scrutinised by anyone. They appeared not to have been touched. However, he failed to open one drawer at the top of the cabinet as he couldn't find the key. He searched through his pockets and his keyring but couldn't find one to fit the lock. In a state of panic, he opened drawers in the dressing table and rummaged through the first without any luck. In the second he saw some paper and moved these to reveal another key. He remembered Jan had returned home earlier than expected one evening and he'd not had time to replace it onto his key ring after having a copy made.

As he checked the filing system of the drawer, he saw some papers were out of date order. She'd been snooping and had been careless when she'd returned them to the drawer. Obsessive in such matters, like his attitude to timeliness, Julian Simpson had to be in control over everything in his life. He couldn't understand why he'd forgotten to attach the key to the key ring when he'd had the opportunity. Maybe he'd had too much on his mind.

With the distraction over and Jan out of the way for a few days, he could remove the contents of all the drawers to another location. He'd have to make sure she couldn't meddle in his affairs again. His plans would have to change. Bethan had completed her part. He hoped Tom Parker would be able to deal with the contents of the parcel. Their joint business interest in Swansea should provide the return he expected.

Bethan caught the ten o'clock train at Paddington in the morning. She sat alone and kept Julian's sealed package by her side for the whole journey. The important paperwork had to be protected. She didn't want to lose sight of it. Pleased he wanted to involve her with his work, she assumed he trusted her. When she arrived at Swansea, there was no-one to meet her. She'd expected Julian to have given a description of her appearance to whoever was supposed to be there. If it had been Tom Parker, he would have known her.

The other passengers had all left the station within five minutes of the train's arrival, and she stood alone on the pavement outside for a further five. As she looked around in anticipation of seeing her possible contact, her telephone rang.

"Have you arrived yet?"

"I've been here for ten minutes now, waiting outside the station, but no-one's here to meet me. How long will I have to wait? I need to catch the bus home."

"Tom Parker phoned about half an hour ago to say he'd been held up. He'll meet you in the hotel opposite the station. Go and get a coffee in the bar. Just go over now."

Bethan sensed a mixture of frustrated anger and panic in his voice, unlike the impression he'd created over the previous month. His attitude surprised her, but she crossed the road and made her way into the bar area as he'd ordered, wondering how long she'd have to wait there.

She assumed no one would notice her with the room full of customers busy in conversation and looked around for a seat. Tom Parker was alone at a table by the window facing the station. He had a half empty glass of beer in front of him. As she approached him, he said, "I think that's for me. Just leave it on the table." She sensed him looking her up and down and eventually he said, "How are you, Bethan, long time no see. London treating you well?" The sarcasm in his voice unnerved her. He still displayed the same arrogant confidence.

He ignored the parcel without even an acknowledgement of its safe delivery and said, "I'll get you a drink."

"No, thanks. I want to go into town and get a bus home."

She left without a "goodbye" and walked towards the bus station, sure he'd been watching her from the bar for several minutes.

Thrown by Julian's attitude, she began to question his motive for beginning their relationship. The flash of anger in his voice when she'd spoken to him on the phone had annoyed her. She had a great deal to think about over the weekend and did not want to be reacquainted with Parker.

She'd hoped spending time away from the demands of London and the unenviable situation she'd created would allow her to reach an objective solution. However, she now wondered if Simpson had intended for her to take the parcel to Swansea from the onset. Why had Parker kept her waiting when he knew her train had arrived? She had a great deal to think about before committing herself to a new relationship with someone she now had doubts about.

Josh telephoned her that evening to tell her about the tragedy, unaware she had gone home to Swansea. Horrified by the news, she agreed to return to London on Saturday to meet him, hoping it would be worth pursuing a possible reconciliation, even on an amicable level. She assumed Julian wouldn't expect her back until Sunday.

CHAPTER THIRTY

Friday, 2 June, 2000

The following morning, Bethan wandered through the shopping precincts in Swansea with her mother.

Mrs. Williams, concerned about Bethan's distant attitude, attempted to find out if her daughter had any worries in London.

At first, Bethan attempted to brush off her mother's probing questions, but eventually admitted she and Josh were going through a difficult time. She told her mother about Josh's phone call regarding Sophie, and her planned return to London on Saturday.

"You do know Josh phoned us the other day to see if you were home. He pretended to be someone else, Richard, who works with you, but I recognised his voice. What's wrong? Have you been seeing someone else?"

"Can we go for a coffee? We can talk about it in the café."

They found one half full of customers, in a shopping precinct, and then Bethan opened up. "I met someone at a concert, someone called Julian." She paused for a few second and looked around the room, guilt encompassing her. "We've been for a drink a couple of times, but it won't go any further." Mrs. Williams made no comment, as if expecting her daughter to elaborate further. "Josh just talks about his music all the time. He's engrossed in it, and sometimes it gets —"

"Boring? What's this new man like?"

"He's not what I thought. He was charming at first, but I'm

not so sure about him now."

Mrs. Williams looked at her daughter in anticipation of what would be revealed next.

"He needed to get some paperwork to an accountant in Swansea and asked me to deliver it by hand as he'd missed the post. He'd arranged for someone to meet me at the station, but the person didn't turn up. He phoned to see if I'd arrived. I told him I'd been waiting ten minutes and wanted to go, but he got annoyed with me and told me to go to the hotel opposite the station, where I'd be met. I dropped the papers off with the person who was supposed to meet me. I think he'd been waiting there for me anyway. I didn't like his attitude."

"Who was he? Did you know him?"

"Someone from the area orchestra I used to play with. Tom Parker, he used to play the cello."

"Parker. Does he live in the Mumbles?"

Bethan nodded.

Mrs. Williams dropped her voice to a whisper and looked around the room, almost afraid to speak. "If it's who I'm thinking of, his father's been involved in the new dockland development, fingers in all sorts—" She stopped and looked around again. "Have you finished, Bethan? Let's go."

She appeared in a hurry to leave and said no more until they'd reached the bus station. "Don't get involved with him, whatever you do. If it's the son, he's into things I can't talk about here. Are you sure it was paperwork?"

"It's what Julian said." Her mother, eager to board the correct bus, instructed her daughter to hurry.

Mrs. Williams didn't push her daughter to engage in uncomfortable dialogue and gazed ahead deep in thought. Once the bus had emptied, she broke her silence.

"How do you know he'd been waiting for you?"

"I don't know. I just didn't see him going in. He was halfway through a drink."

Bethan's father never said anything about his work in the police, but when she mentioned Parker's name he was intrigued to find out about Julian. He made it obvious Parker was as undesirable a character as his father, who assumed he could live outside the law that governed ordinary people.

"Where does this Julian live, Bethan?"

"I don't know, in the east part of London, near the city."

"Are you able to find out?"

"I'll try," she promised, but she'd convinced herself she didn't want to see Julian again. She remembered the party at Tom Parker's house when they were sixteen and suspected she'd been dragged into something she'd regret.

"You're going back tomorrow to see Josh. He's going to need your support now. Just be careful who you meet up with."

Bethan felt relieved she'd not given Julian her address. To continue the relationship with him could possibly place her in danger. Even if she could rebuild the friendship with Josh, she could no longer attend any of his concerts. She'd also have to consider her future in London.

The orchestra achieved little constructive work at Friday's rehearsal. The musicians found some form of solace in each other's company, but Clive decided to abandon it early. The ensemble engagements had to be cancelled, and a decision to continue as a string quartet had to wait until Jan's return from Manchester.

Two police officers were waiting for Josh when he returned to his flat in the afternoon. They interviewed him regarding his activities over the week, repeating questions several times.

"Are you sure you returned here on Wednesday?" the

officer in charge asked.

"Yes, my house mates saw me. You can ask them."

"We already have, and they do confirm you were here early evening, but they didn't see you after ten. Did you go out later?"

"No. I stayed here and practised some pieces for a rehearsal due to be held yesterday. Obviously, we didn't hold it. Clive, our conductor, cancelled when he heard about Sophie. Our colleague, Jan, phoned about eight or just after. She was in her own flat as well."

"Why did she phone? You'd been rehearsing for days. You'd have seen her the following day."

"She wanted to know about a ring tone, how to put a special one on her phone."

"Which one?"

"One by J S Bach."

"Who?"

"The composer. My girlfriend's got it. Well, I'm not sure she is my girlfriend any-more."

"Why do you say that?"

Josh related the events of the previous weeks and how they'd fallen out.

"She's in Swansea for the weekend. I phoned her to tell her about Sophie. She said she'd return to London tomorrow. I'm supposed to be meeting her at Paddington. How was Sophie gassed?" He didn't want to talk about Bethan. "What caused it? She's just moved in. We stayed with her this week."

"We suspect the gas water heater had been tampered with."

"When? It could only have been done after we left."

"It's why we have to question you thoroughly. Do you have a passport?" Josh found it and gave it to the officer. His prints were taken, and the police advised him to be available for further questioning.

Jan phoned him later to inform him what she'd witnessed in the centre of London on Wednesday and her suspicions regarding Julian. "Sorry Josh, but just to confirm, what perfume does Bethan use?"

Although poor with such issues, Josh remembered buying her one for her birthday. Jan had suggested one she herself used.

"Even if his roof hadn't been down, the smell would have evaporated from the last time I was in the car with him. I just think there are too many coincidences." Although he listened to Jan's suspicion regarding Bethan and Julian, he was reluctant to believe her.

CHAPTER THIRTY- ONE

Saturday, 3 June, 2000

Bethan caught the early train back to London. She was convinced Julian's activities had placed her in danger and wondered if he'd pose a threat back in London. He'd bowled her over with his sophistication, but she now suspected what his motive to get to know her had been.

Josh met her at Paddington as arranged, but they showed no physical contact towards each other. They sat in relative silence as they travelled on the District Line south to Wimbledon, even though Bethan attempted from time to time to begin a conversation to demonstrate her sympathy. His response suggested he didn't wish to discuss the events.

As they left the station, she suggested lunch in Josh's local pub. Embarrassed by his silence, she attempted to raise the subject of the ensemble and its future. Aware this venture had little chance of continuing she wanted to demonstrate an interest.

"I'll have to wait until Jan comes back from Manchester," he said.

"You think a lot about her, don't you?"

"Course I do. She's a good friend. She's devastated as well about Sophie. Thank goodness she's got Julian to console her."

"Oh?" she said, attempting to demonstrate her innocence.

"I've not even met him, to be honest. I did see him once meeting her last year at Charing Cross station."

"That's where—" Bethan began but stopped mid-sentence,

165

her mind in turmoil, still reluctant to admit to the affair.

"Where what?"

"Where you rehearse, isn't it?" she asked as she regained her composure.

"No, but it's the closest station to it. It's where I saw them meet last year when they started seeing each other. Probably wouldn't recognise him again. Whenever he came to see her play, he'd take her for a meal afterwards. They'd never stay behind to socialise."

Ravaged with guilt, she lost her appetite, but she finished most of her meal to display an element of innocence. She suspected an attempt to trap her as he pushed his food around his plate, taking the occasional mouthful.

He left half his meal on the plate and suggested they should go to his house. She noticed tears welling up, and in a mixture of loyalty and confusion, grabbed his hand across the table.

"I'll get the bill, and we'll go." He forced a smile, pulled his hand away, and rose to go to the bar. In a quandary, she guessed what would happen if they went to his house. He'd raise the subject of Julian again.

While waiting to pay, he heard a phone ring. Disturbed in his train of thought, he looked across the barroom in the direction and saw Bethan looking at her phone. She returned it to her bag without answering. He gathered someone had phoned her, but he'd not heard the J S Bach ring tone. Josh assumed she'd been instructed to change it to something less noticeable.

As soon as they arrived at his house his telephone rang. Jan's name appeared on the display screen, and he made an excuse to leave the room to answer the call, claiming Clive had promised to phone to discuss the next concert. Jan burst into a tirade of criticism and abuse when he told her he'd met Bethan at Paddington and was in his flat.

"What the hell is she doing with you, Josh? This is a bloody mess. You get rid of the bitch now. Get her out of your life. They deserve each other."

Bethan's telephone rang as they were talking. Her mother's name appeared on the display.

"Somebody's just phoned for you on the house phone. I told him you'd just gone back to London. He sounded annoyed. He wasn't local, by the sound of him. How many of your friends knew you were down here?"

"Only Julian. The one I told you about."

"Where are you now?"

"With Josh."

"Are you going to see Julian again? Has he been to your house?"

"No, Mum. Look, Tom Parker, who I met at the station, knew I was down, but the only people who knew I was coming back to London early were you and Josh. We're trying to sort it out. Didn't the caller say who he was at all?"

She knew it had to be Julian. It couldn't have been anyone else, but she knew she'd not given him her parents' home phone number. She'd never divulged their contact details to anyone in view of her father's work. "I'd better go, I'll phone you later." She checked her phone. Both her parents' mobile numbers were store,d as was her home number, so she'd recognise the caller. *Julian must have copied them without my knowledge.* She sensed her level of vulnerability had increased in those few seconds.

Josh realised Jan's suspicions were correct. He moved away from the door where he'd stood to overhear Bethan's conversation. He'd heard enough.

"You're right," he said. "What are you going to do?"

"I'll have to move my things from the flat. Can you help me? He can be her problem now."

"Where can you move to at such short notice?"

"I have other friends I can move in with. I'll sort it out over the weekend. I've anticipated this happening. Don't tell the bitch about my plan to move. She'll probably tell him."

When Josh returned to the room, he noticed Bethan's agitated state. Now aware of her infidelity, he was ready to challenge her.

"Anything wrong?" she said, attempting to display a level of innocence.

"Perhaps you'd better tell me the truth, because quite a few things don't make sense. You'd better phone home again. You've got more important news to tell them, especially about Julian. It was the name you said on the quiet while I was on the phone. He knew you were going down to Swansea, didn't he? You'd planned to meet last Wednesday afternoon in town. Stay with him in some sleazy hotel before going down on Thursday. I am right, aren't I?"

She failed to answer. Her silence confirmed her guilt. She'd been caught out and had no option but to admit to what Josh had said. Hoping he would forgive her, she remained tight lipped regarding the weekends away. She suspected any respect he might have left for her would disappear in an instant.

"When did you meet?" Josh asked.

"At one of your concerts."

"The last one you attended was weeks ago, how?"

"We were sitting next to each other."

"The weekends you said you were away, you weren't in Swansea. I know because I spoke to your mother last Saturday. You both went home each night, because you've just told me Wednesday was the first night you'd stayed with him."

She nodded in agreement.

"It's not true, is it? Please, if you're going to tell me, at least tell me the whole truth."

She had no option but to admit to the affair. He'd detected a flaw in each excuse she'd made.

He paced around the room.

The vulnerability she felt had increased. How would Josh react once he knew the whole truth?

"I'm right, aren't I?" he asked as he stood above her.

She didn't respond.

"Caught the train down in the morning?"

"I'm going to move back to Swansea in the summer." she said.

He walked over to the window to look out. "Why? Is it because of what happened between us in Cardiff?"

"He just caught me unawares, when I was least expecting it, I just got swallowed up and one thing — "

"Led to another," he finished. He hid his face, but she guessed he was crying. Whatever she had done, he wasn't ready yet to dismiss her from his life yet.

Although they shared the same bed, it wasn't how he'd envisaged spending the night with her. Aware of her affair with Julian, he didn't know how to react. Neither of them was able to sleep, and he got up to go to the kitchen. He wanted to occupy himself, to make a drink. But he fumbled with the kettle and spilt most of the water onto the floor. Bethan joined him and mopped up the mess he'd made. Afterwards they sat to drink the tea she'd prepared.

"Are you going to see him again?" he asked.

"No. I don't want to."

"You seem certain."

The fact she'd delivered a package for him had to remain a secret.

CHAPTER THIRTY-TWO

Sunday, 4 June, 2000

Bethan left the house in the morning, their relationship now over. London had provided her with many opportunities and experiences, but she'd never be able to afford a place on her own. The city drained her of her salary and more every month. Josh would have been an ideal partner with his regular music demands, but she'd destroyed any hope of reconciliation.

As she put her work papers to one side, she looked through her window at the gritty streets, and contemplated her uncertain future. Moving back to Swansea had to be her escape route. She searched through the Times Educational Supplement and saw several jobs advertised in the Swansea area. A letter of resignation had to be presented to her headteacher the following morning. She hoped it would be enough notice to finish at the end of term. Even though Tom Parker had entered her life once again, she had to make sure he wouldn't pose a threat, but she had nowhere else to go. With her father in the police force she'd have better protection.

Josh contacted Jan to confirm what she'd suspected. In the meantime, she'd already arranged to move out of her flat the following Tuesday. Another colleague had offered her a temporary room in her house in the outskirts of West London, and Winston had volunteered to help her move her belongings. Josh also offered his help. She assumed Julian would be at work and wouldn't be aware of her plan until he returned home in the evening.

Chapter Thirty-three

Tuesday, 6 June, 2000

The three musicians met at the entrance of the flats in the morning. Winston found a convenient parking space to load the car, and they took the lift up to the second floor. An eerie silence greeted them as they stepped into the stark, impersonal corridor.

"Do you see many of your neighbours?" Winston asked.

"I haven't, but Julian claims he does, a colleague from work. I've not seen any evidence of anyone apart from — " She wondered how genuine the two visitors the previous week had been and said no more about it as they reached the entrance to her flat.

After they'd opened the flat door, the three walked through the clinical entrance hall. As they entered the living room, they saw several black bin bags bursting with contents on the floor. Jan checked one, intrigued to find out what rubbish Julian was throwing out. To her horror she found it contained some of her clothes. She opened another to find some more of her belongings. All her possessions had been bagged to be disposed of.

"The bastard, he's chucking me out anyway."

"Made it easy for you," said Winston.

Josh looked around the room and saw several photographs of what he assumed were family members on a shelf. He saw no evidence to show Jan had ever been Julian's partner. He picked up one displaying four men, two older and two youngers.

"Is this him?" he said.

"Yes, it's him." Jan pointed to Simpson, but Josh's attention focused on the other young man.

"Who's this?"

"A relative I believe and their fathers."

"Do you know his name?"

"Tom, why?" Josh put the photo back onto the shelf without any care, and it fell to the floor. "Leave it," she said, but Josh looked down at it and stamped his foot to shatter the glass.

"I sense some hate," said Winston.

"Deservedly so," said Jan.

"More than you would understand," said Josh.

Jan checked both the bedroom and bathroom, but nothing of hers remained. All trace of her had been removed. "Okay, let's go," she said, aware she'd been used. She failed to understand why Simpson had invited her to live with and wondered if it had been to present a respectable front.

Within ten minutes, all the bags were stowed in the back of the estate as Jan's possessions were now safely stowed, Josh said, "Get in."

"Not yet, I need to check something else." She ran back into the building and returned to the flat for one last look around. She felt the urge to examine the filing cabinet she'd snooped in and pulled the handle. The empty drawer slid out with ease. It no longer contained the paperwork she'd seen before. Upon inspection, she discovered all the other drawers had been unlocked and emptied. Whatever they'd contained had been moved and possibly destroyed. Desperate to find evidence to suggest the reason, she looked under the bed and through the dressing table, but failed to find anything suspicious, not even the key she'd used to open the drawer. All she saw out of place was a violin case propped up against the wall next to the cabinet. *Not mine. Probably Bethan's. She's welcome to him.* She thought no more about it. As she stood in the room, pondering over what she'd discovered, her phone rang. Josh's name appeared on the display. She pressed the accept button and heard his voice.

"Get out, now. I think he's just driven in. It's a BMW sports. Use the staircase." She put her phone back in her pocket without a response and ran out to the corridor. As she reached the top of the stairs, she heard the lift door open. Two steps at a time, she raced down to the ground floor, through the entrance door and into the car.

"Go, Winston. I've seen enough."

He drove towards the gate, expecting Jan to use her fob to open it.

"Stop, I need to see if any post has been delivered. I'll be quick," she said, and leapt out of the car. As soon as she reached the office she blurted out. "Number one-four-four."

"Sorry, Miss, what's the problem?"

"Has any mail been left here for us at one-four-four?" The security guard checked the locker room where post unable to be delivered to residents' flats was stored. She kept her eye on the security screen for a sighting of Julian's car.

"No, Miss, nothing for your address today but Mr. Simpson's already called in. He does most mornings at this time. She thanked the guard and ran back to the car.

"Drive, Winston. Just drive." She leant over from her seat to open the window and point the fob at the gate's sensor as her phone rang. She looked at her phone display. "It's him," she said.

"Don't answer it," Winston said as he drove through the

gateway.

"I have to. I've got to put him to bed once and for all." Her attention turned towards her ex-lover as she spoke to him on the phone, "I know all about you and Bethan so I'm off. Don't try to —" Jan went silent and obscenities could be heard coming from the phone for several seconds, and then, nothing. She took the phone away from her ear, pressed the 'end call' button and placed it on her lap.

"Drive towards the Blackwall Tunnel and M25," she said having regained her composure. Winston didn't need telling twice. He drove with purpose and didn't give way if fifty-fifty decisions had to be made regarding other motorists.

Throughout most of the journey she sat in silence, only giving instructions when directions had to be clarified. Thoughts about Simpson raced around her mind. His motives for moving her in still puzzled her. It wasn't for sex, although she had regarded it as a healthy side of their relationship. Her relationship with him had been a sham from the start. How many other girls like Bethan had he met to take away on those long business weekends? The situation demanded many answers.

Winston pulled the car into the driveway of Jan's new lodgings in New Malden, her temporary address until she could regain some of her old independence.

On Wednesday Jan travelled back to Manchester. Josh arranged to join her on Thursday for Sophie's funeral.

CHAPTER THIRTY-FOUR

Jan met Josh at the station in Manchester and took him to a nearby wine-bar. After a few lunch-time stragglers finished their meals, it began to empty. She found a seat as far away from the window as possible and Josh bought two glasses of wine.

"I feel safe up here," she said as he joined her with the drinks.

"Have you heard any more from him?" he asked.

"No, what he said on the phone put paid to it all, but in all honesty I'm relieved. I've tried to make sense of everything. I'm convinced Julian isn't what he says he is. Those two characters who called round the other night shouldn't have got in to the complex, only residents are able to get in. They didn't look as if they were. Why had they called at our flat? Apparently, he returns to it in the mornings, possibly to collect his post. I've never seen him when I've been home. He used to phone me in the daytime, obviously checking up. He thought I was here in Manchester on Tuesday."

"Yes, but why had he packed all your things in bags?"

"He must have known I suspected him of something. Bethan must have told him she'd admitted to you about their affair. Last Wednesday night I tried to look for some clues about him and found some invoices and paperwork for his company. I went back to the spare room on Tuesday to check if I'd left any of my things there and tried the drawers. They were all empty. Everything had been moved."

"He knew you'd been snooping."

"I thought I'd put everything back in its place because he's so fussy."

"Why would he have invoices for the company he works for at home?"

"God knows, unless they've run out of space."

"Those offices are huge. They've got plenty of room. It sounds as if he's been buying items through the company for his own use and hiding the proof of purchase from his bosses. He's an accountant, he can hide figures. Did you see what they were or from where they'd come?"

"I don't remember any names just some signatures I couldn't read."

"What's the name of the firm he works for?"

"It's JK Chartered Accountants, an easy name to remember. It's what he told me, ages ago."

"Have you still got the number he gave you for his office?"

"Yes, but it's wrong. I couldn't get through from the hospital when I tried to tell him about Sophie."

Jan's parents were a couple in their fifties and proud of their daughter. They were devastated by Sophie's death, a friend with whom she'd gone to school. They'd been inseparable. They welcomed Josh and insisted he eat a meal before showing him his room for the night.

Later the two musicians visited Sophie's mother's house, where they found Mrs. Carter still unable to believe her daughter had died. Tears ran down her cheeks in a grief she failed to control. She sat in silence for minutes before composing herself to welcome her daughter's best friend.

"We'll have to have an inquest on Jan," she said. You'll be called, and you too, Josh. Is your boyfriend coming up?"

"No, we're not together anymore." Neither Jan nor Josh elaborated about the end of their relationships. It wasn't the time or the place to discuss their own personal lives. Their disappointments bore no comparison to Anne Carter's. Yet her response took them by surprise.

"Good, I didn't like the look of him, but his name's familiar. Perhaps you should move up here now, don't want the same to happen to you."

"What do you mean?" Jan asked, intrigued by the comment.

"Julian Simpson? I remember Ruth spoke about a boy with the same name when she played in the schools' orchestra. Some issue about another boy, but I can't think now."

Jan, although desperate to speak to Sophie's sister about Simpson, realised it wasn't an appropriate time. She hoped the opportunity would arise before returning to London.

They both returned to Jan's house by nine o'clock and after supper, her parents went to bed. "I've got something else to tell you Josh. Prepare yourself for a surprise. You see, Sophie and I had been lovers. She'd never had a boyfriend for any length of time when younger."

Josh remained quiet. He'd suspected their involvement since the night he'd spent with both of them in Putney.

"Were you still—when you were with Julian?"

"We'd always been fond of each other in school. We went on holiday together when we'd finished our *A* levels. Nothing had ever happened, but we'd always thought. A crowd of us from the sixth form went to Magaluf. We shared a room. Boys were boys, show-offs, didn't fancy any of them, disappointed at first, but not really. She and I got on even better. Relief the exams were over I suppose. Maybe we put the boys off, I don't know. Nobody even tried chatting us up, perhaps they'd suspected before we had as well. Anyway, one night we'd had too much to drink and went back to our room. We talked about the boys, how we didn't fancy them and began to console each other. We joked we didn't like boys. We kissed and ended up — well I won't go into the details."

"But Sophie kissed me passionately after our night together, I thought you were angry."

"She tried to put me off Simpson. She saw how I was with you that night. You had to be better."

"Why?"

"She tried to warn me away from him for some reason, never telling me why. I assumed she was jealous and had wanted me for herself. She was also emotional. When she'd been satisfied, she was very emotional. She said you were very different to other men, not a bloke's bloke as she used to tell me. I think if you'd been a bit older, she might have questioned her own sexuality."

"I felt it better with you than with her," Josh said.

"Josh, please don't say anything now, I loved her dearly but was never sure about my own sexuality either, I knew I wanted more. I'll get a drink." Her emotions in turmoil she went to the kitchen, an excuse to be alone for several minutes.

Josh regretted what he'd said and paced about the room, angry with himself for assuming she was attracted to him. Although he wanted to hold her, in his frustration, he wondered why she would even consider him an emotional attachment. She was three years older than him.

Jan returned with two hot drinks which she placed on low tables each side of the settee.

"I'm sorry Jan, I shouldn't have — "

"Shut up and hold me for God's sake!" They kissed without hesitation, as passionate as any he'd experienced, and his mind drifted back to the night at Putney. The emotion was intense, more than any he'd encountered with Bethan, and before either could restrain themselves, they ended up on the floor, as did their clothing. Afterwards they lay exhausted in each other's arms.

"Do you think your parents will have heard?"

"No, they sleep like logs, let's go up."

"Won't they mind?"

"As long as you're in your own bed by six. Please, just hold me, they won't know, but be quiet." She kissed him again. "Now I can with no guilt, you know all about me. Just accept me for what I am, but don't expect too much from me." He looked at her and understood they could enjoy each other's intimacy, but only for the time being.

"Did Sophie's mother know about you two?"

"I don't know. Now shush and just touch me." They needed to be close to each other that night.

Josh awoke at five and crept to the room prepared for him. Breakfast was a silent meal as Jan's parents gave each other a knowing look.

CHAPTER THIRTY-FIVE

Friday, 9 June, 2000

Sophie's school and university friends, who Jan had not seen for some years, joined her family and orchestra members at the funeral. No one was able to comprehend the circumstances surrounding her death. Afterwards, all those who wished to attend met in the church hall near Sophie's home for refreshments. Sophie's sister, Ruth, approached Jan after the funeral. She wanted to find out more about Jan's relationship with Julian Simpson. The two stepped outside the church hall, away from the friends and colleagues.

"Sorry we didn't say much yesterday. You must be as upset as we are," she said.

"We were close, always had been. It's been a terrible time. Your mum's holding up well."

"Thanks for being with her in London."

"It was the least I—"

"Sophie was worried about you and the man you lived with."

"Yes, she'd tried to put me off a few times, I thought she was—"

"Jealous? No, don't worry, I knew how close you were, she told me. No, it wasn't that."

"I don't understand?" Jan said. She hoped Ruth would enlighten her.

"Julian Simpson, what did he look like? Was he tall, dark hair, from this area?

181

"Yes. He said he came from Warrington but had moved to London a few years before Sophie and I did.

"Did he ever say anything about playing the violin?"

"He did. I met him after a concert. It was just before we began the small ensemble. He told me he'd played in school but had given up after he'd left. He'd been too busy, or so he said."

"If it's the same person I'm thinking of I'm not surprised. Have you got a photo of him?"

"God, no, I'm sure I threw them all out."

"Perhaps in your bag?"

Jan opened her bag and rummaged through, "Oh, yes," she said as she pulled out a small photo taken in a booth. "I didn't realise I still had it. I thought I'd thrown out everything to remind me of him."

"Let me see. Is this recent?"

"Well almost, he's clean shaven now but more or less the same."

Ruth looked at the photograph. "Yes, it's him. I remember those cold eyes. He was in our area orchestra when we were in the sixth form. He managed to get in, although I don't know how. He broke a lad's arm in rehearsal one night. They were only seventeen. It was some argument or other, about who was to play what. The lad told us much later, Simpson had wanted to play with the first violins, and they should change places. The other lad refused. It wasn't up to him. It happened during a break in rehearsals. Simpson asked the other lad outside to talk about it. They both went and we heard a cry almost as soon as they'd left us. Simpson claimed they'd been messing about, but the other lad was in so much pain, he could hardly speak. He was rushed to hospital. It was a compound fracture. The conductor kicked Simpson out immediately, he wasn't that good a player anyway. Before he left, he lost his temper in front of us all, and smashed his violin on the floor. Afterwards we just wanted to find out more, but everyone just closed ranks. We couldn't even find out from which school or sixth form he'd come, and we heard no more. He was being protected somehow."

"He was never aggressive with me, just very controlling. But he'd often go away on business, so I'd see Sophie quite often. I stayed over with her when he went away. A short time ago he began an affair with Josh's girlfriend."

"That must have been pretty awkward for you both."

"Yes, but I think Josh's accepted it now, didn't at first. But you'd told Sophie about Simpson I take it?"

"I know this is a big place, but I asked her to describe him. She'd not met him. Said he never socialised after a gig. I was suspicious when she told me his name, and he was from this area. Now I've seen his photo, I'm certain it's who he is. Your friend Josh seems pleasant enough, a bit locked up in himself though. Nothing going on is there?"

"No, we're good friends, look out for each other. I don't want any complications with a serious relationship. It could prove awkward."

Ruth said nothing, but looked knowingly at her, suggesting she didn't believe her.

CHAPTER THIRTY-SIX

Summer 2000

Jan and Josh returned to London over the weekend. They had several rehearsals for a concert arranged for the following Friday. Jan noticed Josh's lack of enthusiasm. He appeared removed from the orchestra's environment. After it ended, she suggested they go together to a quiet bar for a drink, to ask if he needed some more time to regain his composure.

"It's okay, Jan, I'll be fine. I just need to sort out what's happened, just like you must. The more we can play, the more engagements we can get, the better. To take us out of ourselves. Will you come back to my place tonight?"

Although they enjoyed the intimacy of sleeping together, in public one would have assumed they were platonic friends. The arrangement suited Jan.

Josh met Bethan once more before the end of her school term. She confirmed she was leaving London, with the excuse she found it too expensive. She'd applied successfully for a teaching post in Swansea but made no mention of what she suspected about Simpson. Josh and Jan continued to spend time in each other's company after rehearsals and concerts. "I think she's regretted the whole incident, but I don't want reconciliation. She'll be two hundred miles away. We'll be out of each other's way. It's for the best," he said.

"What about when you go home?"

"I've no intention. The trust has gone. At least you and I are getting on."

Jan didn't want to hear this, not wishing to make another commitment. "Please, I've told you not to expect too much from me. I may not be able to stay here. Julian's too close."

He agreed but deep down he wondered how he would deal with another disappointment.

At the end of July, Jan announced she'd be moving to Manchester. She'd applied for a post in an orchestra there during the week of Sophie's funeral. The paperwork she'd discovered in Simpson's flat suggested his involvement in something sinister. She wondered if he'd lied about where he worked. The telephone number he'd given her was wrong, and she suspected he'd be a greater threat than she'd anticipated. Simpson's comments on the day she'd left his flat had convinced her to be as far away from him as possible. Desperate to forget her past with him, she looked forward to leaving London. Her salary would be far less, but her expenses would be less demanding.

Once she'd moved back to Manchester at the end of August, Josh withdrew into his shell once more. It was the only defence mechanism he could access, as well as white wine and strong beer. She telephoned him several times, but he was dealing with his own demons. He felt as if he was reliving a situation he'd experienced at the end of his final year in Cardiff with Vicky. Memories of his time with her had often crossed his mind even when he and Bethan were at their happiest. But he assumed she'd settled into a permanent relationship with her boyfriend.

Over the summer months, Bethan moved back to Swansea, to teach in a small school on the outskirts of the city. Her hair, dyed auburn instead of its natural black, guaranteed as much anonymity as possible. She needn't have worried about Tom

Parker. His influence in the city had been curtailed during the early part of the autumn. She found out later his business ventures had been of a criminal nature, importing class A drugs into South Wales. Nothing had changed. He'd only progressed to a different level of misery. It confirmed she'd been used by Simpson, but she had no intention of informing Josh how she'd been fooled by him.

CHAPTER THIRTY-SEVEN

Autumn 2000

As the Millennium year rushed through autumn and head-long into winter, Josh's fortunes continued to change. He withdrew into himself and began to shut down. Although he kept in touch with Jan for a few months, his interest in her diminished. He realised how insignificant he'd become as the dark evenings grew longer. His insular character no longer protected his emotions, and he found it difficult to regain his positive attitude.

Jan visited London several times in the autumn but didn't stay with Josh. The two only met in the company of a large group of musicians. It was as if their friendship had been inconsequential. To him, finding solace in each other's company to overcome their disappointments appeared to have been the motivation for their relationship.

When not performing, he'd join his housemates for their Friday relaxation drinks, but his reliance upon alcohol increased. This meant several lost days, and his reliability fell into question. His lateness for rehearsals became a regular occurrence, one unfortunately, the night before a prestigious concert at the Royal Albert Hall.

The orchestra was due to play *Mahler's Third Symphony*, and many extra musicians were employed to augment the orchestra for this lengthy piece due to be broadcast on both television and radio. Although Josh realised the stressful atmosphere affected Clive, he continued to turn up late for rehearsals. At the end of the final rehearsal, Clive approached him to suggest a private word.

"I realise you've had a bad summer but—" Clive began.

"That's a bloody understatement Clive. It's been a shit time."

"I'm worried about the concert tomorrow. You've been late for rehearsals too many times."

Josh said nothing in his defence, and made it obvious by his body language, he wasn't interested in Clive's overall responsibility.

"Don't ignore me Josh, please."

Clive began to raise his voice. "This is an important concert, our reputation as an orchestra depends upon it. We can't have any mistakes or slip ups to make us seem sub-standard. Our audience has paid good money and will expect the best, a flawless performance."

"Are you telling me I'm going to let the orchestra down? Aren't you happy with my playing?"

"Look you're a professional musician. You've learnt with the best and are playing with the best. The work you did with the ensemble was exemplary, some of the best I've heard, but *at present—*"

"Do you think I've lost my edge?"

"It's not what I meant, I'm just concerned you're not engaging with the other musicians, and it's becoming obvious to—"

"Who said?"

"No-one, but an orchestra has to be a team."

"I can't just switch on an off like a light."

"God, Sophie's death hit us all badly, and then Jan moving back to Manchester. It's left a gaping hole in the string section."

"And everything that went with it. I'm off, I don't want to talk about it." Josh walked away leaving Clive to ponder on his violinist's future.

After Josh arrived home, he contemplated what he should do. Although tempted to go to his local, to join his house-mates, he realised Clive would be right, he would be a liability.

Josh turned up the following morning as fresh as he'd always looked. He had a point to prove. The all-day rehearsal began at ten in the morning. The individual soloist and choirs had rehearsed with the orchestra on several occasions and the final preparations suggested a successful outcome. The concert had been a sell-out for weeks.

After Clive's pep talk of encouragement, the performers walked on to the stage, and the music began. The musicians, choirs and soloist performed with total cohesion to ensure its success. Clive knew the orchestra's reputation had been enhanced and attempted to congratulate every performer afterwards, but saw no sign of Josh.

Most of the musicians went for a drink in a local bar. Their conductor, caught up in the euphoria of the occasion, joined them and asked, "Where's Josh, Winston?" Clive assumed the violinist had joined them. He wanted to reconcile the atmosphere created the previous evening.

"Gone, he was on good form tonight though. The best I've seen him since before the summer."

"I have concerns about him. I don't think his heart is in his work, for obvious reasons. Can you have a word with him?"

"It's not easy to get through, he'd hoped we could have carried on with the ensemble, in another format but I haven't got the time, I have other commitments. The orchestra's as busy as I've ever known it and we're managing well with my teaching. I feel bad because he thinks we're letting him down, but I've made up my mind."

"Oh, does Timothy feel the same?"

"He's joined another group with musicians who aren't in our orchestra."

"Does Josh know?"

"No, we haven't told him."

"Don't you think you'd better," Clive said, concerned about his violinist's welfare.

Winston shrugged his shoulders, and with a look of guilt, said, "He's become so distant and unreliable we can't commit. None of the other string players want to get involved in more work either."

The orchestra played several concerts over the festive season, but Clive saw Josh became more and more detached from his colleagues. He suggested Josh should take a couple of weeks away, a break at home.

"Get home to see your friends. We haven't much on until mid-January. It's always quiet after Christmas.

Josh hadn't set foot out of London since the summer. To meet up with several of his old friends appealed to him. He stayed away from alcohol and visited Owen in Pontardawe.

Pleased to see him, Owen invited Josh to sit in on a performance with his band. Grateful to be included, he accompanied them for a couple of songs. He didn't play any elaborate improvisations to steal any limelight, but everyone who listened agreed they were listening to a musician of a high standard. An element of innocence returned, and he wished he could bottle the comforts of the area to take back to London.

On one occasion he went into Swansea and saw Bethan in a shopping precinct. As he approached her, she dropped her head, ignored him, and walked on. He made no attempt to follow. The chapter with Bethan was now over.

CHAPTER THIRTY-EIGHT

An Old Love Resurfaces.

Sunday, 8 November, 2009

Nobody mentioned Julian Simpson's name in the shop for the remainder of the weekend, almost as if the subject was taboo. Josh knew he had to keep his suspicions to himself. The man had to be the Julian Simpson who'd come between him and Bethan, but he wondered why Simpson had arrived in South Wales. What link did he have to the area? It then became clear. He remembered the photograph he'd smashed in Jan's flat the day she'd moved out. It was one of Julian Simpson and Tom Parker and their respective fathers. They were related. He'd been too preoccupied with the image of Tom Parker and the link between the two men to make a mental note of what Simpson looked like. He'd pushed the events of the Millennium summer to the back of his mind, but now they returned to haunt him yet again. Josh had to get some confirmation regarding the identity of the man attempting to infiltrate his boss' business.

Hadn't he and Jan had problems getting hold of Simpson? They'd suspected he'd been involved in some fraudulent activities. How could he tell his boss what he suspected until he had proof?

He needed to get in touch with Jan somehow. She'd be able to give him some insight into the Simpson's character and habits, but he had no idea how to contact her. Chris would surely be able to advise him, with the advancement of IT.

As Josh travelled with Chris to the rehearsal, he said, "I need to get in touch with someone from my time in London. I've lost her contact details. Not my ex, I hasten to add. How would I go about it? I'm not particularly brilliant with IT, and have never kept in touch with old friends."

"Is she connected to your latest worries?"

"I think someone from my past, I'd rather not know, has turned up." Josh described Simpson's involvement with both Bethan and Jan.

"Where do the boy and his violin come into this?"

"I don't know about the boy, but the violin's so like my old one

"Maybe the boy's stepfather, or someone he knows, bought it. Perhaps you could ask him."

"I don't feel I could. I've only spoken to him once on the phone, and I get the impression he's not very approachable. Anyway, the initials inside have been scribbled over as if its past has been deleted."

"Try *Friends Reunited* or *Facebook*. Do you know where she studied?".

"Northern College of Music."

"That's your first bet. Where's she from?"

"Manchester, but I can't remember where. I only went to her home once."

"Big place Josh, you could always try a search. It could give you an indication of her school and the area. Then try directory enquiries with her parents' name. The internet has provided all sorts of ways to contact people these days.

Sean arrived at Josh's flat for his lesson on Wednesday. He placed the music from the previous week on the stand and began to play. After the first sixteen bars he stopped.

"I've got this far with my Mum's help," he said.

"Let's play it again, and I'll accompany you on guitar to keep the rhythm steady." They repeated the first phrases several times without protest from Sean. Josh was impressed with the boy's perseverance. It was obvious the boy had received a great deal of support at home.

They spent no time with other tunes and Sean demonstrated his knowledge of major scales in flat keys, and their arpeggios towards the end of the lesson. This confirmed Sean could progress through the examination system with ease.

To change the subject, Josh asked his pupil how he was settling into his school and where he lived, but he sensed Sean was reluctant to give away too much information, almost as if he'd been primed. He claimed the village school near his home had an unpronounceable Welsh name. Still unsure about the schools' area orchestra, Josh decided not to reintroduce the subject.

Mrs. Francis remained as elusive as ever when she arrived to collect her son and Josh gazed after the car, still puzzled by her reluctance to be more forthcoming.

On his way home from work Friday evening, Josh visited the library to begin a search for his ex-colleague. He trawled through *Facebook* and *Friends Reunited* and discovered a large number of people in Manchester who shared her surname. Those who claimed to be musicians were the obvious people to contact if a telephone number was highlighted. The first person he phoned had only moved to the city three years before. Several more attempts proved unsuccessful, and he contemplated contacting the orchestra in which he'd played in London. It would possibly have retained her personal information and forwarding address.

He made one more attempt and a familiar voice answered,

one almost identical in tone to how he remembered his friend Jan's. Her mother remembered his name. He explained he'd lost her daughter's telephone number and made the excuse he wanted her help over a musical matter. Jan had an orchestral engagement, but Mrs. Fowler gave him her mobile number. He said he'd call again over the weekend.

When he arrived home, he phoned his parents, only to be told Bethan had phoned them during the afternoon. She wanted to contact him. Enid had given her his number.

"She said she'd get in touch over the weekend. I told her you were working, so she said tomorrow night. I've got her number."

Josh entered it on his contact list.

Intrigued by Bethan's second visit to his parents, but concerned her husband would be home, he decided against telephoning her. If she wanted him, she'd phone.

To clear his head, he put on his coat and walked to his local pub. He planned just one soft drink and to return about nine, to listen to some music, and practise his violin with a mute on the bridge, in preparation for Saturday's engagement.

When he returned to his flat, he noticed a missed call on his phone. Bethan's name appeared on the list of callers, but she'd not left an answerphone message. He pondered over how he'd approach her, how civil he'd be, but dialled her number anyway. She answered after the first ring tone.

"Hello Bethan. You called in to see my parents, what's up?"

"You sound cross."

"Sorry I didn't mean to, are you okay? What's wrong? It must be nearly ten years since I last saw you. What have you been up to? Mum told me you were still home in Swansea and had called round."

"Can we meet up? Where do you live? Your mother told me you'd moved back to Cardiff."

"I work most days, in a shop here, but I've got a gig in

Cardiff tomorrow evening. I doubt if you'd be able to get here—what would your husband say?"

"He's not home, so it's not a problem."

"We could meet up before the gig and you can catch the train back to Swansea."

"I've got a car, so I can meet you anywhere, even where you live. I can pick you up from work, if you want. I need to see you." He surmised she was either in danger or had a worry to concern them both. It had to be related to the fateful summer of the millennium year.

"I finish work at five. I can contact the others in the band and ask them to meet me later at the venue, rather than go down to Cardiff with them. Let me phone Chris to sort out the lift and I'll call you back."

In response to Josh's call Chris asked, "So who are you meeting?"

"My ex, from Swansea."

"So, you've made contact with one."

"Both."

"See you at the gig. Don't be late." Chris said no more. He knew Josh would reveal all when he was ready.

.

Apprehensive about meeting Bethan, he spent the day busying himself about the shop to avoid making conversation in case he let slip he'd made contact with a past girlfriend. He was determined her presence wouldn't affect his performance at the gig. He had to focus on what the musicians had prepared. He'd rebuilt his confidence in the two years he'd spent in the area and didn't want this interruption to distract him and spoil the cohesion of the band. His aim to regain a professional status in the music world meant he had to blot out all other influences. It would allow him to make an impression at these public performances, irrespective of the genre of music the band played. He hoped meeting Bethan again would be without complications, but the coincidence of both her and a Julian Simpson turning up simultaneously aroused his suspicions.

As he'd been caught in a heavy downpour on his way home from work, he decided to shower, glad Bethan hadn't turned up. His stomach churned as he stood in the shower, and a part of him felt he should have ignored her request to meet. Another time when he wasn't playing would have been more convenient.

At quarter to six she still hadn't turned up. Josh decided to wait just another five minutes before phoning Chris to collect him. To keep himself busy he switched on the kettle to make himself a coffee, the solution to alleviate his impatience. But as the water boiled, he heard the doorbell being rung. This must be her. Ready to greet her as an old acquaintance whose respective paths had had no great bearing or influence on each other, he opened the door. Bethan smiled at him. Her attractive features caught him unawares and he felt his resolve weaken. He wanted to stretch out his arms to hold her but knew he shouldn't.

"Hello Josh, I'm—"

"Please, don't say anything."

They looked at each other, the attraction still evident. They embraced, and Josh held her head against his shoulder. Her arms around his waist, she turned her head to face him. Their faces drew closer but before their lips met, he said,

"This mustn't happen. I was going to be strong." But her voice, her appearance, still held an attraction.

"So was I. Do you still—?"

"Probably, always will I suppose," he said, guessing what she'd attempted to ask. "But we need to go. I've got a gig tonight."

"Your mother told me you'd left London."

Josh sensed her reluctance to let him go as she continued to hold on to his waist.

"What are you doing now? I take it you're still involved in music." She turned to look at his violin case and amplifier by the door. "Where are you playing tonight?"

"In a club in Roath."

"Not classical. How's the lovely violin of yours? Have you still—" She remembered him exchanging the Hoing for the Andre Coinus.

Not wishing to resurrect the past he interrupted her.

"I haven't got it anymore." He remained quiet for several seconds, reluctant to tell her how his life had changed since they'd known each other in London. "I'll tell you the whole story one day."

Josh knew he shouldn't let her into his emotions ever again, however difficult holding her at arm's length would be. But she was married, and any weakness on either of their parts could end with a great deal of regret for both of them.

"Can we go now?" he said and moved her hands from his waist.

As soon as they'd set off, he said, "Is something wrong? My mother told me you'd called round."

"Wanted to know where you were. I don't know who else to speak to." The comment puzzled him. Why would she want to discuss her worries with him?

"I think my past is coming back to haunt me," she said.

"Join the clan. I've had a few suspicious moments regarding mine as well."

"In what way?" she said and turned to face him.

It began raining again, and Josh, concerned about Bethan's concentration level, noticed her lack of attention to driving. The wipers, set to maximum speed, cleared the water from the windscreen, but the torrent of rain demanded greater attention.

"Watch the road and tell me yours first, it's why you wanted to see me."

"What happened between us years ago, I'm sorry. I want to say I've regretted it ever since."

He decided not to mention Julian Simpson's possible involvement in the shop for the moment. He needed to hear her concerns first, assuming she hadn't wanted to meet up with him just to apologise.

"No, I regret what it did to us, meeting Simpson. He involved me in something if it hadn't been for my father, I could have been in serious trouble."

Josh's interest increased but felt it best to let her continue.

"Do you remember I went down to Swansea the day your friend died? I met Tom Parker at the station. Simpson had asked me to take a package down to give to him. Simpson said he should have posted it, it was to do with his work, or so he told me." There were several seconds of an embarrassing silence, and Josh waited in anticipation for it to be broken. He sensed her reluctance to continue and asked,

"What do you mean?" Bethan still failed to proceed any further with her explanation, and they continued the journey in silence until they approached a petrol station.

"I'm going to pull in here to get some fuel." She got out of the car to fill the tank.

He waited for her return, intrigued to find out what Simpson had used her for. It had to be unlawful if her father had been involved. A previous link between Parker and Simpson had been confirmed with the photograph he'd smashed in Jan's flat. What revelation would come next?

Once she returned to the car, she started the engine and continued.

"Tom Parker was nothing to do with Simpson's work. He told me Parker worked for an accountancy firm."

"Wait a minute, how were you persuaded to carry a parcel

to Tom Parker, a parcel of what anyway?"

"He asked me to deliver a parcel of papers to a firm of accountants in Swansea. I'd been led to believe they were to do with their business. He'd arranged for Parker to meet me at the station, but no-one had arrived to meet me off the train. Simpson phoned to tell me to go to the bar opposite the station. I wanted to get home. His attitude towards me changed. I realised then he'd probably used me. Parker had been waiting in the bar anyway. He'd been watching me through the window. He took the package, and I left as soon as I could to catch the bus home. I came back to see you early, your friend had died, and it all went pear shaped."

"Killed," Josh corrected her.

She looked at him unsure what to say.

"Yes, I remember," he said to break the silence, "but it had gone pear shaped long before." He couldn't resist the dig.

"What do you mean killed?"

"The inquest returned an open verdict. She'd been gassed. They'd found evidence of intruders. Weren't you interviewed the following March?"

"Yes, but no-one said anything about a murder. I was just questioned about where I'd stayed overnight."

"With Simpson. They questioned him too, but we heard no more."

"Nor me."

After several silent minutes she continued with her explanation. "Tom Parker brought a pile of ecstasy and cocaine into South Wales in the summer. As one of the ringleaders, he was sentenced to fourteen years. Not a first offence by any means, which is why it was so long. My dad found out about his recent release."

"What's it got to do with you?"

"I told my dad about Simpson and me at the time and how I'd been conned into bringing a package down by train. We realised later it was probably some of the ecstasy or cocaine. I don't know how my dad did it, but he had enough evidence to convict Parker without involving me, otherwise I wouldn't have been able to teach anymore. Now I'm sure Parker will try to get at me. My parents have been getting strange phone calls from someone claiming to be a loan company. Apparently, I'd borrowed some money in two thousand, when I lived in London. I've paid off everything, student loan, credit card bills. I clear those every month. I don't know what they're on about. My dad's retired now and hasn't got the same access to things."

"But Parker wouldn't want to get at you. It happened years ago."

"I gave him the package, remember. I had it with me on the train for three hours."

"But how would he know your parents' phone number?"

"I've no idea, they're ex-directory. He never came to my home."

"What about Simpson? Did you tell him?"

"He knew I came from Swansea and was aware I knew Parker—" She paused, realising he could have accessed her phone when they were sleeping together. She hoped Josh's sensitivities hadn't been affected and continued. "I tried to get hold of Simpson to finish with him, but I only had his mobile number and couldn't get through to him. He disappeared without a trace after he'd used me, without any care. I'd been an absolute fool and was worried he'd find me in Wandsworth, another reason I had to leave London. What about your friend Jan, did she stay in touch with him?"

"She moved out. Winston and I helped her. When we got to her flat, he'd bagged all her stuff. We only had to carry it to the car, almost as if he'd closed one chapter and opened another, which we'd assumed was you. She'd suspected his involvement in something underhand, and you've just confirmed it. We tried to find out where he worked, but by the time we got the number and phoned the company, he'd disappeared, he didn't work where he'd said anymore, if he ever had at all. Where does Parker live now anyway?"

"Probably back with his parents. His father's a bit ruthless when it comes to business. Involved in new developments in Swansea. Like father like son."

Josh recalled the night of the party at Parker's house.

"Yes, we went to a party once." She sensed his animosity. "It was a long time ago."

"We were always destined for failure, didn't matter how many times we tried," Josh said.

"Yes, I suppose so." The air of disappointment in her response confirmed how she felt about him.

By the time they reached Cardiff the rain had stopped. They found a small café on the City Road and ordered a light meal. She felt obliged to ask Josh what he'd done after they'd parted.

"What happened to the ensemble, didn't you find replacements?"

"The rest of us didn't have the enthusiasm to carry on."

"When did you leave the orchestra? I thought you enjoyed it."

"I fancied a change, went to play with an opera company for a while."

"What about you and Jan? You liked her a lot, I could tell."

"I suppose I did, but she moved back to Manchester that summer. She felt vulnerable as well, especially after what had happened to Sophie. Anyway, the opera company wasn't what I wanted either. After a concert one evening I met up with Sue—Sue Ellis from the schools' area orchestra?"

"Yes, I remember her. You were together for a while in Cardiff. Did you get back—?"

"No. She was a music critic, wrote for one of the

broadsheets. She wasn't very complimentary. She still bore a grudge about us. I tried other types of music as the classical field had no further opportunities and ended up back here just over two years ago. I enjoy playing with the band."

She listened without interruption, surprised by how his classical career had taken a downward turn. "How's your past catching up with you?" she asked, remembering Josh's earlier comment.

"I've got a pupil whose violin I think I recognise. It's identical to my old one, the Hoing I had as a teenager — you must remember it. You played it often enough."

Bethan remembered persuading Simpson to buy Josh's old violin. His comment confirmed Simpson had probably moved to South Wales, to continue the link with Tom Parker. She was reluctant to tell Josh what had happened to the instrument after he'd sold it — it would alienate him. She needed his help now, more than ever. Their lives had become linked again.

After the meal, Bethan drove Josh to the venue and helped him carry in his equipment. As she left, she kissed him on the cheek in front of the other band members. She drove home aware she'd have more to contend with than she'd thought, and hoped she had an ally.

Dave looked over at Chris, intrigued by Bethan's public show of affection. He'd not seen Josh with a female interest before.

"I can't tell you," Chris said, "it's none of our business." When he had a moment, he approached Josh, out of earshot of the other two.

"Your ex, I assume."

"Don't worry Chris, I've no intention."

"Not what she thinks."

CHAPTER THIRTY-NINE

Sunday, 15 November, 2009

R elieved he'd overcome his initial reaction to seeing Bethan, Josh needed to telephone Jan with the information
he'd learnt about Simpson. For once Bethan hadn't made him
feel inferior. It had been the emotion he'd lived with since the
summer of the millennium year. Jan had been as much a victim as Bethan had, albeit in a different manner. How many
more girls like Bethan had Simpson used?

On his way to work, Josh turned on his phone to make the
call and noticed a missed one from his boss but chose to ignore it. Jan greeted him by name, pleased to hear his voice,
and after they'd caught up on the intervening years, he introduced the topic of Julian Simpson.

"What makes you think it's him?"

"He's approached my boss, claims he's got a clothes factory, and wants to supply our shop. He came to one of our
gigs a couple of weeks ago. Strangely enough, he asked my
boss about me and where I'd played before. Luckily, I hadn't
mentioned my past life as a musician when I started in the
shop. I remember you'd said he'd been a musician, used to
play the violin."

"Had been, played in an orchestra with Sophie's sister
Ruth in the sixth form, until he was thrown out."

"What for?"

"Beating up another violinist, broke his arm."

"This guy seems aggressive as well. Creepy, to say the

least."

"What does he look like?"

"He's tall, much taller than me, got a neat beard. Trouble is I only saw him once in London and from a distance, so I can't be sure. There's another thing I've found out. I've met Bethan."

"Oh, that's interesting. Does she want to get back with you? I hope you're not. Sorry, it's none of my business."

"No, it's not that, it's more complicated. She's convinced Simpson used her to transport drugs to Swansea to his cousin Tom. He was the guy in the photo with Simpson, the one in your flat."

"Oh yes, I remember. The one you smashed. Why does she think that?"

"She carried a package from Simpson to Parker, believing it was business paperwork. Tom Parker was gaoled that summer for dealing in coke and ecstasy, and he's just been released. He was dealing as a teenager."

"So, she was fooled as well. What's the problem?"

"She thinks Parker may want to take it out on her."

"She was a fool to agree —" Jan stopped.

Josh sensed her regret for the comment.

"When I find out more, I'll get back to you." He checked his watch, and explained he'd have to end the call. The conversation had taken longer than planned and he had two minutes to get to work.

He found the shop's front door locked when he arrived. No-one had turned up. Terry was always at the shop at least half an hour early, but it appeared empty. Josh unlocked the door and made for the office, but he saw no sign of his boss.

After he'd raised the window blinds, he checked his watch again in the hope he'd not have to serve a customer. He phoned Terry's home number, but no-one answered.

Within seconds, Nathan rushed in full of apologies. "I'll tell you later, let's get the till sorted." They rushed to put everything was in place for customers.

"What's the matter? Your father's never been late since I started here."

"I was out with my girlfriend last night and stayed over. I had a call from my mother this morning to come and get the keys for the shop. I wasn't due in until one this afternoon. I got to the house about ten-thirty and tried to phone you to let you know Dad wouldn't be in, but you were engaged."

"What's wrong with him? Is he ill?"

"No, she said he had a meeting at mid-day, couldn't come in, I don't know where, but I assume it's at the golf club."

"Did he say who?"

"No, he just told me to hurry up, as the shop needed to be opened and you didn't have access to the safe. My mum said he'd tried to call you earlier but couldn't get through."

"No, it was off. I'd turned it off last night before the gig we had in Cardiff. I turned it back on this morning. I had to phone an old friend. The call took a while, which must have been when you tried to get through. Did your father say who he was meeting?" Josh hoped Nathan could remember a name.

"A new supplier or something."

"He hasn't mentioned the name Simpson, has he?"

"Not to me."

The shop closed at four. Terry didn't make an appearance, neither did he telephone.

CHAPTER FORTY

Monday, 16 November, 2009

Josh arrived at work at ten to nine to find Terry in the stock-room, the floor covered with sweatshirts.

"Busy Mr. Evans? I'd have come in earlier to help, but I didn't realise you needed to do this."

"Can you pass me the flat-packed boxes behind the cup-board so we can sort them into different items and sizes? I didn't realise we had so many. It'll take us months to shift this lot."

"We always keep a good stock because of the regular trade. Huw Rogers always has plenty to keep us going."

"The recession's hit people hard here. They won't be able to afford our prices, someone else may take over."

"Is another shop opening?"

"Possibly."

"Simpson?"

"I can't say any more." Terry's evasive comment confirmed Simpson had coerced him to accept his offer.

Josh did not want to upset his boss, who appeared to be under a great deal of pressure. He couldn't understand the reason why this man Simpson had pinpointed Terry's busi-ness with such aggression. There didn't appear to be any ad-vantage in having done so.

Josh opened the shop at nine o'clock, while Terry contin-ued to carry out the job he'd begun. Terry's earlier comment regarding honouring Huw Rogers' contract had now been ignored.

No conversation of any length occurred between the two for the remainder of the day and Josh was relieved he only had to work in the morning the following day. Time spent in Cardiff's music shops was a distraction from the atmosphere in his own.

Sean arrived for his lesson on Wednesday with his old three-quarter sized violin. It was obvious he'd not practised as much as Josh had come to expect.

"Gone back to your old violin Sean?"

The boy appeared disappointed. Over the weeks both teacher and pupil had built up a rapport and Josh had enthused about the quality of the boy's musicianship. Although Mrs. Francis had supported her son by paying for private lessons, the boy's access to the Hoing violin appeared to have been withdrawn.

Josh accompanied Sean to the car at the end of the lesson, and as he opened the door, Mrs. Francis turned her head forward. It was obvious to Josh she didn't want to make eye contact with him. He could only make out her silhouetted profile.

"I don't think Sean's been able to practise a great deal this week, Mrs. Francis. He's gone back to his old three-quarter sized violin. I don't want to appear pushy, but he's an incredibly talented player and shows a lot of enthusiasm. Has he not been well?" Josh hoped his approach would break down the barrier between them, but she displayed reluctance to discuss the problem and said nothing in response for several seconds. It prompted him to believe he'd overstepped the mark. He'd intruded into their private lives.

"Thank you, Josh, we're fine," she said eventually, continuing to look through the windscreen. He was surprised with her response. It suggested she'd not been offended. She'd addressed him by his first name. He hoped the barrier between them could be broken down.

Josh noticed Sean put his hand out to touch hers before he closed the door to allow them to drive away. He suspected a problem in the Francis household. Sean's violin lessons were a possible escape from an unpleasant atmosphere at home.

As mother and son travelled home Sean asked, "Why did Josh call you Mrs. Francis?"

"Did he? He must have mixed you up with another of his pupils, dear." Sean looked at his mother. He knew the mistake shouldn't be divulged to his stepfather. How many times had she said not to say too much about his lessons when they were home? She always discussed these in depth on the journey, but as soon as they arrived at the house, she'd say, not to talk about them to her partner. He wouldn't be interested.

The following afternoon two strangers entered the shop. Josh greeted them in his customary welcoming manner. Without a word they made eye contact to suggest he had no right to acknowledge them. It was obvious the two had no intention of buying anything. Their size deterred him from attempting to engage with them any further. They gave the impression they were capable of defending themselves without a problem, in any physical conflict. To Josh's relief Terry Evans joined him in the shop, but he saw his boss' demeanour change as soon as he saw the two. He suspected they were connected to Simpson. They removed shirts from their hangers and draped them over other displays as if on purpose, to annoy. Five minutes later they left without a word, and Josh stepped out from behind the counter to re-arrange the clothing.

"Thank you, may I leave you in charge for a few minutes?

I'm going to make a cup of coffee," Terry said. He didn't offer to make Josh one.

Josh suspected Terry was being subjected to a protection fiasco. Some more information regarding Simpson had to be acquired. If he'd dealt in ecstasy and cocaine, he wouldn't have been alone. He hoped Bethan would be able to enlighten him.

Once Josh arrived home, he phoned her, to find out if she'd been aware of anyone else Simpson had contact with. She claimed she didn't know of anyone apart from Parker. Although he described the incident in the shop, she didn't appear interested. She changed the subject and asked Josh about the new pupil and his family. Josh proceeded to describe how Mrs. Francis had approached him. She listened without interruption.

They continued to talk for over ten minutes. Josh was intrigued to find out why she was prepared spent so much time on the phone to him.

"As a matter of interest is your husband still away?" he asked eventually.

"He's away on the rigs, won't be back until just before Christmas. It's not a problem, you can contact me anytime. We should meet up again soon. I enjoyed seeing you." He wasn't sure how to, but arranged to meet her on his next day-off.

He finished the call and wondered if his response had been appropriate. Although his heart strings played a strange tune, he hoped he could trust his reluctance to re-kindle what he'd insisted would never happen.

Friday had a busy turnover of customers, and Terry attempted to sell as many uniforms he could to reduce his stock. Josh had not seen his boss attempting such a hard sell to parents before.

At five minutes to closing time the two characters from the previous day entered the shop again. Josh sensed Terry's apprehension and decided to stay beyond his normal working hours.

"I'll go when everyone's gone, Mr. Evans."

"Thanks," Terry said no more. The two men targeted the displays again much to Josh's annoyance. Terry made no attempt to intervene or ask them to leave as he would have done with customers who attempted to stay later than the normal shop hours.

They left at five thirty and Josh began to re-adjust the presentations back to their original places. Terry stopped him.

"You go, Josh. I know you're busy tonight."

Another gig in Cardiff had been booked and agents from recording companies had arranged to watch the band. Josh wanted to protect his boss from Simpson, but realised he needed help from another source. He needed to discover Simpson's true identity first.

Josh put his violin through its paces at the gig, and at times lost himself inside his complex improvisations, much to the delight of his band members. They knew his extraordinary talent was key to their continued success as a well-received band in the area. Josh knew the punters had come to expect a flawless performance with the band's cohesive attack. He was aware they were being watched by influential people in the music business. His energy and ability had spurred them all on to reach a presentation to excite the audience. Afterwards the four musicians discussed possible opportunities with some studio time to lay down tracks for a CD.

Josh hoped he could escape the humdrum existence of the last two years. He could leave the worry of the shop. He knew a return to a full-time professional status would demand a single minded and selfish approach, whatever the outcome.

His new violin proved to be the cathartic stimulus essential to strive for a return to his trained-for status. He decided he no longer needed his old instrument, but it had to be re-varnished before it could be sold.

An opportunity to play to enthusiastic audiences would allow him to escape from the Simpsons of this world. Bethan had to be ignored—it would have been a pointless liaison. Although frustrated, he no longer wanted, or needed a frivolous relationship. He wanted a more secure one, with an element of permanence, someone he could trust.

CHAPTER FORTY-ONE

Saturday, 21 November, 2009

His phone rang as he walked to work. The display indicated Bethan's name, but he chose to ignore it, the euphoria of the previous night still fresh in his mind. He needed a single-minded approach to pursue what he craved, without any distractions. Her problems would have to be dealt with by her husband.

She phoned him again as he reached the shop, but he ignored her call yet again. Within minutes he heard his phone's text alert and he suspected her desperation to make contact. He knew it had to be her but took his time with a customer who'd approached him. Once the shop had emptied, his inquisitive nature prompted him check his phone. Her message was a request to meet at 5:30. He ignored it at first, but by lunchtime another text with the same message arrived. He wrestled with his conscience, and as he had nothing to lose, phoned her.

To meet her would give him the opportunity to tell her of his reluctance to involve himself in her present problems. The responsibility would have to be either her husband's or her parents'. He no longer wanted to be drawn further into a web of deceit. He'd spent half the night reliving the performance which suggested the possibility of a professional future in music. Terry would have to sort out his own problems with Simpson. Why couldn't his boss say *No* and be done with it? Surely Simpson didn't have a hold over him. Terry would have to contact the police.

After the call, he went to the mini market to buy a sandwich and a local newspaper to read over what remained of his short break. He placed the newspaper on the table in the shop's stock room and began to eat his sandwich. Terry joined him as the shop was empty and picked up the newspaper. He flicked it open to the second page, but within seconds he put it down, and walked back to the shop without a word. Terry's reluctance to say anything prompted Josh to pick up the paper before he'd finished eating. Turning over the first page, he saw a heading.

Fire Destroys Clothes Factory

Reading on he understood Terry Evans reaction.

A clothing factory in Newport was destroyed in a fire last night. The fire brigade was called out to deal with a large fire. Huw Rogers, the owner, was interviewed and revealed he was telephoned by night security guards to report the fire. Several fire engines attended and eventually extinguished the flames which at some point reached fifty metres into the air. Nearby homes were evacuated, and residents were moved to the local community centre. No more details regarding the fire are available at present due to our publication deadline. A further report will appear in Monday's edition.

If Julian Simpson had instigated the arson attack, his ruthlessness had no limits. He'd stop nothing at to achieve what he wanted. Simpson posed a greater threat than he could have imagined. Josh returned to the shop and showed his boss the article.

"Oh," Terry said after several seconds. Josh sensed his boss' denial about Simpson's involvement.

"What about the uniforms?" Josh said.

"We're lucky Simpson's turned up." Terry turned his face

away from Josh and removed cash from the till.

"Does it mean your decision's been made for you? We'd better get in touch with Huw Rogers, just to let them know we're concerned, we have his home number on file." Terry Evans didn't answer and took no further part in any conversation with Josh for the remainder of the afternoon.

Josh realised he'd have to reconsider his attitude towards Bethan. It was obvious she needed him more than he needed to ignore her.

He rushed home and changed, ready to meet her, but she didn't turn up outside his flat at the agreed time. As he paced around the living room, he peered through his window from time to time, and became more and more frustrated. He checked his watch and considered the possibility she'd had an accident.

Bethan eventually phoned and asked him to meet her at the local railway station rather than his flat. The more he thought about it, the more convinced he became she knew more than she'd already admitted.

He failed to see her car outside the station so he waited underneath a streetlight, so he could check his watch. His phone rang after a minute and Bethan's name appeared on his display.

"Where are you? I'm at the station," he said.

"About fifty yards up the road, you just passed me."

"Why didn't you stop me?"

"I wasn't sure it was you until you answered your phone. I'll flash my light so you can see where I am." He looked back along the direction he'd walked and saw a pair of headlamps flash once. The car was parked in darkness, away from streetlamps.

As he opened the passenger door, he saw her in conversation on her phone. It was obvious Bethan was appeasing someone's concerns. Josh guessed it was her mother. After a minute the call ended. She put down the phone and stared ahead not acknowledging his presence.

"Where shall we go?" he said to break the silence.

"I don't care, anywhere. Somewhere where we won't be recognised, we're very conspicuous here." The call had obviously unnerved her.

"OK, let's go down to Cardiff. It's only twenty minutes, as good as anywhere."

The outskirts of the city offered several budget restaurants to welcome families, and they found one where they assumed they could remain anonymous. Although the car park was nearly full, Bethan found a space near the exit into which she reversed her car.

"You wait here, and I'll go in and find a free table." Josh said.

As he stepped through the doorway, he could see the room was full. He turned to leave, but as he did so, he spotted Sean Francis with two adults engrossed in reading their menus. He considered approaching them, hoping his presence wouldn't be treated with alarm by his mother. However, facing Josh, with his head slightly bowed to read the menu, sat a man who had to be Sean's stepfather. Josh reconsidered immediately. It was the Mr. Simpson he'd served in the shop several weeks before, he was sure of it. The man also appeared to have the same build as the one who'd approached his boss at the dance. It confirmed Josh's suspicions. They were both the same person. A woman he assumed was Mrs. Francis had her back to him. To approach her now was out of the question. He turned away from the family and walked towards the door.

He couldn't believe this man could be connected to Sean and Mrs. Francis. *Why had she requested the tune Sean had subsequently wanted to learn? And why is she so keen to retain her anonymity?*

This had to be forgotten for now. To confirm the man's identity as the man who'd used Bethan in London was now his priority. If willing, she could provide the answer.

Once he reached the car, he sat next to her in silence, contemplating how to persuade her to walk into the restaurant and verify what he suspected.

"Well, are there any free tables?" she asked, impatient to find out if they'd have to wait to be seated.

"Have you got a scarf or a hat, or both with you?" he asked.

"Yes. Why?" She reached to the back seat and held them up. "I thought we were going in for a meal. We haven't got far to go to the door, or is there a queue?"

"Just shut-up and listen for a moment. I want you to put them on to disguise your appearance. I've just seen my star pupil with a couple. The man looks like someone whose been troubling my boss in the shop. His name's Julian Simpson."

They looked at each other for a few seconds, each one expecting the other to speak. Her silence spoke volumes as she turned away from him and stared through the windscreen. Her reaction convinced Josh she was probably aware of Simpson's presence in the area, but he needed her to identify him before he could challenge her.

"I want you to go in, look around and see if you recognise him. It's pretty full of kids, so you won't look out of place if you walk out. He's sitting near the window around to the right as you walk in through the doorway. Do you want to do it?" After a moment's hesitation she agreed.

Bethan put on the hat and wrapped the scarf around the lower part of her face. On this cold November evening, her appearance wouldn't be conspicuous. Josh watched her as she walked towards the door. Once she'd entered the restaurant, he moved over to the driver's seat, suspecting Simpson would possibly notice her. He started the engine in the belief it would be necessary to drive away from the carpark without delay. Although he had no licence, he could drive. He'd not had the opportunity to pass his driving test.

Bethan felt nervous about coming face to face with Simpson. She was aware of his ruthlessness. Once inside, she looked around to give the appearance she wanted a table. Although she had a good idea where Simpson was seated, she scanned the entire restaurant. As she turned to face the direction she'd been instructed, she spotted a young boy about ten or eleven with a couple. Without warning, her scarf slipped down her face. The man lifted his head to attract the waitress' attention, and Bethan saw him looking directly at her. They both recognised each other. It was Simpson, the man she'd known in London. He acknowledged her presence with a cynical smile but didn't move. She didn't wait to see what he would do next but turned to open the door.

She saw the car's headlights, and heard the engine running as she ran towards it. The passenger door was open, and she guessed Josh had changed seats. As soon as she jumped in and closed the door, he pushed the gearstick into first and released the clutch to drive towards the exit. She glanced back towards the restaurant door expecting to see Simpson but there was no sign of him.

They drove on in silence until they'd reached the nearest service station by the motorway.

"Well?" he said, his heart still racing. "I think we'd better change seats."

"It was him, bloody cold eyes. He saw me, too. He remembered me immediately, almost as if he's looking for me. The chilling look he gave me was full of malice."

"He didn't follow you out, though. Probably waiting for a

more convenient time when his partner's not with him. Now you can take over. The boy with them is one of my pupils. Wait, Sean's mother said Julian's cooking tonight. It's all clear now, why hadn't I remembered?"

"What are you talking about?"

"I tried making conversation with her one evening after Sean's lesson, and she made the excuse she had to go as her partner had a meal ready. Jan often mentioned he'd have a meal ready for her when she arrived home. A tenuous link possibly, but a correct one. What was Simpson like as a time-keeper?" Josh asked, looking for a reason for Mrs. Francis' reluctance to discuss Sean's lessons with him in her hurry to leave.

"He hated being late or anyone being late to meet him," she said, remembering how he'd reacted to her lateness on one occasion.

Josh suspected a problem in the household. Mrs. Francis was always in a hurry to get home. He remembered her appreciation of his musical skills, as she'd dropped her guard to display this at the Halloween dance. Simpson had watched without emotion. Josh wondered if he'd punished her for her display of enthusiasm.

The evening's discovery prompted Josh to want to avenge the decline in his fortunes in London even more, but it would be easier said than done. He suspected the two men who'd made a nuisance of themselves at the shop had to be involved with Simpson. He was no match for either.

Emotionally exhausted, Josh suggested he and Bethan should travel to Roath, in the city, to eat. Once they'd found a restaurant in which they could appear inconspicuous, she told him a loan company had phoned her parents again.

"It's what my mother wanted to talk to me about when I met you at the station. They've had five calls from them this week. She said it sounds like the same person every time. As

I said before, I'm solvent. I haven't got any debts. My husband earns more than enough, hence my new car. It's got to be Tom Parker, or Simpson, trying to get at me. My mother said he sounded forceful and threatening. I can't think how they got my number."

"From your phone, when you were sleeping." Josh said. She didn't respond. Her embarrassment was obvious by her silence. "Where do you work?" he said after a period of silence. He needed to change the subject.

"In a school in Morriston."

"You're not Miss Williams any more, I take it. No, don't tell me in case."

"In case of what?"

"Just in case. You'd better change your number. Tell your father what's happened. I take it he's not in the police any longer, but must have contacts. What about your husband?"

"God, I daren't tell him about any of this. What would he think?"

"You'll have to tell him when he's home next."

"But I'd have to tell him I've been seeing you."

"You haven't been seeing me. Tell him I'm an old friend from schooldays. I assume you haven't told him about us anyway." She shook her head.

They continued to eat in silence, Josh, deep in thought about the way Bethan had deceived him in London.

"What are you thinking about?" she asked.

"Nothing." Now was not the time to vent his feelings. He suspected Simpson was using the shop, and his presence, to locate Bethan. Simpson could take his time. He was in control.

After they'd finished their meal, she drove him home. On the way, Josh asked her to take a detour via Terry Evans house, out of curiosity. Josh noticed three cars in the drive, one he recognised from elsewhere. "Strange, Terry owns a

Jaguar and his wife a Peugeot, but that's a BMW at the entrance. Go to your parents' house tonight, in case you're followed. He may have your registration details."

"Can I come in for a quick coffee?" she asked as they pulled up outside his flat, "I need some caffeine before going home." Not in a position to refuse, he promised himself it wouldn't be any more. Simpson would be aware she'd driven to his flat, and he didn't want to keep her any longer than he needed.

Before she left, he asked one more question. "Did you ever tell Simpson you were in a relationship with me at the time?"

"You're dragging up the past again Josh, it's gone, whatever I did, please don't go on about it again."

"No, this is important. If you didn't, there's a slim chance he won't be able to link you to me."

"No, I didn't. But he must have known about you through Jan. He attended concerts."

After she finished her coffee she rummaged through her handbag and placed her phone on her lap. "So, you think he accessed my phone contacts?"

"Probably. Someone claiming to be Winston, our cellist, phoned my parents in the summer with an offer of a job. He wanted my phone number. He told my mother he'd phone me. Winston never did, not even socially, even if he'd found someone else, which I thought was strange. Check if you've still got my parents' number.

"Course I have, I phoned them the other week."

"It's clear what's happening. He accessed my parents' number from your phone and pretended to be Winston, now he's contacting your parents. You'd better go. Your car will be recognised."

As Josh escorted Bethan to his front door, she turned to face him, and wrapped their arms around him before kissing him on his lips. It wasn't what he wanted to happen as he knew it would be difficult to control his emotions, but he couldn't stop himself focusing on her presence. The fracture of their past relationship was temporarily forgotten.

"You're right. It's probably not safe for me to stay," she said releasing her embrace.

Josh, unsure how to respond, put his hands out to hold hers and saw her eyes moisten. "No Josh, I must go now." She pulled her hands away from his and took her keys from her pocket. "I'll call you." He opened the door and she touched his cheek before stepping out into the night.

The road was quiet of traffic, and as she reached her car he called, "Text me when you get home." Without a response, she got in without a backward glance. An hour later his phone alerted him with the message, 'I'm home xxx.'

Chapter Forty-two

Sunday, 22 November, 2009

By the time Josh arrived at the shop the following morning, Terry and Nathan had prepared the till. Reluctant to speak, Terry went to the office. Josh gestured to Nathan to ask whether his father was fine.

"I don't know. "I'm not sure what's happening. Something's not right." Before Josh could respond, Terry returned to the shop. Josh sensed an uncomfortable atmosphere which prompted him to break the silence. He wanted to find out more regarding stocks of clothes.

"Is there any more news about the fire in Newport?"

"Nothing, I'll call them tomorrow, we'll find out more then."

As the conversation finished, the two unwelcome characters who'd entered the shop the previous Friday walked in. Josh realised the pointlessness of greeting them and busied himself. He opened a drawer of bow ties and began to tidy them, hoping they'd leave before he had to think of another meaningless task. To his relief, they left within a few minutes.

"Weren't they the same people who were here late Friday afternoon and left the rails in a mess?" Josh asked.

"Were they? I couldn't tell." Whatever hold Simpson had over Terry Evans. Josh had to keep his nerve. It was pointless informing his boss what he'd confirmed the night before.

Josh contacted Bethan after work to discover she'd already discussed Simpson's appearance with her parents. It had been greeted with alarm.

"They suggested I move back home for the time being," she said.

"If it makes you feel safer."

"But it'll be more awkward for —"

"For what?" Josh realised what she had in mind. "You've got to keep safe. You mustn't come here again."

"You can come to see me though?"

"When I have time off."

"I can collect you. From anywhere."

"I'm off next Sunday." As soon as he said this, he realised what would probably happen.

The next day Josh asked his boss if he'd heard from Huw Rogers.

"Mr. Rogers is OK. I contacted him at home last night. I told him I'd look around for a temporary supplier when our stock runs out. Once he gets his operation up and running again, we'll get back to him." Josh remained quiet, but it prompted him to change his plan for his Tuesday afternoon off.

At lunchtime, he bought a newspaper and scanned through the pages to look for the article regarding the fire.

'The speculation is arson was the cause as evidence discovered suggests this.'

The remainder of the article included photographs of the burnt-out shell. To discuss the matter with Terry Evans was pointless.

Josh began to sandpaper his old violin in the evening. He rubbed the back of the instrument until he'd removed the varnish in preparation to re-stain it. The task took his mind off his concerns as he waited for Chris to collect him for the regular band practice. The physical effort to clean the instrument he'd played for the last eight years was more therapeutic than he'd expected.

The barn where they practised offered little heat, and they abandoned the rehearsal. Dave promised a better heating source would be available before the following week.

"Any luck finding your friend in Manchester?" Chris said as he drove Josh home.

"Yes, it was a great help, thanks. I wanted some advice on a piece of music I'm working on."

Several reasons why Simpson would want to find Bethan crossed his mind as he continued to remove the old varnish from his violin. It didn't seem to make sense. However, one possibility he'd previously overlooked became obvious. He needed some clarification and telephoned Bethan.

"I'm being a conspiracy theorist, but I need you to be honest with me. Did you take anything out from the package you gave to Parker?"

"For God's sake Josh."

"Told you, you wouldn't like it, but it's important. You see, if Simpson had sent less dope down to Swansea than he'd claimed, he's blaming you for having removed some."

"Go on, I'm not with you."

"Dealers aren't honest. They'd stab each other in the back to make a profit. Parker possibly thinks you set him up as well, believing you'd opened the parcel to find out what it contained, and told your father. I'm looking for a valid reason why Simpson would want to get to you. Was your father involved in the case? If so, maybe he has a score to settle. You got to tell him what I suspect."

Josh knew he was playing devil's advocate but couldn't be of further use to her without her father's intervention.

"But I never told either of them about my father's job. I'd tried smoking grass as a teenager, so telling someone like Parker what my father did wouldn't have been wise. Some of my closest friends knew, but not exactly what Dad did. Anyway, he kept me right out of the case."

"But you didn't contact Simpson again when you returned to London, did you?"

"No."

"Then he suspects you'd opened the packet."

"Which I didn't."

CHAPTER FORTY-THREE

Tuesday, 24 November, 2009

Josh had made up his mind the previous day to go to Newport. He normally went to Cardiff to browse around the music shops on his afternoon off from work, but this particular Tuesday he wanted to meet Huw Rogers. First of all, he visited a music shop in the town and bought a manuscript book, violin strings, sandpaper, and some instrument varnish. Once he'd left the shop, he walked towards Huw Rogers' factory.

As he approached the burnt-out shell, he saw its charred remains would take some time to rebuild. Delivery drivers he recognised stood outside the gates, their livelihood threatened without warning.

"Mr. Rogers has kept us on for the time being," one said. "A hell of a lot of our stock has gone. Fortunately, our warehouse has some clothing, enough for a month's sales, but after Christmas, who knows?"

"Is the boss about?"

"Yes, he's coming over here now," said another, pointing to Huw Rogers. "We're not allowed to go in, as it's too dangerous. They'll have to pull the building down."

As Huw Rogers joined his employees, Josh introduced himself. "Sorry about your factory, any idea what happens next?" he said.

"We pull it down and start all over again, it's all I've ever done. How's Terry? I haven't heard from him for a while."

"Yes, he's fine," said Josh. Huw Rogers' last comment

confirmed Terry was aware of the reason the factory had been destroyed.

"Tell him we'll soon be back in business."

Josh didn't mention his meeting with Huw Rogers in work the next day. The less Terry knew what he suspected, the better. Simpson's name didn't crop up in any conversation between the two. At lunchtime, the two men who'd visited the shop before walked through the doorway and made for shirts on the display rails. They rummaged through and dropped several onto the floor. Josh stepped out from behind the counter to pick up the clothes.

"We've not finished looking yet," one said, "at least allow the customer to finish before you interfere." The other pulled two shirts from the rail and dropped them onto the floor and stood on them.

"Excuse me sir," said Josh, "I'd like to pick those up, before they get in your way." As he said this, the shop door opened. The man Bethan confirmed was Simpson walked in, He looked at Josh as if he was a fleck of dust to be ignored.

"Is someone being a nuisance Mr. Evans?" He grinned at the two characters, who by now had stopped their activity. This convinced Josh the whole episode had been planned. "Looks as if I came in at the right time," Simpson continued, as he watched them walk through the doorway. Josh picked up the shirts, the better option than thanking Simpson for his intervention. He noticed mud stains on the clothing and folded them.

"We can't sell these, Mr. Evans," Josh said, avoiding eye contact with Simpson.

"What a waste. A word in private, in your office." The anxiety didn't leave his boss' face as he accompanied Simpson. A steady stream of customers ensured Josh's concentration had to be directed away from the incident.

Half an hour later, Simpson walked through the shop. He ignored Josh and left. Terry Evans spent the afternoon in his office while Josh dealt with customers alone. Little communication occurred between the two, even when the shop closed at the end of the day.

Sean turned up for his lesson with his old violin. He again failed to display the enthusiasm he'd shown in his earlier lessons.

"What's up Sean, not had time to practise? You've probably got a lot of homework, haven't you? The last year before secondary is always tough." Josh said, attempting to show some empathy towards his pupil. He hoped his pupil might open up about his home environment. "You realise you're good enough to become a professional musician one day." He could see the boy's confidence had been dented. "Let's have a look at *Lord Inchiquin*. We can cover a couple of tricky bits I want to go through, if it's okay."

Sean didn't object but his half-hearted attitude displayed his lack of enthusiasm.

"Is there something wrong with the other violin?" Josh asked. He wanted to find out the real reason for Sean's despondency.

"No, I'm not allowed to use it anymore. Mum and my stepfather had a huge row about it. His sister has moved down as well, and she took his side. She said I was a spoilt brat. Mum stayed in my room all night. I didn't see him this morning before she drove me to school." Josh listened without interruption, surprised by Sean's willingness to discuss his problems at home.

At seven o'clock Sean packed away his violin without warning. "I have to go. Mum has to be home soon. Thank you, Josh. I hope to see you next week." He gave Josh the regular payment in an envelope and waited for him to open the door.

Sean walked, his head down, towards the car. Mrs. Francis drove off as soon as he got in.

When Josh arrived at work on Thursday, he saw a notice on the window. Terry had announced a sale on school uniforms. "We won't get any more from Huw Rogers for a while, Mr. Evans. Once these go at a lower price we'll be without stock for months."

"They're not selling fast enough. We've got to get rid of them. Ten pounds in the till is better than twenty on the shelf." Josh didn't reply. He suspected the stock had to be sold to make room for Simpson's merchandise.

The rest of the day passed without the intrusion from unwanted customers. The sale of school uniforms increased over the next two days, diminishing the stock to half its previous amount.

On Friday night the band had an engagement in Cardiff, supporting a London based outfit. As Chris and Josh travelled to the venue, they discussed the hope of the breakthrough into the music business, to change their futures. Josh had rehearsed at every spare moment to ensure perfection.

The performance, an exhausting one, as he'd channelled his emotions into his playing, had been flawless. He craved the opportunity to lose himself in his music as an alternative to losing control of his private life. His virtuosity reached cathartic heights. Nothing restrained him on this stage. His band members allowed him free reign with the knowledge his classical experience would take them to uncharted areas, but always with a safe return. They all revelled in the excitement of these moments, their recent willingness to experiment, displayed their enthusiasm to push the boundaries of their own abilities.

"Everything OK, Josh? You're quiet tonight, emotions

came out on stage," Chris said as they drove home.

"Got a bit of a problem at the shop, nothing I can't handle."

"If things go well after tonight, we could all be giving up the day job." Chris said.

"I could cope. In fact, I'd welcome it." Josh began to open up and they discussed the gig and the songs they'd chosen but agreed some more original numbers were needed. "I'm not working this Sunday I'll try out some new tunes, we can look at them at Monday's rehearsal."

The following morning Bethan phoned Josh to find out if he could see her over the weekend. As they'd agreed not to meet in the Cardiff area, she suggested she'd meet him in Neath the next day. It would ensure they were away from possible danger.

CHAPTER FORTY-FOUR

Sunday, 29 November, 2009

Josh believed Simpson had coerced either his partner or Terry to reveal where he lived and suspected his empty flat would invite intruders. After much deliberation he decided to take his new violin with him, to meet Bethan. He placed his old one on his bed in full view of any intruder. It would serve a purpose. Although he'd planned to varnish it to sell for the best possible price, that would have to wait. His hid his guitar inside his wardrobe.

As he reached the station, he spotted one of Simpson's accomplices near the entrance, reading a newspaper. Josh knew he would be followed. He bought a return ticket to Neath, hoping his pursuer hadn't heard his request. However, as he predicted, the man followed him onto the platform. He watched the overhead digital clock as it progressed through the minutes and seconds, until the train's arrival time appeared.

Much to his relief, the train stopped, with a door adjacent to where he stood. He boarded a carriage without looking to see if the man had also stepped onto the train. But as he peered through the window, as the train pulled out of the station, he failed to see Simpson's accomplice. He guessed the man was following him.

Josh had to change trains at Cardiff, and he boarded the link to Neath. As he did so, he turned to see Simpson's accomplice stepping onto the next carriage. Fortunately, he saw an empty seat near the exit, and hoped it would provide him with an advantage when he arrived at his stop. He texted Bethan to meet him at Port Talbot, the station before Neath, where he could hopefully leave the train unnoticed. Unfortunately, as the train pulled into Bridgend, the next station, the man had moved to a seat in his carriage. Josh now wondered how to escape. He'd have to leave the train in a hurry. His exit would have to be timed to the second.

The train stopped at Port Talbot, but Josh sat motionless. He waited for the sound of the guard closing doors, and as it became louder, he stood and moved towards the exit door. It was open, and he jumped onto the platform. As he landed, he turned and pushed the door closed. The guard gave him a condescending look.

"Sorry I must have dropped off to sleep," Josh said. The guard didn't reply and signalled the train to leave. As it pulled away Josh glanced in through the carriage' window and saw his pursuer make an attempt to reach the door.

He left the station and saw Bethan standing by her car. When he reached her, she kissed him on the lips. Her appearance, a smart red skirt and a blue woollen sweater underneath a thigh length, black, leather jacket was guaranteed to attract his attention. She looked as appealing as she had done years before.

"Why did you change stations?" she asked.

"Someone's been following me. I didn't want to make it obvious I was meeting you."

"You've brought your violin?"

"I didn't want to leave it behind in the flat."

"Why? Are you worried someone will break in?"

"I don't want to take any chances. Meeting you like this could be awkward in future."

"Let's make the most of today then."

Why does she want to see me? Did we take our reacquaintance to another level last Saturday? Of course, we did. She doesn't appear like a person in danger, eager to discuss her worries, but as a girl-friend, pleased to see me, to spend the day with me, as lovers do.

She drove towards the Swansea valley, towards the scenic waterfalls that enhanced the beauty of the area, to guarantee its popularity. Once they arrived, they took the path that led to the Henrhyd Falls, and within twenty-five minutes they arrived at a spot where they could see the sublimity of the waterfall ahead of them.

"We used to come here," she said.

"I know, in another lifetime."

She put her arm through his as they stood side by side. No words were spoken. As she turned to face him, they embraced. Tears ran down her cheeks and Josh held her in silence. Aware she'd planned this meeting for a reason different to discussing her worries, he assumed she wanted to intensify their level of intimacy.

They looked at each other and eventually their lips met. Her passion could not be disguised, but Josh pulled himself away.

"No. We can't fool ourselves this is going anywhere."

"I know," she answered in embarrassment, "I just needed—"

"No, we mustn't. Someone's going to get hurt and I don't want it to be me again."

Unsure of what he wanted, he turned to look at the waterfall, to focus on the flood of the river as it wove its way through the surrounding woodland. He knew why she'd brought him to this particular place. They'd made love several times on the very place they now stood.

They both sat on the cool grass and began to sob, their emotions in turmoil. The events of the millennium year flooded back to his consciousness. It had been the year the media had proclaimed one should celebrate a new era, a new century. He'd had nothing to salute, no flourish of trumpets and no hallelujah chorus. For him it had signalled a downward spiral in his fortunes.

The last two years in London and the two he'd lived near Cardiff had seen him rise from his depths of despair, but he was frightened the inglorious past he'd experienced would haunt him again. Bethan had attracted him at the beginning. She'd been the first to kindle his passion, and a magnet still attracted them to each other. But was it love? He'd hated her for what she had done, but he knew he wanted to make love to her again but was unsure of the reason. Could it be revenge, or the need for intimacy? He knew she would welcome him entering her.

She placed her hand in his, but he wanted to retain control. He didn't want to be deceived by her again. But for the afternoon, he was prepared to accept the solace each could provide for the other, whatever their motives. They sat huddled up together for warmth, conquering all outside influences. Soon however, their hands searched for each other's intimacy and he lay between her legs. She welcomed him with unbridled passion as he climaxed inside her, both willing partners in their unreserved release of emotions. A tearful outburst by both followed, as they held each other. He knew they'd both been Simpson's victims.

An immeasurable amount of time passed as they sat arms entwined in each other's warmth and emotion. As they stared in silence at the waterfall, it illuminated the flow of life, to release its misdemeanours in the blink of an eye.

Very soon however, he began to feel the physical coldness of reality. The lateness of the November day enveloped him, and he suggested returning to the car.

Despite what had happened, Josh attempted to predict his destiny. He had a great deal to consider. To begin another relationship with Bethan, however intense they'd become, would be too complicated.

"I need to see your parents about Simpson and Parker," he

said as they set off. The threat posed to both had to be eradicated. She agreed. It was the only chance of resolution.

Bethan's parents welcomed him with warm embraces. They'd always been pleased to see him when they'd been together in their relationship. Circumstances were now different, but they were grateful for his support, however awkward it appeared to Bethan's marital status.

"All we can do is to keep an eye on the shop. Let us know if anything more unusual happens. I think I know what may be going on," Bethan's father said.

Neither Bethan nor Josh made any indication their relationship had been rekindled, but Josh noticed a look of suspicion in her mother's eyes.

Bethan drove Josh to Neath railway station. "Thanks for today," she said, as she reached out to hold his hands. He sensed an electric charge throughout his whole body and their moist lips met. A memory, not dead, never forgotten.

"Yes, you too." He could say no more. What had happened between them during the afternoon had given him a great deal to consider, far more than he'd anticipated.

"I want to see you again. I'll ring," she said. They embraced and held each other for several seconds.

Simpson's phone rang. He looked at the display and turned to Sean's mother from the comfort of his armchair.

"I want to take this call in private, and it might take some time." Simpson's sister remained seated and smirked as the boy and his mother left the room.

"He got off at a different station," a voice said the on the phone.

"Not Swansea? Must have been Neath."

"I'm on the platform at Neath, waiting for the next train

back. He got off at Port Talbot before I had a chance to follow him. She wasn't on the platform."

"You know what to do when you get back don't you?"

"Don't worry." Simpson put his phone down and turned to his sister.

"You still think she opened it, don't you?" she said as Tom Parker walked in and sat on the seat vacated by Mrs. Francis. Simpson acknowledged his presence with a nod and addressed them both.

"Of course. How else would it have come to the police's notice? He had to be involved as well, just to get back at me. I saw her last weekend, but it wasn't convenient to approach her. I had the kid and his mother with me, still that'll be over soon. Stoller will lead us to her at a suitable time."

He stood and walked over towards the doorway through which Sean and his mother had left.

"They've gone," Parker said. Satisfied they weren't in the next room, Simpson continued, "But then, once we find where she lives, we can close that chapter as well. An ex-lovers' tiff, it will be easy to disguise, but nothing must happen until after Christmas. Revenge will be worth the wait. Then we can move on. Our priority is Saturday. We'll get it out of the way first. I couldn't believe how useful the shop would be. Evans was easy to deal with."

Both mother and son knew when to make themselves scarce. If they didn't comply with Simpson's wishes, the atmosphere in the house would be unbearable. She needed to escape the toxic atmosphere of which Sean had become aware and took her son from the house. The strange visitor who'd turned up at regular intervals had arrived yet again as they both sat in the kitchen. It had been a signal to leave. The man's social skills were non-existent as far as she was concerned.

Whenever she'd mentioned this to Simpson, his reply had been, "He's family."

She had to take Sean away. It was crucial to select the correct time. She had no idea where Simpson went when he left the house. He would leave without warning. Reluctant to keep Sean off school, a place of safety, she had to plan their escape for a convenient time, to put enough distance between them and her partner. She'd hidden the car's spare key in her compact case and had left another of a similar appearance in its place. Sean would learn about her plan at the last moment.

Josh stared without focus as he sat on the train. He had a great deal to think about. Were he and Bethan destined to be re-united? Should he pursue her and put their past as far behind them as possible? Was it what either of them wanted? Would she have contacted him if the circumstances in which she'd found herself been any different?

He'd not experienced a relationship of note since he'd moved from London, but to make a commitment to her would pose problems, he knew it. He was deluding himself. She'd expect more than he could offer.

As he stared through the window, the darkness outside allowed him to examine his reflection. A pensive stare at his image prompted him to wonder how he could take positive steps to change his life, to ensure a future for which he craved. The infrequency of gigs with the band frustrated him. Everything depended on what the agents would suggest in mid-December. He hoped they'd accept the band in its present format. His private life appeared to be out of his control again, and he needed his music more than ever.

Now that he was solvent, recognition in his chosen field would give him the confidence and renewed aspiration to succeed as he had done before. This was his opportunity for a second chance. He'd been a misfit for years. He would be thirty-three in January. He didn't want to end up as an odd eccentric musician nobody else wanted beyond the performance. Bethan wasn't who he needed, but he couldn't dismiss her from his thoughts. She'd given him a reason to express his emotions other than to music.

He remembered he'd promised to work on some new songs over the weekend, but all he could only reflect on his own situation. He took out his notebook and jotted some lyrics.

I left my home when I was just eighteen,
But city lights weren't as bright as they seemed.

He continued for two more verses, and the beginning of the last, highlighted what he hoped his future would provide.

But I'm older now and feel the lines of my age,
And tired of acting on any old stage.

It was all he could write for the time being. He hoped he could finish the verse before the following evening's rehearsal.

He wasn't followed home but knew Simpson would ensure repercussions for his earlier action at Port Talbot. He suspected these would take place at the shop in the week. He had to be wary.

As soon as he walked into his flat, he sensed someone had broken in during the day. Upon opening his bedroom door, he failed to see either his old violin or its case on the bed. They were on the floor. Although the instrument was undamaged, the four strings had been cut.

Feeling vulnerable, he turned around, half expecting to see the intruder waiting for his return. Relieved to discover he was alone, he sat on his bed and took several deep breaths. After checking each room, he returned to the bedroom to place his new violin on his bed, glad he'd taken it with him. His guitar, in the wardrobe, hadn't been touched.

In need of a drink, he went to the kitchen to make a cup of coffee. The thought of preparing a quick meal left him. Caffeine would be enough. As the kettle boiled, he checked the entrance door. It showed no sign of a forced entry. Whoever had broken in had picked the lock. The landlord had a key, but he'd not made a copy for anyone.

Nothing, apart from his old violin, appeared to have been touched. It didn't take a great deal of guesswork to work out who'd instigated the break-in, and why. Informing the local police was pointless. Whoever had entered his flat would have worn gloves. It was a warning. He had to contact Bethan and her father.

Both phone calls were unsuccessful, so he left a message for Bethan, believing either one or the other would call back the next day. The lyrics he'd written on the train, although introspective, appeared to relate to his present situation.

I don't need any of this. He'd been warned and needed to think of an alibi to justify why he'd got off the train at Port Talbot. Questions would be asked at work the following morning. Several ideas came to him, but he settled on one he felt would be believable, to Terry Evans at least. A sleepless night was a distinct possibility. It was essential to place obstacles behind both the outside and bedroom doors. Anything but tired, he needed to calm down, to relax, and picked up his guitar to play some familiar tunes.

Several jazz chord progressions began to materialise to complement the lyrics he'd written earlier. It wasn't the usual style his band mates played, but hinted at a possible new beginning, for him, at least. A fresh approach to stimulate him was essential. He wondered how the band would react.

CHAPTER FORTY-FIVE

London: Through A Haze

2001

Josh returned to London mid-January, determined to regain his former enthusiasm to be an integral part of the orchestra. His time at home in Swansea had allowed him to place the acrimony between him and Bethan into perspective. Clive noticed a more composed musician than he'd witnessed over the autumn. However, one of his students at the university where he lectured had begun to show an interest in him.

The perceived innocent approach to discuss the finer points of their tutorials after the other students had left became a regular occurrence. To others, she seemed to have become enraptured with him. By Mid-February, he'd begun to feel uncomfortable about these post-tutorial meetings. She demonstrated the appropriate body language, making it obvious she wanted to bed him. Fresh from home but not so innocent, she knew which buttons to push to attract his attention. It wasn't an unreasonable age gap, but he suspected his position demanded a sensible distance between them.

He didn't want an involvement with a student at the university. As a student himself, he'd witnessed such relationships develop beyond the tutor/student arrangement, and the embarrassment when tutors had decided the trysts should finish. Although unaware of any rules regarding lecturers in relationships with students, he knew they could become unhealthy.

One afternoon as Josh sat alone in the refectory checking his seminar notes over a cup of coffee, she approached him with a line of music to be arranged for piano.

"I'd like you to look at this please. Can you tell me what style I should arrange it? It seems too modern to be arranged in a classical style as you requested." Uncomfortable with her lack of understanding of body space, he took the score from her. He turned away to view the music in the light from the window to avoid her physical closeness.

"What's your main instrument again, Molly?" Although aware she played the cello, he wanted to emphasise he had little interest in her as an emotional attachment. "A cello," she said, annoyed he'd not remembered.

"Then you shouldn't have a problem with the bass clef, and I'm sure you must be au fait with the treble, given the solo playing you must have done."

His abruptness, designed to dissuade her from being too familiar, didn't impress her. She snatched the score from his hand and marched out.

Hopefully that'll sort her out.

Before he left at the end of the day, Josh stopped at the head of music's office to mention the incident. He'd built up a good working relationship with John Fanthome and wanted to pre-empt any fallout from the incident with the student.

"Come in, I'm glad you've called by, sit down." Josh took a seat and gazed around the room, this, the second time he'd been invited into John Fanthome's office — the first at his interview. He looked around the room at the various photographs on display highlighting successes of past students either playing as solo performers or as orchestra members. The university had a proud record of instrumental success from where many had progressed to become respected solo performers.

John placed the paperwork on his desk in order, concentrating through his grey bushy eyebrows on the task he wanted to complete before he directed his attention towards Josh. John knew the reason for Josh's visit but wanted to hear his colleague's version of events first. Once he'd finished, he looked up. "How can I help you Josh?"

"I've just had an uncomfortable moment with one of the students."

"Molly Smith? Yes, I've some idea about it. She called round to see me earlier."

"Oh, I didn't realise. I just wanted to let you know. I gave her some sensible advice about a task I'd set, and she stormed out on me. But in all honesty, I've begun to feel uncomfortable in her presence. It's as if she has another agenda. I don't know what the university's policy is on staff and students in relationships, but as long as you know, I'm not interested. I saw the fallout from these several times as a student."

John looked at Josh with his archaic academic hat placed firmly on his head.

"As a student, when I began this journey in higher education, the lecturer would close the door for a tutorial. It left everybody to jump to their own conclusions. Now we're wary, most just wouldn't do it. Staff are made aware of the need to keep away from situations they may regret. I apologise if we've not made this clear to you. It's not illegal, as long as you're prepared take the consequences. The young madam is tempting you, is she?"

"No, I just thought she was trying it on with me. I don't want to get caught up in something to compromise my position here."

"Sensible. Let me look at her records. We keep them on all our students. Now we've got these new computers, we can access all our students' progress with ease." He turned in his chair towards a screen and keyboard and typed a few details. "Ah yes, most interesting, she's on the film presentation course, got in through clearing, but she's being monitored. That's all I can say for now." He paused for a few seconds and turned back to face Josh. "I'm not sure why she's with you. Does she give a problem in her group?"

"She does try to make her presence felt in front of the others in an overconfident manner. I can cope with her at present. Other students are far more constructive about their wish to learn."

"If she's free at those times, I'm loath to stop her unless she creates a problem in the tutorials. Take your coffee elsewhere in your breaks. Remember your responsibilities to the ones who want to learn from you. Now if you'll excuse me, I've got to meet the vice-chancellor." He stood and moved towards the door to let Josh out.

As Josh travelled back to Wimbledon he gazed through the bus window. He suspected his student had another agenda and had pre-empted the incident. He hoped John had believed him and the problem had been solved. He took out a novel from his bag and turned to the marked location to carry on reading, but his level of concentration failed him as he thought about Molly Smith. He wondered if he should have been more pleasant towards her and had not acted in such a defensive manner, but he couldn't turn back the clock.

On Josh's visit to the university two weeks later, John Fanthome stopped him in the corridor. "A minute before you start." Josh stood and waited in anticipation. "Molly Smith, I've moved her from your group, she made a formal complaint about you, so I began an informal investigation as it were."

"You didn't let me know."

"No, because I wanted to speak to you face to face and haven't found a time convenient to us both. I don't intend to take it any further. I've had a word with some of her fellow students. Apparently, she's boasted she was going to bed you — it was the phrase she'd used. She's not a very popular young lady here by all accounts. She's done nothing to warrant a formal warning, but her friends, more importantly, your friends on this occasion, took your side. She implied you'd asked her out on several occasions. This only came to light after the incident you reported to me, so I'll give you the benefit of the doubt on this. Now if you'd not come to me about it, I may have had my suspicions, but as it is, you have my support. I assume of course you can refute the accusation."

Grateful for John's intervention, Josh wondered what the motive behind his student's behaviour could be.

The relaxed atmosphere in the tutorial as a result of Molly Smith's absence encouraged each student to contribute without fear of conflict. Josh played the arrangements he'd set, on the piano to display the variety of styles adopted by his students, and each one explained his or her choice of harmonic form.

"I see you've all modulated to the dominant at the correct place."

"Nobody too dominant here today," said a young male student. Josh gave a wry but embarrassed smile, having noticed the overall support throughout the room.

At the lunch break he went to the canteen to take his midday meal and sat next to some of the other members of staff. As he ate, he heard a voice above the sonorous hum of the meal-time conversations. He looked up and saw Molly Smith make her presence obvious, speaking to a fellow student with a loud voice. She looked over at Josh and fixed a stare to unnerve him before she left the room. He felt the perspiration run down his back and wondered if another issue had to be dealt with.

Before Josh left, to carry out another seminar, John approached him, to request a meeting. Nothing untoward had happened since the morning. He hadn't spoken to Molly Smith. His tutorials with the students had been both constructive and amicable. However, he soon found out she was determined not to be beaten.

The university vice chancellor had approached John in the morning. The matter had taken a cruel twist.

"She now says you attempted to assault her." The look of incredulity on Josh's face confirmed his unwillingness to believe the accusation. "It happened one night when you were out in Wimbledon, or so she says." Josh couldn't remember seeing her on his own patch. "She said you'd asked her to your house, and when she refused you became angry with her and took hold of her wrists."

"But she wouldn't know I lived in Wimbledon. I don't think I've told anyone here where I live."

"Well she knew, somehow. Have you chatted up or met someone from the university?"

"In my local pub just down the road I meet lots of people, it's a popular place. I go there most Friday evenings if I'm not with the orchestra, but I'd remember her."

"What's the name of the pub? This could be crucial." Josh told him and added,

"I never go on my own unless rehearsals finish early, and I pop in for one drink on the way home from here. I'd planned to go in for one today, as I haven't got a rehearsal this evening."

"It's where she said she'd met you one night. If we change the day you come when young Miss Smith isn't timetabled to be here, maybe I can appease the vice chancellor. The other students will be in agreement, they're very supportive of you

"If the university's prepared to believe a liar, I'll have to consider if I want to work here any longer. I'll be grateful for a good reference and I'll be out of your hair. The other students, the proper musicians, who want to learn, appreciated what we did today, be fair to them at least. Who is she, anyway? What influence does she have?"

"The university has to take every accusation seriously, Josh."

"It was her parents, wasn't it?"

"I appreciate what you are saying, but I can't tell you any more than I already have. I'll be sorry to see you go." John gave the impression he had no control over the situation, his options gave him very little choice. He stood and offered Josh his hand.

Josh left the campus unable to comprehend the accusation directed at him. He attempted to recount the occasions she'd followed him to discuss the tasks he'd set. What had been her ulterior motive? Had she'd expected the advancements to be reciprocated?

Most events went over his head when engrossed in his music, and he could be insensitive to other people's feelings. But this was a bewildering act of revenge. It was an accusation of aggression. He wasn't aggressive even in drink. True he found one or two pints would allow him to relax and help him strike up a conversation with a female he found attractive, but he knew he hadn't met Molly Smith anywhere other than at the university. Maybe she'd followed him and had seen him in his local. He couldn't disprove the allegation without an admission from her.

On his way home he stopped at his local and drank too much for his own good. At the end of his session he was refused service, and he staggered home, leaving his violin in the bar. The instrument was placed away out of reach of other customers, to be collected at a later time.

As a result of his drunken state, he missed the next day's orchestra rehearsal. It was only later in the day he noticed several calls from his conductor, Clive. He'd apologise at the next rehearsal.

His house mates aware of his worries, confirmed they'd not witnessed him having had a causal relationship of any kind with a Molly, or anyone who appeared to have been an eighteen-year-old student.

"I'm certain I haven't brought anyone back."

"No-one since the summer, just your friend Jan, from the orchestra. A Molly Smith, about eighteen? Not your style anyway." Carol confirmed.

"Okay, I'll contact the university tomorrow to see if I can get my job back."

At nine the next morning, Josh telephoned John Fanthome to apologise and to confirm his housemates knew nothing about a Molly Smith.

"I understand your concern and I've spoken to some of her fellow students who have been out with her. They weren't very forthcoming but looked puzzled when I mentioned Wimbledon. There are far more lively places around here, and in the university." John said.

"Where did she get the name of my local from?"

"No idea, I'll have a word with the vice chancellor again, hopefully today, but I do think it would be better to change your timetable anyway, just to protect you. People know their rights far more today, but then we see some who forget their responsibilities to others, if you understand my meaning. You wouldn't believe what we have to deal with. People make allegations, some genuine I must add, but others after a quick pay-out. I'm glad my career is nearly at an end." Josh agreed to meet him the following Wednesday.

He made his way up to town for the lengthy rehearsal prior to a concert due to be held on the Saturday on the South Bank, a venue they'd performed in many times. When he arrived, he noticed a less than cordial Clive.

"Back to your old habits Josh, I'll have to have to consider your position here."

"But Clive, I've had a problem at the university where I teach and I've had to sort it out,"

"What? Can't keep your trousers on?"

"Clive. For God's sake. What are you insinuating?"

"You tell me." Josh could tell his conductor had lost his patience with him. He knew he should have rung him the previous day to apologise for his absence. "I thought you were recovering after some time at home. You had been. Perhaps London isn't good for you."

Josh attempted to explain the problem he'd encountered but Clive was less than sympathetic.

"Is there any truth in it? I recommended you to John. He's a good friend of mine, and I don't want you to let him or me down."

"I'll take my place then," Josh said, aware Clive didn't want to waste any more time with him.

"Last chance, next time I'll have to release you." The comment shocked him. Clive had become impatient with him. Shaken by the ultimatum, Josh didn't socialise, either during the break or after the rehearsal had finished. He turned up in good time for the concert arranged for the weekend but didn't stay for a drink afterwards. He felt himself he needed a change, and bought a magazine highlighting other options in the music business. One caught his eye.

Chapter Forty-six

March, 2001

Josh met John Fanthome at the university the following morning, but as he walked through the main entrance, he spotted Molly Smith talking to two male students. When they saw Josh, they stopped and focused their attention on him. He realised it was pointless approaching her to challenge her allegation, and continued walking until he reached John Fanthome's office, glad of the coffee on offer.

"Thank you for coming in at this time. How is everything with you at the orchestra?"

"I want to move on. An opera company is looking for more musicians. I shall tell Clive today. I feel I need a change. It's presenting *Orfeo ed Euridice*. I didn't realise my knowledge of opera was so limited. I've listened to Puccini and Verdi and we used to perform Gilbert and Sullivan's operettas at school, but this is so dramatic. Some of the melodies are well known to me, but the emotion is so electrifying."

"I'm glad you like it, most punters arrive at their appreciation of opera later, so don't expect too young an audience, not that you'll see each other as you'll be in the pit. Be prepared for a few unexpected conventions as well, such as a female in the role of *Orfeo*, a male character. You'll enjoy it. I wish we could attempt some of them here with the more enthusiastic singers."

"Is it a request?"

"No. I've had a word with the vice chancellor, and he's

discussed the matter with the governors. He's very sympathetic, but I suspect someone's leaning on him to terminate your contract at the end of this term." Josh sat in silence unable to understand why the decision had been made. "Are you sure you've not approached her in the past, possibly last term?"

"I've thought long and hard about this, and I have no recollection of meeting this girl outside the university, definitely not in Wimbledon. I do meet girls when I'm out, but not this one."

"It's a mystery to me as well. How would she know where you drink?"

"I've even asked my house mates if they remembered me bringing anyone young back to the house, and they drew a blank. She was very forward with me for a few weeks. I gave her more attention because I felt she wasn't grasping some elements we'd covered in the tutorials."

"I sympathise with you, but can we change your timetable for the remainder of the academic year?"

"I can come in on a Thursday or a Friday morning."

"Can you come both, every week?" I have another group of students whose tutorials have had to be shelved due to illness." John appeared to want to help as much as he could, aware of Josh's unjust treatment. "Until the end of the summer term. The governors needn't know we can extend your contract. The girl isn't due to be in lectures on those days, she's just scraping through. Let's play it by ear."

"When can I start the new times?"

"Next week, I'm sorry about this, but I can't be more helpful."

Josh called in at his local pub on the way home, but as he opened the door, he saw Molly Smith at the bar with the two male students he'd seen with her at the university. He didn't want to cause any trouble and turned to leave. It was pointless attempting to discover her motive to cause his dismissal. He arrived at his house within five minutes in a distressed state, noticeable to his housemates.

"What's up Josh?" Carol asked. Once Josh had explained, Phil suggested they should all go for a drink.

When they reached the pub, there was no sign of the girl and her two companions. Josh asked the barman if he remembered serving the three strangers earlier.

"Yes, when you came through the door. I saw you turn around and leave. The girl asked who you were. I told her you sometimes popped in for a drink on the way home from work."

"Did she stay long afterwards?"

"No, they finished their drinks and went within five minutes or so, the three of them."

"Do you know them at all?"

"No, I don't remember seeing them before."

"Unfortunately, I know her."

"Oh, someone you'd rather not be acquainted with?"

"You're right." The barman smiled at Josh. "And no, I haven't, fortunately."

CHAPTER FORTY-SEVEN

Early April, 2001

Josh was invited to join the opera company as soon as he completed his audition. Despite a drop in salary, he accepted the position. Once he'd secured his new post, Josh gave his letter of resignation to Clive.

The opera, due to open at the London Opera House at the beginning of May, presented several conventions new to Josh, as John had explained.

The principal soprano, Julie, in the role of Eurydice, attracted his attention. She'd encouraged him with a subtle flash of her eyes at rehearsals, but not so as to attract the attention of their colleagues including Colin, the conductor. Josh noticed Colin's roving eye focussed upon her as well but thought no more about it. In their brief conversations, she'd insisted Colin shouldn't be aware of their covert flirtatious behaviour. He didn't approve of relationships within the company.

After one rehearsal, they arranged to meet in a pub, away from the prying eyes of the remainder of the company. Two drinks later, she asked him to accompany her home to her flat in Hammersmith.

"I've a ground floor flat I share with someone. It's not far out of your way, and I don't like travelling home on my own." Josh guessed what would happen.

Within seconds after inviting him in, she began to unbutton his shirt. They made for the bedroom and undressed to enjoy each other's sexual needs. After frenzied foreplay he entered her and they both climaxed within seconds of each other. Two sweaty bodies, both satisfied, rolled onto their backs. Within minutes however, she began to excite him again.

"I want you," she demanded. His attention aroused once more, frustrations of the previous months were released.

At ten thirty she stood to put on her dressing gown.

"You'd better go now, my flatmate will be home soon, working late until eleven." He assumed she shared the flat with another female and left, satisfied their tryst wouldn't be discovered, for the time being. He looked forward to more evenings with Julie but was prepared to allow it to develop at its own speed. He was convinced his choice to work with this company would be a pleasant affair.

Congestion on the underground the following day resulted in him arriving five minutes late for the next rehearsal. As he walked into the rehearsal room, he turned to face the conductor to offer his apologies. However, he saw Colin engrossed in his music score, pencilling in notes, with Julie at his side. She appeared to be doing the same with her own copy of the music. They ignored Josh's presence, and he took his seat.

Before Colin turned his attention to the orchestra, Josh noticed Julie's smile was focused on the conductor. He reciprocated and stroked her arm, the mutual affection towards each other obvious. Josh failed to lip read the response Colin had made.

"Wonder what they're discussing." Josh turned to his fellow violinist Paul as he said this.

"Probably what they're having for dinner tonight."

Josh was stunned. He now realised the identity of Julie's so-called flatmate.

Although his past was far from innocent, most of the girls he'd slept with had demonstrated an element of coyness, requiring persuasion before they'd submitted to him.

"You've been sniffing there, haven't you? Don't think I haven't noticed. Keep away, before someone else does." Paul looked at Josh to wait for an answer, but Josh returned his gaze, feigning innocence by shrugging his shoulders. With no verbal response from his colleague, Paul continued. "I know far better sopranos than her who would have done the job, but they were overlooked. I'm friendly with one or two, and they couldn't believe she'd got the role. Take my advice, keep right away from her. If Colin thinks you're interested, you'd better keep a low profile."

"Oh shit." Josh said.

"What have you done?"

"I went back to her flat, last night."

Paul looked at him in disbelief.

Colin silenced the orchestra in preparation to play the overture. As it reached its conclusion, he demonstrated his displeasure and began to berate the string section. Josh turned to Paul and said, "I thought it went well, didn't you?"

"Shut up," Paul whispered in response.

"I believe you said something Josh. Is your violin in tune? I noticed you were late arriving. It sounds flat, get it sorted." Josh checked his instrument to make sure it was in concert pitch — no adjustment was necessary.

"Now we'll try it again." Colin continued.

They played the overture twice, after which it was agreed to proceed to the first soprano aria. A few noticeable mistakes crept in, as Julie had difficulty reaching the higher notes. No criticism was made, and Josh now understood Paul's comment.

At the break the two violinists continued their conversation about Julie's ability to sing the role. Josh was now no longer sure his move from Clive's orchestra had been a wise decision.

For a number of days Colin appeared preoccupied and didn't berate individual sections or members of the orchestra. Josh assumed Julie had been playing away again.

The opening night was well received, and an appreciative audience appeared impressed, given its reaction to the presentation. Both cast and orchestra were satisfied and were up-beat about the performance. However, reviews in the media the next day were mixed. One, in a respected broad sheet, slated the sluggish string section. Colin, who was furious with his orchestra, read the article to his musicians prior to the second night's performance. Josh felt the conductor's attempt to demoralise them before a performance was unfair, especially as the soprano soloist was the weak link in the company.

"Hell, I've worked with all sorts, amateurs as well as professionals, but nobody as unprofessional as this," Josh said.

"You'll get used to him," Paul said.

"Who's the critic who wrote this piece anyway?"

"A Sue Ellis, freelance writer. She worked in publicity here briefly."

"Do you know her at all?"

"I met her once at a party. From your neck of the woods I think."

"Oh!"

"What's up?"

"Is she about my age?"

"Yes, mid-twenties." Before the conversation could continue, the musicians were brought to a halt.

"First violins, big improvement on last night or people will be asking for their money back."

Josh had respected the fact operas were emotional. Now he understood the performers on the stage weren't the only prima donnas.

The finalé attracted a tremendous applause, and the mezzo-soprano who played the role of *Orfeo's* character was given a standing ovation by the entire audience, but the weakness of Julie's voice didn't attract the same response. The strings had played well with the correct phrasing and intonation. They'd followed every beat conducted, so no blame could be directed at them. Josh approached Colin to offer his congratulations. He didn't want to slink away in an antisocial manner.

"Well done Colin, I think we can safely say we saw an improvement on last night to nullify the critique. By the way, who wrote the review?"

"A youngster up from the Swansea area. I spoke to her when we were putting together the programme. Her name's Susan Ellis."

Josh suspected the critique had been directed at him, more as a personal attack as opposed to a musical one.

"Is she a musician to write such a qualified article as the one you read?"

"Of course, Josh. She's a flautist. She worked here until six months ago, a multi-talented girl. You can always rely upon her."

"You'll have to introduce us. I'd love to have a chat with someone from home." Susan Ellis still held a grudge. He'd have to be pleasant to her if their paths crossed. It would be the only solution to improve the critiques, to be fair to the other musicians.

Chapter Forty-Eight

The Inquest

May, 2001

The inquest to determine the cause of Sophie's death was held at the Coroner's Court in Croydon. Her neighbour, aware of her profession as a musician, testified he'd heard movement in the corridor in the early hours of the morning of her discovery. He assumed she'd returned late after an engagement. As he'd broken the door frame to enter her flat, it had been difficult to assess if the door had been forced during the night.

CCTV records confirmed Jan had reached her flat at five on Wednesday afternoon. She was recorded leaving early the next day. Josh's housemates had also testified to the police he'd been at home in Wimbledon all night.

Jan listened to evidence from the landlord, police, safety inspectors, fire crew, and the hospital doctor, aware she would also have been a victim had she stayed over. When she gave evidence, she stated she had keys to the flat as she often stayed with Sophie when her ex-boyfriend Julian spent time away on business.

"I left Sophie on Wednesday. Josh and I had been rehearsing with her for a few days. I stopped off in London on the way and –" she hesitated. She looked over at Josh, aware of his thoughts.

"And what?" the coroner asked.

"I saw Josh's ex-girlfriend. She'd arranged to meet my ex. They were having an affair. Neither of us knew."

"Is this relevant to this case?"

"No, but you wanted to know what I'd done."

"Did you go to your flat after you saw the ex-girlfriend?"

"Yes, until the next morning."

"You said in your statement you'd had visitors, at what time?"

"At about ten fifteen, but I didn't answer the intercom, I only turned on the video camera to see who'd rung the bell. I couldn't see their faces, as their heads were covered. Residents rarely contact their neighbours, so I assumed they were strangers. But if they were, they shouldn't have got into the complex, as only residents have access to the place. Fobs like this allow them entry." She held up her own fob and apologised for not returning it when she'd left the flat. To avoid Julian on the morning she'd moved out was her priority. The coroner instructed the police to assess whether her fob was an illegal copy.

"The CCTV record shows two hooded people entering the complex at nine fifty-five. Did anyone have access to your keys to Miss Carter's flat?"

"No, I kept them with me at all times."

"Did your ex-boyfriend know Miss Carter?"

"No. In fact she told me they'd never met, not even after concerts he'd attended. It would have been the only time they'd have had possible contact. He always used to wait outside the concert hall after a performance and take me for a meal, or to a club."

"So he never met any of your colleagues?"

"No."

"Did Miss Carter know him?"

"Only that he was my boyfriend. As I said, they'd never met." She remembered however, Sophie had not been happy

259

about her involvement with Julian. Ruth had explained why at the funeral. Jan had often talked to Julian about Sophie, and her sister Ruth They'd played in the schools' orchestra. Perhaps she'd hit a nerve.

"Did you know where your boyfriend was on the night in question?"

"I assumed he was working late, overnight, as he sometimes did. He phoned to tell me so, but we found out he'd spent the night with Bethan Williams, my friend Josh's exgirlfriend." Jan looked at Josh as she answered. His bowed head demonstrated an obvious embarrassment.

"Do you have any contact with him now?"

"No. I don't even know if he still lives in London."

Josh, questioned about his whereabouts during the week, had nothing to add to his original statement. The coroner asked him for Bethan's home address so she could be contacted and questioned. Not having mentioned her in his original statement, he'd assumed it would have no bearing on the case.

The investigating officer concluded his evidence on the first day, leaving the case open ended.

"Any person entering a room leaves a trace of his or her presence. Traces of Miss Carter, Miss Fowler and Mr. Stoller were found in the flat, but we can eliminate both Miss Fowler and Mr. Stoller from our investigations. The landlord has testified the flat was cleaned to remove all traces of previous tenants before Miss Carter took up residence at the address. However, the forensic team have discovered strands of hair belonging to another person in the kitchen. Unfortunately, we are not able to match these to anyone on our database. Not even the previous tenant. This suggests another person made his or her way into the flat in the early hours and tampered with the gas boiler."

This revelation suggested Sophie had been murdered, but

without an obvious motive. Her mother burst into tears. Ruth failed to console her. Although everyone connected to Sophie knew she had died in suspicious circumstances, the final statement was still devastating. The coroner expressed his condolences to the family and adjourned the inquest to reconvene a week later.

On the second day of the inquest, the coroner stated the fob Jan had presented the previous week was genuine and had been returned to the security staff. Julian Simpson no longer lived at the address he'd shared with Jan. He'd moved to Chester. He'd been located and questioned regarding his whereabouts on the night. He confirmed he'd spent the night with Bethan at a hotel in central London. He also confirmed a past colleague, with whom he'd lost touch, had lived in the same complex, but drew a blank when asked about the two visitors. Other residents had no knowledge of visitors on the night in question. Simpson's old employers confirmed he'd resigned his post that summer.

Bethan had also been questioned in Swansea and had confirmed their night together. The hotel's CCTV had recorded they'd returned to the hotel at eight forty-five. They'd left the following morning. Jan, alarmed to hear where Simpson lived, hoped Manchester would provide her with enough anonymity to remain safe, even in the orchestra.

After all the evidence had been delivered, the coroner summed up and instructed the police to continue investigating the case. The finality of the inquest was upsetting for Sophie's family. Solving the crime appeared nigh on impossible.

CHAPTER FORTY-NINE

June 2001

With *Orfeo ed Euridice* due to run over the early summer months, Josh had to postpone some of his private pupils until the opera had run its course. Three weeks after it had begun, Colin asked Josh to join him in the bar after the performance. Colin had mentioned an old friend of his was keen to meet the new violinist. Josh thought no more about it. He felt the orchestra had played well, but Julie had been the cause of some tricky moments.

The role of *Orfeo* had been sung by Helen, an understudy, one of the chorus members. She'd sung the part in another opera company, so was familiar with the role. As it was her first night, Josh suspected the Julie had attempted to upstage her.

He stepped out from his dressing m and saw Helen in the corridor. It was obvious she was upset, believing her performance had been spoilt. With a great deal of effort, he persuaded her to accompany him to the bar. "Come on, I don't fancy meeting one of Colin's friends on my own. Why don't you come with me? Just one drink."

She agreed, somewhat reluctantly.

As Josh and Helen entered the crowded bar, they saw Colin and Julie, drinks in hand, deep in conversation with a blonde female, with her back to them. Her formal appearance suggested she was well connected in opera circles and had attended the performance out of interest. Reluctant to have to make polite conversation, given the possible conflict between Helen and Julie, he walked towards an empty space at the bar. To buy drinks and move to an anonymous part of the room was a priority. He wanted to cajole Helen back to an acceptable level of confidence. She was due to deputise the following night as well.

The blonde woman turned around, and Josh recognised her. "Sue, I didn't expect to see you here." Although he felt uncomfortable seeing his old flame, he acknowledged her, appearing pleased to see her. Her response, however, was less than cordial. "It's Susan, actually. Didn't Colin tell you about me? How remiss of him." As she spoke, he detected the cynicism in her voice. Her Neath accent had all but disappeared. "And I see you're with tonight's understudy, and you are?" she directed her attention towards Helen.

"This is Helen. She had to fill in at the last moment. I thought she covered the part well," Josh said, noticing Helen's reticence.

"Yes, it is a tricky part, very demanding, especially for a novice like you," interrupted Julie.

"Excuse me, but I'm just going to get Helen and myself a drink." Josh sensed the comment had annoyed Helen and wanted to protect her from further insults.

"We're fine, thank you Josh, just in case you're offering," Susan said.

He guided Helen towards an area of the bar from where he could attract the barman's attention. As he ordered the drinks, Susan moved over to stand by his side with her back to Helen, to block her out of the conversation.

"How nice to meet you after all this time. Must be five years since our paths crossed," she said.

"Must be. I assume it is you who writes the critiques in the newspaper. You could have been kinder regarding the last one you wrote about us. I'm surprised Colin's as friendly towards you as he is."

"Oh, Colin and I have an understanding. Julie's told me a few things about you. Helen's your next conquest, I assume." Helen looked on red faced with embarrassment.

"Excuse me. We're going to sit down. Helen's had a demanding night."

"Of course, I won't join you. It was interesting seeing you again though. Oh, by the way I'm here in my professional role as a journalist as well, as I was all evening."

Josh and Helen found two vacant seats. He was relieved they could escape from Susan, but he sensed Helen's anger.

Helen recognised the animosity between Josh and Susan. She also wanted to be as far away from Julie as possible. Julie's comment had angered her. "Novice, I'll give her novice, the bitch. She shouldn't even be part of this company. She can't hit those top notes at all, she hasn't a clue. I wouldn't even give her a job in the chorus. What the hell has she got to have convinced him to give her the role? I can guess."
Josh said nothing. He didn't want Helen to be aware of his evening with Julie.
"I take it you and Susan know each other?" She watched his nervous reaction. He held the glass to his lips as if in a hurry to leave the bar. When he placed it back on the table his fingers turned it as he stared into its contents.
"It's obvious there's animosity between you two. I take it she want's revenge for something."

Josh felt embarrassed by the situation, but knew he'd have to explain what had happened. "Yes, we're from the same area. We went out together when we were younger, until I went to Cardiff. We didn't finish on good terms, my fault entirely, I met someone else, but it's a complicated story."

"She seems bitter."

"Is it obvious? I didn't think she would be any longer, but I was wrong."

"What's her professional role?"

"She's a journalist by all accounts, a music critic. She must have written the first review. I don't know why she's here again, but she seems on very friendly terms with Colin. What's his relationship with Julie, apart from the obvious?"

"Latest bit on the side. He tried it on with most of the chorus when he joined us. I told him he was wasting his time, knew what he was like before he even approached me. He's powerful in the business so gets away with it. I'm surprised he asked me to sing the role tonight, but I've done it before, so it wasn't a problem, until we got onto the stage."

"Julie?"

"Please don't repeat it."

"How long has he been with this company?"

"Eighteen months, but he won't be long, got his sights on ENO. I've seen a few come and go. He's the slimiest I've ever known."

"You must remember Susan Ellis, then."

"Vaguely. She worked here until a year or so ago, but I didn't take much notice."

Josh wondered how close she'd been to Colin. "We'll go as soon as we finish these," Josh said, "I feel a bit awkward." He noticed three pairs of eyes scanning the room, to end up looking in his direction. He couldn't stand it any longer and asked, "How are you getting home?"

"I'm getting a cab, it's fifteen minutes. You?"

"Tube, District line, I'll be home in twenty. I'd better say goodbye to her. I don't think I'm very popular, judging by the atmosphere."

"I think you'd better. Don't sink to their level."

He approached Susan and tapped her on the arm. "Good to see you again, I have to get home, I'm teaching tomorrow morning at nine thirty. Hope to see you again."

"Yes, Josh." Her cold steel-blue eyes demonstrated her emotions better than her vocal response.

Relieved to be out in the air, he walked Helen to her taxi.

"Thanks for looking out for me tonight. It's a shame the meeting didn't go well. I'll be more prepared tomorrow evening," she said as she got in the cab.

A quiet house greeted him on his return. Although Susan had unnerved him, the company of his housemates the following day helped him push the experience to the back of his mind.

Helen's portrayal of *Orfeo* overshadowed Julie's attempts the following night. This was confirmed by the audience's reaction to her performance. Josh winked at her as they met in the corridor afterwards.

"Fancy a celebratory drink?" he said.

"No thanks, Josh, but I really appreciate your support last night. I'm meeting my boyfriend. He came to see me tonight. I think he'll be pleased even if I've annoyed Julie."

A less than complimentary critique of the performance written by Susan Ellis, appeared in one of the Sunday reviews. Julie's performance was hailed as exemplary, but Helen's performance had been hampered by sluggish manner in which the string section had accompanied her. With more cohesion in the orchestra, Helen's performance would be far more fluid if asked to deputise again. Josh wrote his letter of resignation in the afternoon.

He turned up for Monday's performance at six-fifteen, early enough to make sure he could spend a few minutes discussing how he felt with Colin before he gave the conductor the letter. As he passed Julie's changing room, he saw the door open. Colin was deep in conversation with her. Josh knocked, to attract their attention.

"What do you want?" Colin asked.

"A quick word, please. The review in the paper yesterday was totally unfair towards Helen and quite untrue. The string section wasn't out of time. We followed your every beat. Given the opportunity, Helen's an excellent understudy and could well take over the role. Don't you remember the reaction to her performance on Saturday night? She's sung it before anyway. You knew that, otherwise you wouldn't have asked her."

"You're making advances on her now are you, you bastard. Julie's told me how you tried it on with her, didn't get very far did you? We have no room for people like you in this company."

"No. I don't want to be part of it either, here's my resignation letter. I'll play till you find a replacement, the sooner the better."

"I've got one, tonight. So you can go now."

"What? Just like that?" Surprised by the comment, Josh stood dumbfounded. He regained his composure before leaving the dressing room. He had nothing to lose "It was the bloody soprano, you," he said, pointing at Julie. "You cocked it up. You couldn't keep in time with the phrasing. You stayed on notes for too long to delay Helen's entries, probably on purpose. In your position, Colin, it's her you should be sacking. She won't do anything for your reputation. I thought Susan Ellis, would have been a more astute critic, if I remember anything about her writing skills. You can tell her from me. Oh, by the way, I suggest you ask Julie the truth regarding those advances." He couldn't resist this parting shot.

As he walked towards the theatre exit, he bumped into Helen. "I've just resigned,"

"Why?"

"I'm not needed."

"It's the review in the paper, isn't it?"

"Part of it, but the journalist's getting her revenge."

"He will be leaving, why don't you sit it out?"

"Too late, take good care, see you around."

Josh sat on the tube to take him back to his watering hole to contemplate his future. Tuesday became a lost day.

CHAPTER FIFTY

Summer 2001

O ver the summer, Josh's private pupils cancelled their lessons, and his university work came to an end. This threatened his ability to honour the rent on his room. Music magazines advertised posts in West End musicals, a genre he'd never considered before, but they attracted his attention. It was work.

He attended one for a popular show on the West End. Unfortunately, it had to be postponed for two hours, and to kill time he decided to visit a nearby bar. One drink became more, before he returned to the audition. As he entered the room, he failed to see the panel members look at each other. Each one's face displayed disappointment. One couldn't avoid the smell of alcohol on his breath.

Several had recognised his name from his previous work and were surprised he should be auditioning. After a less than convincing performance, he was advised to apply elsewhere.

His frustration began to get the better of him, and he decided to busk in Central London. He believed a railway terminus with a steady footfall would attract the attention of a greater audience. As he stood at the entrance of Waterloo Station, he gazed around at the faceless commuters rushing to destinations known only to themselves. In a more successful time, he had been one of these, ignoring all other travellers. This morning he had to attract their attention, to make them pause and search their pockets for loose change or more.

He knew he had the skills to impress an audience, but this was different environment to the ones in which he'd entertained appreciative audiences. Although a seasoned player in concerts and orchestra pits, he was now face to face with people with other priorities. He wondered if he had the skills to appeal to these unsuspecting rail travellers. He'd always played behind an invisible wall, separating him from his audience. But that wall no longer existed, and people rushed past each other, desperate to be elsewhere.

Faceless travellers, eager to reach their destinations, weaved in and out of each other's paths. They sidestepped to avoid collisions and to protect their personal body space. They demonstrated no interest in his renditions of the classics and world music, unknown to the majority, however masterfully they were played. Some even kicked his case with no word of apology. They'd not expected to have had to avoid another annoying busker. He stood in their way. With several coppers and a few pieces of silver in his case, he soon realised this method of making money proved to be far more difficult than he'd anticipated.

Within five minutes, a member of the transport police approached him. He didn't waste any time giving his opinion what Josh should do. "Move along, Sonny, before I take your earnings from your case and put it in the charity box, not that you've got much in there. All these people have got to get somewhere, and you're in the way. Learn something we all know, will you."

Josh felt deflated and left the station to make his way to Covent Garden. Here street performers vied with each other for spaces to entertain for whatever financial rewards they could obtain from the myriad of tourists.

He spotted a vacant spot and unravelled his music stand. A part of him now wished he'd kept his old Hoing and had bought a cheap but adequate instrument for this purpose. He opened his book of J S Bach's tunes and began to play. Several people stopped to listen, and the odd passer-by tossed a coin or two into his case. As more people showed their appreciation, his confidence grew.

After half an hour, his performance was disturbed without warning. Another musician carrying a guitar case approached him.

"This is my fuckin' spot, what are you doin' in it?" he said as he placed his case on the pavement. Josh continued until he'd reached a suitable place in the music to finish. As he played the final phrases, he noticed the guitarist closing his violin case. "I said, what you doin' 'ere? Piss off, this is my spot, I play 'ere every day you posh fuckin' bastard, fuck off somewhere else." In his impatience, the guitarist attempted to grab the violin, forcing Josh to step back out of his way. Josh was reluctant to react with any aggression. He had a four-thousand-pound instrument in his hand.

"Sorry, I didn't realise, what do you have to do to get a spot?"

"Check it isn't someone else's like every other fucker 'ere. Now fuck off." Josh felt embarrassed by the guitarist's attitude. He wanted Josh to move and didn't care his outburst had attracted the attention of passers-by. To argue with this seasoned hustler was futile, and Josh wondered how he'd survive in this new, hostile environment. To do so he would have to become far more ruthless with this type of competition.

Josh picked up the coins from his case and stuffed them into his pocket. By now the guitarist had put the strap over his shoulders, and had begun to play with an attitude, the opposite of how he'd approached the violinist.

Now deflated, Josh walked on to where he heard an ensemble of musicians playing at the entrance to a restaurant on the lower floor of the busy concourse. Here he saw a string quartet entertaining a large crowd who stood on the balcony above, as well as the diners in the area below. This appeared to be a popular venue, and he walked down the stairs to approach the owners.

"You're wasting your time," a voice called out, "this is ours for the next hour."

"I'm just looking for the possibility of a spot sometime."

"You need to be part of a group, and it's more than playing, you need to entertain. It's what people want here. You don't look like you could."

Josh became even more disillusioned and walked towards Leicester Square, where he attempted to entertain groups of tourists more interested in soaking up the commercial atmosphere of the West End. After he'd played for several minutes, someone threw a coin into his case. He now realised how sheltered he'd been within the enclosed safety of an orchestra. A few minutes and fewer coins later, another busker approached him, claiming the spot.

On three more occasions he encountered the same reaction from other entertainers. As a result, he decided to try the underground. The congestion of rush hour commuters intensified by the minute, and his presence hindered their movement. Consequently, a member of staff moved him on.

By late afternoon, frustrated by his inability to perform in any one place longer than several minutes, he returned to Wimbledon. The loose change he'd collected totalled twenty pounds.

This less than successful attempt at earning what he'd hoped, made him realise his lifestyle would have to change. Would he want to go through the abuse and the inconvenience with which he'd been treated on a daily basis? It wasn't the ideal way to live his life over the summer. The possible damage to his expensive violin posed another problem. He needed to make an effort to get a steady position with an orchestra and not to blow his chances with an overindulgence of alcohol. However, achieving an acceptable level of sobriety was easier said than done.

CHAPTER FIFTY-ONE

The Andre Coinus Is Sold

October, 2001

Josh's precarious survival as a busker over the summer allowed him to scratch a living on the streets. But he often encountered several unpleasant situations similar to the one he'd faced in Covent Garden. Desperate to find other musicians with whom he could network and be accepted, he visited pubs where he could jam with others. These sessions led to the occasional engagement with either a jazz or a rock band. In each case however, payment, at the landlord's discretion, meant more being spent behind the bar.

He attended further auditions for productions in the West End, but being his own worst enemy, they resulted in little success. When his private pupils resumed their lessons, his income increased. It ensured he had sufficient funds to honour his rent payments. It wasn't an ideal way to make money, but limited opportunities in the professional music scene left him little choice. He failed to organise himself to perform on the underground without interruption from another busker or staff member, and with the threat of a cold winter, playing in the open air proved less than inviting.

Reluctant to use his violin to play in the streets, he wished he'd bought a cheaper instrument, had he known his future.

The Andre Coinus hadn't brought him any luck, and with little money, he worried how long he'd be able to manage on his meagre earnings. He reflected upon his declining status, which, coincidentally, had begun with its purchase.

By the end of October, he made up his mind to sell the violin, the final twist in his failure to succeed as a prestigious musician. His accomplishments and acceptance as one of the elite the serious musical field no longer existed.

One cold Saturday morning he set off to find a music shop in London where he could negotiate a realistic price for his instrument. He'd paid three thousand eight hundred for it, and another thousand for the bow. The sale of both would ensure his place in the house would be safe for at least another few months.

As he sat in the tube train carriage, clutching the violin case, he gazed at the expressionless passengers who travelled to their destinations, oblivious to anyone's predicament, but their own. He reflected on how his success had diminished. Again, he wished he could have been satisfied with his more than adequate Hoing, but that time was now over. The insecurity facing him forced him to withdraw even further into the shell of his solitude.

With four thousand five hundred pounds in his pocket, the price reached between him and the dealer, he bought a cheap instrument for two-hundred and fifty pounds. He also bought a flexible cover to conceal the case, so on any return to his parents, the decline in his fortune would not appear so drastic. The surplus he paid into his bank account.

CHAPTER FIFTY-TWO

Rock and Alcohol

2002

Christmas came, and Josh tumbled into 2002 with little hope of lucrative work. His bank assets, buoyed up by the sale of his violin, disappeared far quicker than he'd anticipated, and by February, he found it difficult to afford to live in the shared house. He didn't wish to claim unemployment benefit as he still had six private pupils, each paying twenty pounds an hour. One hundred and twenty pounds a week barely covered the rent.

He looked for work in music shops and hoped he could find one in town where his expertise would be useful. As he was competent on both piano and guitar, he felt he could give customers expert advice on which suitable instrument to buy. He visited several music shops in the Charing Cross, Leicester Square area and described his musical background to each of the owners. Fortunately, one in Denmark Street offered him part-time work three mornings a week. This gave him an extra ninety pounds. He found it a useful place to work and met various musicians eager to find others with the ability to play at a high standard.

Josh began to play on the semi-pro rock scene by the summer of 2002. However, the amount of alcohol he drank continued to increase, and he found it difficult to control the habit.

If at home in Wimbledon on a Friday, he would join his housemates at the local, but only after he'd consumed at least one bottle of cheap wine beforehand. Two or three pints would push him over the top, into a state to cause embarrassment.

When he performed, he kept a bottle of wine at his side. At first, the band members who'd employed him were amused by his antics, but they soon lost patience with the looseness of his playing when drunk. His mistakes threatened the cohesion of the group's performance and they frequently fell out.

For a year or so his lifestyle continued to revolve around work in the music shop, his private pupils, and the semi-pro rock music environment. One by one, his housemates moved, and he began to feel abandoned. New tenants were reluctant to accept his erratic behaviour and asked him to leave.

By 2003 he was lucky to still be employed in the music shop, and very few musicians wanted to include him in any impromptu sessions. As he staggered across a road one evening, his mobile phone fell from his pocket and was crushed by a car. He had very few contacts left in London and felt a mobile phone monthly contract, his old one completed, would be pointless. This he replaced with a pay-as-you-go handset but failed to install the numbers of his old acquaintances.

In mid-December he moved to a bedsit in Wandsworth, a small room on the first floor of a converted house. It had limited furniture, a single bed and wardrobe, and overlooked the backyard of a restaurant. From this, the pungent smell of cheap cooking oil contaminated his room if his window remained open. This meant a choice of eitherliving in a stuffy airless environment or allowing the pervading odour to contaminate his belongings.

The accommodation, one-hundred and fifty pounds a

month less than his room in Wimbledon, would be his home for the foreseeable future. However, his private pupils no longer wanted lessons due to the extra travelling costs, so his income diminished even further.

Fortunately, he found a music shop in Clapham that wanted an assistant to work every day. His expertise in classical and world music attracted interest from the shop's manager, and Josh was employed to promote these genres.

As he lived and worked in the same area of London, his transport costs were almost eliminated. It also gave him the opportunity to explore the different ethnic cultures of the area and embrace the different types of music on offer in various bars and clubs. He felt he had been transported back in time to his teenage years when he'd been involved with the variety of music he'd experienced in the folk festivals. He made the acquaintance of people with whom he could improvise. This encouraged him to take greater responsibility for his wellbeing.

The local pub rock scene attracted his interest, and from time to time he asked to join in with impromptu sessions, as he had as a student. Local musicians began to invite him to join in sessions, which made him happier than he'd been since the Millennium. By the end of the year, he'd been invited to join a local folk-rock band, which gave him back his old confidence as a player. He still played his cheap two-hundred-and-fifty-pound violin, but made it sound like an instrument four times its value when played through a PA system.

His versatility enhanced the band's overall sound, as he played both guitar and piano when available. The band achieved a respectable level of popularity in and around South London, and he soon began to regain his self-respect.

He regained his ambitious streak again and wanted to expand his possibilities, to reignite his initial career and return to his trained for professional status. He'd found the energy to compete with the young bucks who wanted to make names for themselves.

CHAPTER FIFTY-THREE

A Topsy-Turvy Relationship

2002

As the year progressed, the group secured bookings in venues further afield. He tried to convince his bandmates to search for engagements at some of the large open-air festivals over the summer months, but to Josh's annoyance, they were reluctant to play to audiences of thousands. Their experience in the dark atmospheres of the spotlighted contemporary pub rock scene hadn't prepared them for this potentially new sea of faces that would see them in the broad daylight of sunny afternoons. Josh had to respect their wishes, as each member possessed a secure and lucrative occupation outside the band.

Now twenty-eight, with years of alcohol abuse and disappointment behind him, Josh felt he'd wasted London's opportunities. More mature and aware of the politics within the music business, he needed to find another avenue where he could use his skills. He explored the local newspapers and discovered adverts for experienced musicians to accompany several amateur musical and operatic groups. Financial returns were limited, but it gave him the opportunity to meet others he could use to network and find orchestral work once again.

Over the summer months he worked with two amateur operatic companies. One of Gilbert and Sullivan's favourites — *The Mikado* — was to be presented in Greenford in June.

Oklahoma, a popular musical, had been planned for a September presentation in Wimbledon.

The musical director of *The Mikado* called four orchestra rehearsals, so Josh didn't have the opportunity to get to know the cast members until the after-show party. This topsy-turvy event turned out to be an interesting affair, as he attracted the interest of each of the Three Little Maids. Each one had brought her partner, and all three males made it clear their little maids were off limits. Amused by the reaction, he directed his attention towards Josie, the orchestra's oboe player. Impressed by his musicianship, she didn't require a great deal of persuasion to stay with him overnight. She appeared a safer and more attractive prospect.

He felt confident he'd found a regular partner with whom he could identify. They met two or three times a week over the summer months, Josie, however, proved reluctant to take their relationship beyond the sexual attraction. He suspected she had another romantic interest behind the scenes, but an admission wasn't forthcoming, just vague information another man had been in the background before they'd met.

One evening, when they'd arranged to go for a meal together, she didn't turn up. She made an excuse she was meeting friends. When they next met, Josh could tell from her mood she'd not been truthful.

"Am I just an option, an alternative?" he said. "Because if so, I won't be able to put you first. I've been in this position before, and it hurts." Josie failed to answer him and walked away. They would not meet again until September, in the Wimbledon Musical Society's production of *Oklahoma.*

Three weeks before its presentation, Josh turned up for the first orchestral rehearsal. It seemed strange to be back in Wimbledon, but he kept away from his old haunts. He was a reformed character. Alcohol was off limits. Once he'd introduced himself to the show's director, he was given his score.

The other string players regarded him and his violin with suspicion—they recognised its value. But he tuned to concert pitch in a matter of seconds and proceeded to play the first sixteen bars of one of Bach's partitas, then placed the violin back in its case. "That's better. Seems in tune," he said to himself, but loud enough to be audible to the other members of the orchestra. The silence in the room was deafening, the cast, and the musicians who had already arrived, looked at each other, impressed by what they'd heard. The musical director smiled

The popularity of the show, a recent West End production, ensured a sell-out audience each night. After the last performance the cast and musicians attended an after-show party. Josie had brought a male friend and kept away from Josh. He'd spent most of the time engaged in small talk with some of the cast, too embarrassed to speak to her. Frequently he looked over towards her and saw her turn her attention from him in a manner to suggest she also regretted the outcome of their earlier relationship. At the end of the evening she approached him, to bid him a good night.

"I'm sorry. I wasn't entirely honest with you."

"I'd guessed you were seeing someone else anyway. So, you're with him now. I assume he was the other guy when we were together."

"Yes, you were right. I'd been seeing someone else at the same time, but I finished with him once and for all on the night I didn't meet you. I'd hoped we could have carried on. But when you talked about options and putting you first, I felt guilty. You just threw me. I didn't know how to respond."

"Do you want us to meet again?"

"I couldn't go through it all again. It was good to see you again, though." She put her hand out to shake his and left. He caught the last bus home alone, wishing he'd followed his heart and not his pride.

Although his band resumed their engagements in the autumn, they were not as regular as he'd hoped. Debt, controlled by ruthless credit card companies, was a constant worry. To make ends meet became more difficult.

By Christmas, his impatience boiled over. His fellow musicians were reluctant to pursue more regular gigs, and the band folded. Replacements, enthusiastic about increasing the workload, were soon found. Josh, however, realised the band needed more rehearsal time before seeking engagements, and he often demonstrated his annoyance at the quality of sound.

In early February, he decided to search for the orchestra where he'd begun his music career and bought a ticket for one of its performances at the South Bank later in the month. The concert consisted of pieces by Gerald Finzi, the rarely played violin and piano concertos. These were followed by Vaughan Williams' *Sinfonia Antarctica*, composed for the film based on Scott's quest to reach the South Pole. Winston still played his beloved cello and Josh enjoyed the intensity of his performance. Timothy's viola however was absent — he'd obviously moved on. Once again Josh pined for the old Hoing and happier days. Moved by the emotion of the music, he regretted how he'd allowed his life to spiral out of control.

Aware the members of the orchestra would meet in the bar afterwards, he bought a drink before they arrived. Winston was delighted to see him, eager to find out how his career had progressed. Josh didn't elaborate upon his experiences post orchestra. He didn't feel the need. Winston noticed his choice of drink, no more large glasses of wine — non-alcoholic by choice and necessity. Clive also demonstrated his pleasure to see his past maestro, and the three spent fifteen minutes together. Josh asked about possible vacancies in the orchestra, but Clive was unable to offer him anything. They exchanged telephone numbers in case an opportunity presented itself, but he made no mention of the quality of his violin. He hoped the problem could be overcome if need be.

As the year progressed, Josh's band secured more gigs. It gave him the income to be able to live a less frugal existence than he had for a number of years, but his debts didn't diminish as quickly as he'd hoped. The band continued to play in the immediate area, but success further afield eluded them. Most evenings were spent either rehearsing or performing. The other musicians however, showed little sign of improvement.

By the end of 2006, frustrated with both the effort he'd made to make a living in this musical environment and the quality of his band, he decided his survival depended on a fresh start elsewhere. The city lights weren't as bright as they had seemed when he'd moved to the capital, but he knew he'd contributed towards the dimming of its brilliance. He had to make one more effort to achieve some level of success. This could only be achieved by leaving the city, but he had no idea where to go.

In the spring of 2007, he travelled home to explore the possibilities of a return to South Wales. He didn't want to stay in Swansea. Success would be better achieved in Cardiff. After a week with his parents, he travelled up to the Welsh capital to look for an ordinary day job. He hoped it would allow him time to explore musical opportunities. He also had to find inexpensive accommodation.

Within a week, he discovered work in a clothes shop, in a town several miles north of Cardiff. It was a job he found more convenient than interesting. He didn't mention his experience as a classical musician who'd played at the highest level. It was inconsequential in his opinion.

Fortunately, he found a flat in the same location, an inexpensive area to live. The rent was less than twenty-five per cent of his wages. Once he'd settled, he advertised for pupils to supplement his income. He also searched for fellow musicians with whom he could play on a regular basis. Although he felt he was drifting without a musical challenge, he'd placed his life back on an even keel. However, the telephone call from Mrs. Francis resulted in a future he could not have predicted.

CHAPTER FIFTY-FOUR

Identities Revealed

Monday, 30 November, 2009

Josh took a long time to get to sleep as the time rolled on past midnight. The lyrics he'd written played on his mind as he stared at the ceiling. He no longer wanted to act on any old stage. The lines of his age, as he'd intimated, demanded a rapid recognition of his talents.

He was no longer confused by the degree of intimacy he and Bethan had experienced the previous day. He had to place the situation in perspective. Although he was flattered by her attention and her willingness for intimacy, she was married. Admittedly, she had reminded him of the intensity of their previous relationships, but he had no wish to wait for convenient opportunities. Convinced he'd made the correct decision, he sat up in bed and grabbed his notebook. The fourth verse was complete.

How wise we become with each passing day,
No reason for dreaming our lives away.

When Josh arrived at the shop, he found the door locked and had to let himself in. As he closed the door, he heard the sound of activity from the stock room. Terry was struggling to stack boxes on top of each other to create more floor space.

"Having difficulty?"

Terry Evans grunted a response. He was out of breath.

Josh ignored this and took over. He lifted boxes still on the floor one by one, theb placed them on top of the others already in stacks of three. Although slight of build, he'd retained an element of fitness. His wiry frame belied his natural strength. Between them they completed the task before they opened the shop.

Josh felt obliged to begin a conversation with his boss to overcome an embarrassing silence. He suspected Simpson would have told Terry about the incident at Port Talbot and knew he'd have to mention the journey.

"I caught the train home to see my parents yesterday. I haven't seen them for a while," he said.

"Which station do you use? Neath, isn't it?" Terry's response confirmed he'd been aware of what had happened, but Josh had prepared an answer he believed to be plausible.

"Yes, but they're moving to Port Talbot and wanted me to see the house. I nearly forgot, thinking about a new song, and almost missed the stop." He hoped the conversation would stop there, but Terry continued.

"Oh. When are they moving?" This surprised Josh. He'd not thought beyond an excuse for his sudden exit from the train.

"Soon, they hope it'll happen before Christmas. It seems a silly time to move, but they want to get in and sorted before the holidays." Josh hoped his boss believed him. To be found out at a later time wouldn't matter. He'd take evasive action. He could move on. Simpson's realm of deceit would be avoided.

Now solvent, with no financial demands, it would be the kick Josh needed to take full advantage of his musical skills. Promise of a more rewarding existence appeared to be on the horizon with his band. However, Terry's next comment surprised Josh.

"Why don't you have this Saturday off? I'm sure your parents will need some help packing boxes."

"Thanks Mr. Evans, but it'll be a busy day a few weeks before Christmas, surely." He felt it necessary to display an element of loyalty.

"No matter, Nathan will be here." Josh had not seen any paperwork to suggest a delivery. Terry wanted Josh out of the way for some reason. With Simpson in control, anything was possible.

A steady stream of customers kept both men busy throughout the day, with limited conversation between them. When the shop closed at five o'clock, Josh thanked his boss for allowing him time off over the weekend. Terry just smiled his response, and nothing more was said.

It was now essential to speak to Bethan's father, whatever he'd decided about his relationship with Bethan. When he arrived at his flat, he checked his phone, but neither Bethan nor her father had responded to the text he'd sent the previous night. He attempted contact again, but no answer meant having to leave an update regarding the time off he'd been given the following weekend.

As he put down his phone, his mother called. Their conversation consisted of the usual small talk about his work and band performances. As they were about to finish, she said,

"Oh Josh, I had a call from an estate agent this afternoon, advertising its services. They suggested a twenty-five percent discount on its fees. I told him we weren't moving."

"Did he say anything else?"

"No, he just apologised for having bothered us. Never known them touting for business before. He didn't sound local." Josh knew it had to be Simpson.

"What was his company called?"

"He did say a name, but I don't remember it, I was so

surprised by the call." They ended the conversation, and Josh considered what he'd heard. Simpson had contacted his parents. It had to be him, proof the so-called phone call from Winston over the summer had been a scam as well.

Chris collected him for the band rehearsal at seven o'clock, and armed with both his guitar and violin, they went to the practice venue. This was the distraction Josh needed.

"You've got both instruments tonight, what are we in for?"

"Some ideas came to me yesterday on the train."

"So, you went to Swansea."

"No, I had to see someone else."

"You don't need to tell me, I can guess." Josh looked over at his friend and smiled. There was no need to continue the conversation.

Josh and Chris were greeted with a warm barn when they arrived. Several heaters had been acquired, and the musicians felt comfortable to continue with an extended rehearsal. His first task was to play the new song he'd arranged to gain the band's approval.

Once Josh had finished, Dave suggested the song needed a chorus or middle section. They played around with various chord sequences and lyrics to add to Josh's initial composition and agreed after half an hour on a chorus to be included after each verse.

But dreams are shattered when you build up your hopes
Nothing's what it seems when you untie the ropes.
Locked in a void of insecurity
Desperately waiting for maturity.

He'd made up his mind. He had to be positive about his future and pursue what he wanted. He had a point to prove.

"We'll showcase it on Friday," Chris said.

The band had been booked to play in a venue in Newport and felt it necessary to gauge the response to the song.

"That song had an interesting chord sequence. Where did you get the ideas for the words?" Chris asked as they travelled back to Josh's flat.

"I'm not sure, they just came to me yesterday after—" He quickly changed the subject, believing he'd exposed his emotions. "I want the band to get the recognition it deserves. It's got the potential, worth trying different types of music. Broaden our repertoire. I've always liked jazz, ever since I was a teenager. I thought we could try a different type of chord progression. We can always change the tempo, funk it up a bit. Dave caught on without any trouble. What's his experience of playing jazz?"

"No idea, just known him as a rock guitarist, playing haunting melodies and power chords. So, you are keen to go further, whatever the cost?"

"I think I need it more than ever now."

"What about your ex?"

"Nothing I can't handle," he said, full of bravado.

Once inside his flat Josh checked his phone, but neither Bethan nor her father had responded. Josh's spent an uneasy night attempting to sleep. He could not understand why they hadn't made contact. The fact Simpson had phoned his parents meant an added worry. It was obvious he knew Josh's identity and wanted him out of the way on Saturday.

Josh spent Tuesday afternoon practising for Friday's gig. After a few hours, frustrated by waiting for a response from Bethan's father, he telephoned him. Mr. Williams answered and demonstrated his impatience. Once Josh had explained what had happened since Sunday, he calmed down.

"Then take the opportunity to go home," he said.

In a peculiar way, Josh felt safe for the time being,

assuming any act of aggression towards him, would focus attention on the shop. After the weekend he'd have to be more vigilant.

Mrs. Francis phoned Josh as soon as he arrived home from work the following evening. She wanted to cancel Sean's lesson.

"Is he not well?" The reply wasn't one he expected.

"I don't know when he'll be able to come again."

"Oh, he's getting on well. Maybe after Christmas, we can start again."

"Yes, thank you for your help, Sean's enjoyed your lessons. I have to go, thank you." She wanted to finish the call in a hurry, unable to explain her reasons for the cancellation.

Sean had wanted to go to his lesson, but his mother had a specific reason for not taking him. She asked him to make a list of his belongings he regarded as precious.

"Why do you want me to do that?" he asked.

"We may be moving back to Cheshire. Julian's thinking of moving back, but don't say a word yet. Things aren't working out as he'd planned."

"Do we have to go with him? He gets so angry. He wasn't like this before we came here. I like my violin lessons with Josh, and I've made friends at school."

"We have to go. It may be after Christmas."

"Are we going to see Nan and Grandad then?"

She put her arms around her son and whispered, "So many questions Sean, and yes we shall see them soon." Maybe sooner, with a bit of luck, but I daren't tell you yet. We'll have to pack when he's out, over the weekend, hopefully.

Her plan to leave was gathering momentum. She'd overheard Simpson discussing something regarding Saturday over the phone, and hoped she'd be able to pack the car and leave before he'd notice.

"Josh likes the violin, Mum. He seemed upset when I stopped taking it to lessons."

"Yes, I should think he was."

"Why do you say that Mum?"

"No reason, it's such a good instrument. Julian's lucky to own it, I can't understand why."

"He's not much good on it, is he?"

"No, he shouldn't —"

"Shouldn't what Mum?"

"It should be played more often than it is," she corrected herself, "maybe one day."

Josh telephoned Jan to update her. "Bethan's confirmed it is Simpson from London. He's not alone. He's got two men working for him here. I've been followed a few times, and someone broke into my flat on Sunday."

"Was anything —? Oh." She stopped mid-sentence. After a pause of several seconds she continued. "What did you say? Two men, working for him? What do they look like?"

"They're big, unpleasant looking characters. I wouldn't like to get involved with either of them."

"Do you remember I told you two men called at the flat the night Sophie died? I saw them on the video link. I didn't let on I was in. I hadn't let Simpson know I was home either. He thought I was with her. Oh hell, no wonder he looked surprised to see me."

"What do you mean?"

"When I went to my flat to get my things to go to Manchester with Sophie's mother, he arrived home and looked at me as if I shouldn't be there."

"You don't think he had anything to do with Sophie's death, do you?"

"I didn't think so, even at the inquest, he never seemed aggressive. Her case is still open. No-one's been caught."

"He's been pretty ruthless down here." Josh stopped to consider all that had happened in the last month. "It's adding up now. I suspect he burned down the clothes factory my boss used. He's forced him to buy from a company he claims to own. He's terrorised my boss. He's even contacted my parents pretending to be Winston."

"Whatever for?

"To offer me a job in an orchestra."

"How did he get their number?"

"He must have got it from Bethan's phone."

"So he accessed her phone. The sod had planned to use her from the start."

"It looks like it. Did he ever have access to your key ring?"

"I suppose he could have taken it from my bag to have them copied unbeknown to me, but I always had them with me in the daytime. I'd have noticed if they were missing. I always used to check they were with me, because often he'd be away without warning."

"Swapped your keys when he knew you'd both be home together for a few nights?"

"I don't understand why he'd want to have us killed, though."

"What if he'd found out about you and Sophie? He was with Bethan that night, but his two accomplices weren't. As they had no answer at your flat, it could be them who broke into Sophie's, believing you were with her. My door hadn't been forced, so they could have got into Sophie's without copies of your keys anyway. The police found hair that didn't belong to any of us at her flat. I'm sure they could match a copy."

"And you're going try and get some DNA evidence from them?"

"No, I'm not that stupid, but I can search my flat for some.

This weekend something's due to happen at the shop. My boss has told me to take time off. I had last Sunday off. I only get one a month. He wants me out of the way for some reason. Bethan's father suggested I should go home. He wants me out of the way, too."

"Then don't stick around, get right away. If you've let him know, he's sorted out something. He can't tell you what. Just take his advice."

Thursday and Friday passed with no sign of either Simpson or his accomplices. Josh had to focus on the gig. His future depended on the quality of the performance, with the new song foremost on his mind. His ability to compartmentalise was his saving grace. The jazz undertones and up-beat funky rhythm of the new song suggested a new direction for the band, and possibly him.

The audience reacted with enthusiasm after the song had been performed. The musicians were delighted and began playing some of their other songs in a funky style.

"Your song went down well, any more inside your head?" Chris asked on the way home.

"I can try, the music's easy, but the lyrics are trickier."

"They were pretty deep, sounded almost personal," Chris said.

"It sometimes happens. You just want to write down your thoughts and hope, by reading the words over and over, they'll become a reality."

"That's a bit philosophical."

"Different styles of music appeal to me, I experimented a lot when I was younger. I didn't just play classical music. I listened a lot to Eastern European music fused with jazz and experimented with a variety of chord sequences and modal scales. Perhaps we can work together more often to explore what to write about."

"Could be interesting. You should have enough subject matter, but I've never seen myself as a poet."

"Song lyrics are different. I hope we'll have the time. Let's see how the meeting goes in a few weeks." He smiled and sat quietly, dreaming of the possibilities before they reached his flat. As he opened his door, the reality of the weekend before him brought him back down to earth. To what would he return on Sunday?

Chapter Fifty-Five

The December weather demanded several layers of clothes, and Josh put on an old warm coat, one he'd planned to donate to a charity shop. Its bold pattern and threadbare cuffs, signs of regular wear, would prove useful for what he had in mind. He also placed a beanie hat in his pocket.

From his wardrobe he took out a battered old rucksack into which he stuffed a scarf and a newer plain blue woollen jacket. This time he left his violin behind, believing it would be safe, hidden in his wardrobe. To carry it would only single him out for recognition. Simpson and his accomplices would be too busy to break into his flat, if what he suspected was about to happen. As he reached the station, he noticed one of Simpson's accomplices standing several metres from the entrance, his head bowed, reading a newspaper, as before.

Josh asked for a return ticket to Neath, making sure his request was audible to all around him. When the train arrived, Josh saw the man boarding the train. He hoped he could evade his pursuer when he changed trains.

Once he reached Cardiff, Josh caught a two-carriage sprinter train to take him westwards. He walked the length of both carriages to see if the man was on board. Fortunately, there was no sign of him.

As soon as the train had passed through the suburbs of the city, Josh went to the toilet and changed from his old jacket to the newer one. He put on his beanie hat and scarf, pushed the old coat into the rucksack, and waited by the carriage door.

When the train stopped at Bridgend he disembarked and crossed the bridge to the opposite platform, to board the next train back to Cardiff. He then caught the train to take him back to where he'd started his journey.

He gazed out through the carriage window at the different communities of the city through which he passed. Nothing specifically caught his attention due to the speed at which the train travelled, but he became increasingly concerned he'd made the correct decision. He knew his future would change. Whether it was for the better or not, he'd soon find out. With his mobile phone switched off, he was ready to witness the events unfold without interruption.

To occupy his mind, and to appear as inconspicuous as possible, he bought a newspaper at the station and walked towards the centre of town. Nothing appeared out of place, so he entered a café from where he could see the shop, fifty metres or so along the road. The high street, like so many in the sleepy towns which had lost their custom to the accessible cities and cut-price outlets along the M4 corridor, appeared empty. The shop would not be overrun with customers. It appeared to be an ideal day to make a delivery.

After half an hour, and a prolonged cup of coffee, he began to feel uncomfortable. One of the counter staff asked him if he wanted more refreshments, and he realised his presence required the purchase of another drink. He stood to leave, not wanting to draw attention to himself.

The street appeared quiet, and he assumed the delivery he'd anticipated had not taken place earlier in the morning. If the police had raided the shop, its evidence would be apparent.

It was now mid-day, and he turned to walk towards the local rugby club to kill time. He hoped he'd not have to wait hours for something to happen. A match had been arranged to take place later that afternoon. He approached the club and looked at his watch. It was pointless standing around looking conspicuous. He turned to return to town, unsure what to do next.

In need of warmth he returned to the café and ordered a sandwich and another hot drink. One of the counter staff, who'd begun her shift at twelve, recognised him and engaged him in conversation.

"Not working today Josh?"

"No, I've got the day off. I'm going to see the match, but it's too cold to wait outside, it doesn't start for another two hours."

"Who are we playing today?" He'd not considered checking the fixture list and had to think of a feasible answer.

"Swansea."

"I didn't think they were in the same division," she said, and gave him a strange look. Not wishing to be caught out he replied,

"No, it's a team from Swansea — Clydach." He collected his coffee and sandwich and sat by the window, relieved he'd managed to evade any more questions. He could look out unhindered and take his time.

As he warmed himself, he wanted to see if anyone had attempted to contact him. He pulled his mobile phone from his pocket and switched it on. A message from Bethan appeared on his screen, instructing him not to be anywhere in the vicinity of the shop. She'd obviously been told to warn him to stay well away from the area. He wondered if he should telephone her father to let him know his location but decided against it. It would complicate matters. He'd only intended to witness the events as they unfolded anyway.

He finished his sandwich and stood to order another coffee, but as he did so, he saw a large delivery van stopping outside Terry Evans' shop. The driver stepped out and opened the double doors at the rear. Simpson's two accomplices appeared from the shop doorway and began to carry boxes inside, five in total, each one heavy enough to require two to carry it.

The speed with which they completed the task suggested a necessity to hide the boxes and whatever goods were contained inside them from public view. He had a good idea but was not going to miss what he hoped would happen next. The opportunity to see retribution being carried out on Simpson excited him. He'd played his part.

After the van had pulled away, one of Simpson's accomplices stepped onto the pavement and looked along each direction of the street before returning inside. It suggested the boxes didn't just contain clothing.

Five minutes passed and nothing happened. He ordered his coffee, and another five minutes passed. It seemed like an anti-climax. Unsure of what should have happened, he stayed in his seat pretending to drink an imaginary amount of liquid at the bottom of the cup. As he put down his cup, he saw someone he recognised from his youth walking towards the shop on the opposite side of the road. As Tom Parker reached the shop, he looked around to survey the scene, and disappeared through the doorway.

You're in this as well, are you?

The cocksure appearance of the man still gave off an offensive aura. Josh's suspicions had been confirmed. The large boxes held more than uniforms. No wonder his boss had wanted him out of the way. He wondered what threat had been held over Terry Evans' head.

Josh put on his beanie hat, left the café, and walked in the direction from which Parker had come. He didn't want to be spotted. As he continued along the pavement, three well-built men passed him. They didn't make eye contact but stepped to one side to allow him to continue. Josh stopped to look in through the window of a shop. He didn't pay any attention to the display but turned his head to see two of them enter Terry's shop. The third waited outside and gazed through the window. He appeared to be biding his time, attempting to look inconspicuous.

"Come on Sean, get your things into this." Mrs. Francis had taken a suitcase into his bedroom. "Is your violin ready? don't forget all your music, and what Josh has given you." He looked at her, unsure what she meant.

"Are we going?"

"You've made a list, make sure everything's in, and your clothes."

"How long are we going for?"

"I don't know."

He smiled back at her. He realised they would both be leaving that afternoon.

"Thanks Mum, can we go to see Josh at the shop first?"

"If we've got time, I'll stop where I can park, and you can go in to see him." She found a notepad and scribbled a few sentences, folded the paper, and placed it inside an envelope. "Give him this to thank him."

"Aren't you going to come in?"

"Best not." The two carried their luggage to the car and Mrs. Francis took the key from her compact case. Once they were both inside, she started the engine.

Josh continued to glance along the street in both directions but focussed his attention on the man outside Terry's shop. He appeared to be waiting for something or someone, and Josh saw him check his watch. He turned his back, but Josh saw him take something from his pocket and hold it to his ear. After several seconds the man placed the object, which Josh assumed was a phone, back into his pocket.

Within a minute, two police cars appeared from both directions, and parked opposite the shop, facing each other. The man continued to look in through the shop window and ignored their presence. Three male officers stepped out from one car, and two more and a female officer from the other. They walked into the shop, and it was the last Josh saw of them.

Although he knew he shouldn't be in the vicinity, he was compelled to stay, to see Simpson on the receiving end. The man had been responsible for the demise of what he'd regarded as a relationship with a person to whom he'd been continually drawn.

Several vehicles travelled in both directions as he gazed along the road, but one approached, and caught his eye. A familiar white BMW car, he assumed was driven by Simpson, came closer and slowed down. The driver was looking for a parking space further along the street.

As it drew level with the shop a young woman ran out into its path. The driver failed to avoid impact. The young woman was thrown forward and lay motionless on the road. Josh instinctively raced over to see what could be done to help, but hearing a shout behind him, he saw Simpson running from the shop towards the car in a blind rage. He reached the driver's door and pulled it open, screaming obscenities. Simpson thrust his left hand towards the driver and Josh saw him raise his right hand in a clenched fist, ready to strike.

Josh spotted Sean's terrified face in the passenger seat and realised Mrs. Francis was the driver. Without a thought for his own safety, he kicked the car door with the sole of his shoe as hard as he could. His intervention pushed Simpson off balance, and he repeated this with another kick. Simpson let out a cry of pain, his left arm injured. His attention now focussed on Josh, and he pulled open the door with his right hand as his left arm hung motionless at his side. Despite his injury, he lunged forward and wrapped his right hand around Josh's throat. Josh's smaller wiry frame, dwarfed by his attacker's much larger build, had no defence against the vice-like grip.

"You bastard, turning up where you're a fucking nuisance. I should have finished you off as well as that lesbian."

The man who'd stayed outside Terry's shop raced across the street to intervene. He twisted Simpson's broken arm, forcing him to release the vice like grip on Josh's throat, but the damage had been done. Josh collapsed in a heap on the road. Ambulances soon arrived to take the injured girl and Josh to hospital. Julian Simpson, now handcuffed, was also escorted there, under police guard to be X-rayed. His arm had been broken and his shoulder dislocated, but these would heal.

CHAPTER FIFTY-SIX

Sunday, 6 December, 2009

Josh regained consciousness the next morning. He'd been kept sedated overnight, but as soon as he came round, he felt an excruciating pain in his throat. It took him several seconds to realise he was a patient in hospital. Unable to move his head, he scanned his eyes around the room to the full extent of his peripheral vision. His parents sat on the right side of his bed, and Bethan's father stood to his left. A mask covered his nose and mouth. Breathing was a painful experience. Puzzled to see his visitors, he attempted to remove the mask, but his mother urged him not to.

The events of the previous afternoon began to return to his consciousness. He wondered about the girl who'd been knocked down. She'd run into the path of a car. The driver hadn't been able to avoid her. Simpson had rushed across the road to attack the driver. He'd intervened. Sean's mother, Simpson's partner, had been driving. He tried to remember what she looked like. No, a blank — it had been a fleeting glance. However, Simpson had attacked him as a result of his intervention. He'd tried to kill him. What had he said as he'd tried to strangle him?

The discomfort he felt reminded him of the injuries he'd sustained. He had difficulty breathing. *Why have I got a mask on my face?* He tried to move but couldn't. *Why is Bethan's father in the room?* He then heard his father's voice,

"I'll go and get a nurse, don't move."

A few moments later, a doctor arrived at his bedside.

"You've sustained damage to your trachea, or windpipe. A tube has been inserted to connect the pharynx and larynx to the lungs. It allows air to enter and leave. It helps you to breathe. We hope we can withdraw these tomorrow."

The events of the previous afternoon became clearer. He remembered waiting in the street when all hell had broken loose. He remembered what Simpson had shouted as he attacked him It was as Jan and he suspected. He knew he'd have to contact her and tell Bethan's father.

The doctor sensed Josh's wish to speak, "Please don't talk, you'll find it too painful for a few days, but we'll keep you here until you begin to feel better and can breathe unaided, then you can go home." Josh listened, unable to respond, although he had many questions to ask.

Bethan's father stood to leave and said, "I just wanted to thank you for all the information you'd given us. I'm glad you're all right, it means a lot to us as a family. But you should have listened to me. We must put all the past behind us and carry on with our lives as before." Josh understood this as Bethan's father's way of telling him he and Bethan had to move on.

Terry Evans and his wife walked into the ward later. He couldn't thank Josh enough for his intervention. He told him the background behind the events of the past month. Simpson had imported a large quantity of cocaine in packages, in the boxes. He'd threatened Anne, and Terry had been forced to agree, to protect her. Simpson had also hidden a small amount of cocaine in his house, his insurance to stop Terry informing the police.

In need of a rest, and to his relief, Josh saw a nurse entering the private ward, to ask everyone to leave. As he lay in bed, he thought of Sean's mother, the woman he'd saved from her partner's anger. He remembered her interest in the music he'd played at the Halloween party, and hoped she'd be grateful for his actions. He hoped she had no part in her partner's crimes. Simpson's reaction to her at the scene suggested this. His arrest would surely allow her to drop her guard. She wouldn't want to protect him after what had happened.

When he awoke two hours later, Josh saw Sean by his bed. His mother stood behind him with her hands on his shoulders. He recognised her. Unable to believe who stood in the ward, he closed his eyes attempting to comprehend why she was standing at his bedside. He knew the mysterious mother, who'd been unwilling or unable to reveal her identity before. She appeared relieved Simpson had now been eliminated from her life. Josh remembered how Sean had attempted to comfort his mother after one of the lessons. She'd also been a victim, just like Jan, just like Bethan and especially Sophie. Vicky, the girl he'd loved in his final year in Cardiff, stood before him. He recognised the unmistakable likeness between her and Sean. She smiled at him, and the world seemed right again. He wished he could speak to her, but her smile was enough to lift his spirits. Her lips glistened.

Had her request for the tune at the Halloween dance been a cry for help? It was one he'd often played when they had been together in Cardiff.

"Thank you, Josh, for all you've done," she said.

Sean smiled, apparently not sure what to say, but he appeared happier than he'd been for several weeks.

"I can bring the best violin to you now at the next lesson, and Mum's promised to get me a nice new one for Christmas." Josh was unsure what he meant — he'd assumed Sean's lessons had finished.

Vicky squeezed Josh's hand before they both left, and as they went through the doorway, she turned and gave him one last look. He saw her eyes moisten and guessed tears were welling up inside. She gave a relieved smile and mouthed the words *Thank you, Josh.*

As soon as they'd left, the police officer approached his bed and described the events of the previous day. He explained an officer would ensure all his visitors would be vetted. The delivery of clothes to the shop had been imported via Amsterdam. The boxes also contained the drugs to which Terry had referred. He couldn't elaborate any further until the case was ready to be brought to court, hopefully in the spring. Simpson's comment, overheard by the plain-clothes officer, had triggered another inquiry.

Josh, relieved the circumstances surrounding Sophie's death would be investigated once more, had to contact Jan as soon as possible.

During the week of hospitalisation, he received several visits from his fellow band members and pupils, who joked about him having to keep quiet. By Friday, he regained his ability to speak, albeit for short periods. His father collected him on Saturday, on his discharge, to stay at his parents' home until the following Wednesday.

Vicky visited him several times before he left hospital, and he promised Sean he would continue teaching him as soon as possible at his own flat. He wanted to return to some semblance of normality.

CHAPTER FIFTY-SEVEN

The Violin is Returned

December, 2009

Sean arrived at six thirty with two violin cases. This time
Vicky accompanied him into the flat. "I've been practising
on my new violin." Sean opened a brand-new case to reveal a
new full-sized instrument. "For Christmas. Early." He gave it
to Josh, who examined its quality. Josh smiled and placed the
violin under his chin. He picked up the bow and drew it
across the strings. They were in tune, and rosin had been applied to the horsehair. He looked at Vicky and continued to
smile as he began playing *The Devil Went Down To Georgia*.
After several phrases, he stopped and gave the instrument
back to Sean.

"Your turn to take over," he said.

"You still play that tune beautifully." Vicky said.

"You asked for it at the club. Your reaction changed as soon
as we started playing it, as if — "

"I was trying to tell you something. He gave me hell afterwards. Said he thought he knew you."

Throughout this brief conversation, Sean looked back and
forth at his mother and Josh, clearly now aware they both
knew each other.

"I'll come back later, give me a call when you're ready. Oh,
Sean, you've got something to give Josh." Sean held up the
other violin case in front of his teacher.

"Open it," Sean said.

"This is the one you used to bring. The Hoing, I thought it was my old one when I saw it first." Josh stared at the instrument. Vicky smiled. She sensed Josh's delight at seeing the instrument again.

"It is yours," she said. Josh looked at her, unsure if the confirmation of his suspicions was correct. "You lost this somewhere. When he said he owned a violin, I asked him if I could see it. He took it from its case, and I had a close look at it before I played it. Your initials were on the inside, but I didn't question it as they were the same as his, even though it had been made by the same luthier. I assumed he'd had it as a teenager as he'd said he'd played at school. I took him at his word. When Sean was big enough to hold it comfortably, I looked at it more closely and saw a small scratch on the back, and I recognised it." She looked embarrassed. "Then I saw your name on the card in the newsagent's. I couldn't believe it. I suggested Sean begin lessons with you after I saw your advertisement and asked if he could use it. He agreed without question. When he brought it back after the first lesson, I noticed the initials had been scribbled over. He must have known about you from somewhere. In a mad moment I tried to phone you in the shop to let you know your violin was safe, and I would hopefully get it back to you, somehow, but I was interrupted before you could answer. I was desperate. I had no idea it would turn out like this."

As she was about to leave for the lesson to continue, she turned. "Can we meet tomorrow?"

Josh agreed without hesitation.

CHAPTER FIFTY-EIGHT

A Secret Revealed

December, 2009

Vicky collected Josh from his flat to drive to a quiet pub for lunch. She'd had to move out of the house she'd shared with Simpson and had booked into a cheap hotel until Christmas. Forensic teams needed to examine the property. After initial investigations regarding her ex-partner had been completed, she and Sean hoped to move back to Manchester to live with her parents until she could find work.

Josh needed some form of explanation regarding Simpson, to find out how she'd begun a relationship with him. They'd met two years before. He'd been charming and kindness personified. His accountancy firm often required him to embark on trips away. Josh listened without interruption — it reminded him of the relationship Simpson had had with Jan.

"When I went to see his parents, I couldn't believe the size of their house. It was like a fortress with antiques, artefacts and paintings most people could only dream about, but they were so likeable, and made me welcome. I wondered lately if they were glad he'd met somebody prepared to put up with him, get him off their back. I don't think even they were aware of his secret life. I certainly wasn't. He asked me to move in with him into a flat in Chester last year. I gave up my job at the school, as it was too far to travel. I hoped to find something nearer to where we lived. I didn't mind. It had been difficult, me a single parent. Sean was a pupil at the school where I taught, and I often had to work late. Sean changed schools and started in a preparatory one. Julian appeared to have plenty of money, so I didn't object. Everything became easier for a short time, but within a few months he became very controlling, and would frequently fly off into a rage. It used to frighten me. But what could I do? I was trapped and had no job. I began to teach at Sean's school, but continually looked for other teaching jobs elsewhere. I'd even planned how to escape. Without any warning he decided to move down here before I could sort it out. The fresh start calmed him down temporarily. Sean soon noticed his temper, but now I was further away from Manchester and felt even more trapped."

"Hadn't Sean seen that side of him before you moved?"

"The prep school worked longer hours, Saturdays as well, and Sean played sport on Saturday afternoons, so he didn't see anything, I kept it quiet. Simpson never hit me. Most evenings, he made excuses to go out. I had no idea what he was involved in."

"It's where he made his money. My friend Jan used to live with him."

"He mentioned a Jan, said he'd lived with her, but she'd turned out to be a lesbian, so he'd kicked her out, sorted it all out, he said. I couldn't understand why he moved here, though."

"Easy, it was to renew a link to Tom Parker, a relation of his who's just been released from prison."

"The obnoxious guy who called at the house several times? He said he was family."

"It was close enough and yet far enough away from Swansea not to arouse any suspicion. No more using young girls like Bethan Williams, either."

"Who?"

"Bethan Williams, from Swansea. I knew her in Cardiff. She's a teacher. She trained at the same college as you. I met up with her again in London."

"Yes, I remember her. Wasn't she in my year? I don't understand."

Josh related the events of the millennium year. "She contacted me recently. I'd wondered why, but then it all fell into place. Jan had a close friend called Sophie who was murdered. He as good as admitted to it when he attacked me."

Vicky looked horrified.

"But I can't understand how Simpson had got hold of my old violin. Bethan was the only person who knew where I'd —"

He paused for a few seconds. "Now I realise how he'd got hold of it. She knew where I'd sold it. In her eyes, she must have assumed their relationship was a more intense one. Talk about rubbing my nose in it." He realised he'd been used.

"Legally it's still his," he said.

"I don't think he'll need it for a long time. Luckily for us she turned up when she did. How do you two get on?" Vicky asked.

"No, not at all, although I suspect she —" He paused for several seconds before continuing. "She's far too selfish and shallow. She's married anyway, definitely not," he said with confidence. "If a choice presented itself it would be an easy one to make."

Vicky had a good idea what he meant but didn't respond. She felt awkward and fingered her coffee cup.

After a moment of silence, Josh, changed the subject. He wanted, on impulse, to find out about Sean.

"When you moved back to Manchester, to live with your boyfriend, how long did you stay together?" Josh realised the question was an invasion of her but he needed to know about Sean's background. He wanted to discover the details, however unpleasant it could have been for her.

"I know what you want to find out, I can tell." Vicky said.

Josh thought he'd crossed the fine line between concern and curiosity as he watched her stand. Would she walk away from him? To his surprise she sat on the chair next to his. He could sense her desire to be close as her fingers touched his.

"It's what I wanted to tell you." she said as a smile spread across her face. Her eyes glistened with emotion.

"When is Sean eleven?" His question appeared without prompting.

"The very end of March."

He made some mental calculations.

"So, when you moved back to Manchester, you became pregnant almost straight away and moved in with—"

"Nick?"

"Yes, it's what his name was."

"Josh." Her fingers began to caress his. He didn't withdraw his hand. He felt the old warmth he'd experienced in his final year in Cardiff, as if a mild electric current had passed through his body. "Nick and I were no longer together. He and I had finished in May. He found out about you."

"Why didn't you tell me you'd finished?"

"We had our own futures to sort out. I'd been applying for jobs in Manchester. You wanted to go to London." She paused for a few seconds, "but on the last day we were together—"

"How are you Mrs. Francis?" He interrupted her, anticipating that he'd hear information to change his life, but wasn't sure whether he wanted to know.

"I'm not, Josh. Don't you understand what I'm trying to tell you?"

"Why didn't you let me know?"

"We'd finished, remember. I didn't realise I was pregnant until the end of August. I hadn't met anyone else, but I didn't want to spoil your chances. You were in London, and I wasn't.

I didn't want us to get back together just because I was pregnant. You'd have resented it."

"No, I wouldn't. I wrote to you, and you answered, once. You should have told me. I'd have been delighted."

"I didn't think you'd — You seem — "

"Different?"

"Yes."

"I've had to find out about myself the hard way."

"I read the occasional report in the papers about your orchestra and the ensemble you played in. They were all extremely complimentary. Your name appeared regularly, and then nothing. It was as if you'd disappeared. The orchestra continued to be reviewed, but not your ensemble, or you. I put it down to the music business, and the media being so fickle. By then I'd made a life for myself. I enjoyed my teaching. I wrote a few letters to you but never posted them."

"I wish you had." Tears began to form. He felt her hand on his arm and she leant over and kissed his cheek. The display of affection genuine, he gripped her hand. "I understand now why you had to be so distant when Sean started with me. Boys can be too honest. We get on really well too."

"I know. I couldn't believe it was your name on the card. I was going to teach Sean, because the new school couldn't. But I had to protect him. The less he knew the better. I'd planned to escape to go back to Manchester on Saturday, hoping Julian wouldn't follow me. It's where I was going."

"Would you have contacted me?"

"I wanted to know how both of you got on, see what would happen. But I had to get Sean and myself away from him first. He was unbearable. I didn't know he was anything to do with the shop. I'd planned to stop outside for Sean to say goodbye to you there, he'd asked if he could. I'd written a note with my parents' telephone number for Sean to give to you. Once we were safe, I'd have contacted you."

CHAPTER FIFTY-NINE

2010

Josh realised he shouldn't contact Bethan again. He knew she'd try to wrap him around her little finger whenever she felt the urge, if it meant safeguarding her interests. He regretted how far they'd renewed their past relationship when she'd taken him to the waterfall and wondered how long her marriage would last.

Her husband had been home for two weeks over Christmas, and she telephoned Josh in January, wanting to see him again.

He had no difficulty ignoring the temptation. "I've met someone else," he said. "Someone who's not in a relationship. Someone without any complications. She's not married."

"Who is she?"

"Someone I should have got to know better a long time ago."

"What do you mean?"

"What I say. I have to go." He pressed the end call button and turned his phone to silent.

She rang again and texted several times, but he ignored all her attempts. He knew he'd never be comfortable in a relationship with her. He had no wish to be the other man, forever looking over his shoulder, if a new attraction was within her focus.

The charges against Julian Simpson and Tom Parker were brought to court in the spring. They were both found guilty of importing Class A drugs. Simpson and his two associates were also convicted of arson, regarding Huw Rogers' factory. Bethan's account of the drug distribution in the millennium year wasn't needed, and Josh was relieved not to see her at the trial.

The comment Simpson had made to Josh at the scene of the accident had prompted the police to reinvestigate Sophie's case. Forensic evidence confirmed matches between one of Simpson's accomplices' DNA to the follicle of hair found at her flat in Streatham. Protesting their innocence was futile, and they implicated Simpson, hoping to get a lighter sentence. Although he denied involvement, the jury found him guilty.

Vicky and Sean moved back to Manchester after Christmas. Josh also decided to leave South Wales. The promise of a breakthrough into a lucrative professional status with the band didn't materialise, but he wasn't disappointed. With Jan's help he explored the possibility of work in the Manchester area and secured a post with a professional orchestra in May. Living in the North-West ensured he could mentor his son and renew the close relationship he'd had with Vicky.

You may also enjoy the following from eXtasy Books Inc:

Always Cambridge
HK Carlton

Excerpt

Randy. He'd always been there for me. In fact, I couldn't even remember a time when he wasn't. But Bill Cambridge employed so many men, it was hard to keep track of them all. And given that my father's business practices were questionable at best, employee turnover was great. Around here, you learned not to get attached to people. Chances were they wouldn't be here long. My dad was not an easy man to get along with. Some guys chose to leave because they could not abide the man—others weren't as lucky.

I think the first time I really noticed Randy, I was about nine. I'd begun to wonder why my friends at school didn't have bodyguards around them all the time. Until then, I'd never really given it much thought. I assumed everyone lived the way I did. So, I began watching and listening to my surroundings.

It was then I noticed that everyone else was doing the same. All of my father's men were watchful. They not only kept tabs on my dad, but they were extremely vigilant when it came to visitors. And even more telling, my father's men watched each other. I thought they were all friends up until that day, until I realized not one of them trusted the others. You could see it on their faces. Man to man, they were cordial to one another, but as soon as one turned his back, a cloud of suspicion descended, marring the other's features.

I remember sitting on the edge of the in-ground pool watching and listening. I had decided to learn as many of their names as I could, and maybe even what specific position they held with my dad. I wasn't even exactly sure what it was my father did, but I was pretty sure it wasn't nice. I was bored and alone as usual and it seemed like a good game. April, my older sister by five years, was out. Not that she would have given me the time of day even if she'd been at home. She didn't like me much, but then again, she didn't seem to like many people.

That one, in the ill-fitting, grey pinstriped suit, his name was Buddy. I knew him. As much as Dad tried to keep us separate from them, there were still a few who were permanent fixtures and had been as far back as I could remember. Buddy was one of them. He was almost always at my father's side. His Right-hand man, I guessed.

Then there was Tom. He was just a very big man, tall and wide. I'd seen him shoulder more men than I could count out of my father's path. He would be his enforcer, I supplied.

Then there was Patrick. He was my favourite. He always had a piece of candy for me. But better than that, he was nice to me. He'd bandaged several skinned knees and he always seemed to know when I'd had a bad day at school. And on occasion, I sometimes even got a hug. My father and my sister were not huggers. At times it was nice to have someone hold you tight. It made me feel safe.

That day, I heard other names. Teddy, Jason, Gunner, Phil . . . And as I surveyed the yard, my gaze collided with another set of observant eyes.

His head was bent slightly forwards and his sandy-coloured hair covered his forehead. He looked as if he was ready to pounce right off the bar stool he was perched on. He seemed considerably younger than the rest of my father's associates, but much older than me, probably even older than my sister. He was wearing a worn white t-shirt and jeans, a brown leather cuff around his wrist. Not the usual uniform for their crowd either. I looked away quickly, but not before I saw his mouth quirk up in a grin.

Out of the corner of my eye, I saw him jump from the stool, coming my way. When he reached my position he rolled up the legs of his jeans, sat down beside me and dangled his feet into the warm water.

"Whatch'ya lookin' for, little one?" he asked.

"Nothing," I replied quietly, afraid I'd been caught doing something I shouldn't. I kept my head turned away from him.

"My name's Randy," he said. "You're Holly, right?"

He sounded like a nice boy. I turned to look at him. He was smiling at me. Now that I looked at him up close, he was older. He had stubble on his chin. His grey eyes twinkled as he watched me assessing him.

"How old are you?" I blurted before I could stop myself.

"I'm eighteen. How old are you?"

"Nine," I said, softly again and looked away. Eighteen! Wow! He was practically a man, I remembered thinking.

"Nine. Wow. You're really getting up there, aren't you?" he asked, sounding serious, though his voice made me think he might be smiling.

"I'll be ten in December," I said, trying to make myself sound older then wondering why I'd felt the need.

"Ah, yes, ten, I remember it well," he said, and something in his voice had changed. I looked back at him to see. The grin remained but no longer reached his eyes.

For some reason my usual shyness left me and I asked, "Did something happen to you when you were ten?" I observed him closely, trying to discover what made this seemingly happy boy-man sad.

"You are perceptive, aren't you, little one," he responded, but didn't answer the question.

"Why do you call me that?" Again, shyness, where art thou?

His expression turned severe and he raked his hand through his hair, making it curl and stand up on top. "Oops," he said, under his breath but I still heard him.

"I just wondered," I rushed, not liking that I'd made his smile vanish. "I've heard the other men say little one before. I just wondered at it. Never mind." I tried to make it better.

He looked down at my little hand patting his forearm just above the leather cuff.

I pulled my hand back quickly, mortified that I'd touched him.

To my surprise, he took my hand and placed it back on his arm. He took a deep breath and looked out over the pool. He nodded, as if he'd made a decision.

"Well, you know, all these men are here to . . . uh," he pursed his lips for a moment, measuring his words, " . . . help your father look after you and your sister, right?"

"Mmmhmm," I replied, awed that he was actually going to answer me. No one ever answered my questions.

"Well, we men," he puffed his chest out a bit too proudly, including himself with the elder group. "We have nicknames for you and your sister, so that other people won't know we're referring to you. And your dad doesn't like us to use your real names in public." He tapped my hand reassuringly. "Its just precaution. We're all just trying to keep you safe."

"Oh, like code. So, you call me little one."

"Yep, sometimes we just call you L.O."

"So, if I'm L.O., what do you call my sister?"

Ducking his head, he then smiled broadly. "We call her big one." I could tell he was trying not to laugh and I tried really hard to get the joke.

It wasn't until I said it out loud that I caught on. "That would make her B.O."

Unable to contain his amusement any longer he laughed out loud, a deep affecting sound that made me happy.

"She would have an absolute fit, if she knew that. Not only that you all call her big but that she stinks too." I giggled until my tummy hurt.

As we sat on the edge of the pool laughing together, Patrick approached us from the opposite side of the water. He didn't look happy like he usually did. Ever so slightly he raised his chin at Randy.

Randy scrambled to his feet and rolled down his jeans. As he bent on one knee he said under his breath, his lips barely moved. "I only told you that because you're almost ten and I know you are old enough to keep our secrets." With his sudden scrutiny, I knew he was asking me not to repeat what he'd confided in me.

"I won't tell, Randy," I said, seriously.

His features lightened and he smiled again. "I knew I could trust you, L.O."

He said it so fast as he started to get up I whispered, "That sounded like Lee Lo."

"Lee Lo," he smiled. "I like that." Then he hurried around to the other side of the pool where Patrick stood waiting for him.

Paddy said something to Randy that made him bow his head. His shoulders slumped.

I watched them walk away and I hoped I hadn't gotten Randy into trouble.

It wasn't until I couldn't see them anymore that I realized he'd never answered my question. What had happened to him when he was ten?

ABOUT THE AUTHOR

John Roach grew up in West Wales, where he lives with his wife. After studying Drama and Music he taught for many years. To develop his pupils' confidence he wrote several plays, musicals and orchestrated modern rock, folk and jazz songs for them to perform.

He continues to write short stories and poetry, and this is his first novel to be published. He also plays several instruments in a rock band and sings in a choir. John is often asked to write plays for local festivals. Recently, one of these was broadcast on a local radio station.

Printed in Great Britain
by Amazon